Misty Springs

Casey Fae Hewson

Casey Fae Hewson lives in sunny Marlborough, New Zealand. She loves to write young adult and contemporary romance fiction. When she's not reading, she'll be mountain biking, walking, gardening, travelling and listening to music.

She is the author of *Haven River* and *Aqua Bay*. She is partnered with Bob Boze. Together they have co-written *Light My Way.*, along with a number of short stories and poems.

ISBN: 978-0-473-52606-1 (Softcover)
ISBN: 978-0-473-52607-8 (Kindle)
ISBN: 978-0-473-52608-5 (ibook)

Table of Contents

Dedication

Bob

Once again, thank you for your support, patience, and
encouragement.
I couldn't have done it without you.
This is for you.

Emily curled the fingers she had around the stem of her wine glass. She looked down at her left hand. *What would it be like to have both a ring finger and an index finger?*

The garden party was in full swing. The four-piece orchestra struck up a tune and the leaves rustled gently in the summer breeze.

"This is a great venue for a wedding," Lisa said, flicking back her long blonde hair.

"Hmm." Andrea glanced around at the white gazebos.

"Move over," Marie said to Emily.

Emily shuffled over so Marie could sit on the couch.

"Did I hear somebody mention something about a wedding?" Marie asked.

"Lisa was just saying what a great wedding venue this would be," Emily replied, brushing away a leaf that had fallen on her arm. Her skin glimmered with the sunscreen she'd lavishly wiped on this morning to protect her pale skin.

"Our town could do with somewhere classy for a wedding," Lisa said.

"Hey, Andrea. A good place for you and Vinnie to tie the knot," Marie replied.

Andrea laughed, held up her hand and wiggled her fingers. "I've got to get a ring first."

"I'm sure that won't be too far off. You guys have been together for years."

Emily rested her head on the back of the couch and looked up at the fluffy, white clouds. One looked like a dove. Her mind drifted back to two years ago to an engagement ring that had never reached her finger. The wings of the dove disconnected, then broke in half and the four pieces floated apart. Just like her engagement - broken. The white picket fences – broken. The only happy ever after endings had been when she'd married off her dolls.

"We really should be schmoozing," said Lisa. "There's great potential to pick up some business here."

"Aw, don't." Marie bent down to rub her perfectly manicured foot. "My feet are still aching from yesterday and the day before."

"I could give you a foot rub," Emily offered.

"Oh, yes please. How about after lunch?"

"No worries," Emily replied.

There was very little opportunity for the late-twenty-year-olds to pamper themselves. Lisa, the beauty salon owner, ran here, there and everywhere drumming up more clients for the six-month-old business. Andrea, who was the nail technician, buffed, manicured and painted. Marie was affectionately known as 'The Brazilian'. And then Emily. Massaging. She took pride in the wide variety of massage services she could perform - deep tissue, pregnancy, baby, head, hot rocks and her speciality, aromatherapy.

"Hey, looks like the food and drinks are coming out," Lisa said.

Everyone turned their heads in the direction where the trestle table had been set up. Stiff white tablecloths were held down by big vases filled with hydrangeas, purple daisies and tulips.

The four male waiters caught their attention as they poured wine into glasses and placed hors d'oeurves onto trays.

"Great. I'm starved," Marie said.

"I hope you're not expecting a feast," Andrea replied. "You need about ten of those little savoury thingies to even feel like you've eaten something."

"There are a few waiters I haven't seen before," Lisa said.

Emily squinted trying to make out any familiar faces. She pushed herself up higher on the couch so she could get a closer look. "I don't recognise anyone. It must be some new staff they've employed."

"Well then, it's time to get acquainted," said Lisa, clapping her hands. "Let's find out some more. Who hasn't scored a telephone number in the last few months?"

Emily bowed her head. *Oh no! They were about to play Lisa's get-the-phone-number game.* This was where one of the girls was 'volunchosen' to obtain the phone number for a guy they didn't know. Lisa and Marie had varying degrees of success, mainly resulting in a few one night stands. Andrea, on the other hand, had met Vinnie and their relationship was going strong.

She'd also had some wins. Getting the phone number was the easy part. Following up was harder. She never quite had the courage to ring someone back; the uneasy fear of rejection winning over her again. She hadn't minded this game to begin with, but lately it had made her uncomfortable. It had started out as harmless fun. Now it just seemed childish. And Lisa's win-at-all-costs competitive attitude grated on her.

"Mmm. Who hasn't got a phone number for a while? Andrea?" Lisa asked.

"Whoa. That's not going to help me get an engagement ring from Vinnie."

"True," Lisa replied, "but don't you want to see if you've still got it."

"I've still got it. Pick on someone else."

"Marie."

"It was my turn last time. How about you?"

"I think this thing with Hunter is about to turn serious."

"What?" Marie exclaimed. "After three dates."

"That's serious in my book."

The girls laughed.

"That only leaves you, Emily. And your wine glass is empty," Lisa said.

"Oh no. Not today. I just want to sit and relax."

"Come on, you old woman," Marie said, slapping her lightly on the thigh. "You'll never meet anyone with your constant working and house building."

"I don't have time for a relationship at the moment," Emily protested.

"Relationship? Who's talking about a relationship? It's just a phone number. Not a life time commitment," Lisa said.

Typical Lisa. Her exhilaration was in the chase.

"Yeah, come on Em. We need some excitement before that orchestra puts me to sleep," Marie joked.

"Come on," Andrea encouraged.

"Go Em. Go Em," Marie chanted.

Lisa joined in. "Go Em. Go Em."

"Okay. Okay." Emily put her hands up in protest. She stood up and ran her hands down the front of her floral maxi dress.

"Remember – a phone number," Lisa said, as she waved at Emily.

Emily clutched her handbag close to her side hiding her fingers in the material. Tottering on her heels as they sank into the grass, she walked toward the trestle bar table. By now the other three male waiters were circulating around the crowd offering drinks and food.

Should I approach them? No. Too difficult. Too many people around. It would have to be the lone guy pouring wine into glasses at the bar.

He was about the same height as her, stocky build. Late 20s.

"Hi," she said tentatively.

"Oh, hi," the guy said, looking up.

"Nice day." She wasn't good at social small talk, but put her in a massage room and it came easily as she discussed the best type of massage for that particular person's needs.

"Ah, yeah," the guy said, as he arranged then rearranged the glasses.

"What wines have you got?"

The guy grabbed a bottle and read off the label. "This is a 2014 sauvignon blank." He stumbled over his words.

"Blanc," corrected Emily.

"Pardon?"

"It's pronounced blanc. It's French."

"I don't know too much French."

"Anything else you can recommend. What about a red?" She took a closer look at the guy's name badge: Ricky.

He reached over to pick up another bottle and handed it to her. "Maybe you should read the label yourself."

"A pinot noir. No, I think I'll go with the sav." She handed the bottle back, studying Ricky closer. Something looked out of place. His whole appearance didn't speak professional waiter. His burgundy waiter's shirt was one size too big making him look even stockier. He'd missed the third button and there was a grease spot on the opposite side to his name tag. He somehow seemed out of his depth and he just didn't look the part. Bald head, neatly-trimmed brown goatee. And he couldn't pronounce the types of wines. Yet there was a vulnerability about him lying beneath the toughness.

"Sure thing." Ricky opened the bottle and began pouring the wine.

"Do you do these events often?"

"No. This is my first one."

That explained a few things.

"My name's Emily. You live in Misty Springs then? I haven't seen you around here before."

"Just moved here." He handed her the glass.

"I'd be happy to show you around the town if you like," she said, taking a sip and looking over towards her friends.

Lisa mouthed, 'phone number'.

"If you give me your phone number I'll give you a call sometime."

"That's very forward of you," he growled.

This was not what she was expecting. Most guys didn't hesitate when she asked for their phone number. She hadn't had a response like this in over four months. She gulped her wine, the bitterness catching the back of her throat.

"I'm just being friendly and welcoming," Emily said. Even to her the words lacked conviction. "If you change your mind…"

"This phone number thing's a game, isn't it?"

"Pardon?"

"I've heard about you girls. Trying to score phone numbers."

"I… It's kind of…" A wave of heat rushed over her face and she coughed. She put her glass down on the table. This wasn't working out the way it was supposed to. Was that the reputation she, Lisa, Marie and Andrea had? Andrea was signalling for a refill for her glass. Emily squared back her shoulders. If Ricky was going to play hard to get then so would she.

"I need some refills for my friends. I'll have two pinot gris and a chardonnay." *Let's see how he handles this.*

Ricky looked at her with a blank expression. He turned around to inspect the bottles on the table cautiously picking up a few of them and putting them back down again. He had no clue.

"I think the chardonnay is that one there," she said, pointing to the closest bottle.

He threw her a sarcastic glance.

Another couple had walked up and without waiting for an acknowledgement from Ricky, asked for a merlot and a riesling.

Ricky turned one way, then back, lost in confusion. "I'll be with you in just a moment, sir." He poured the chardonnay. In an effort to speed things up he moved too fast and knocked over the glasses.

Feminine laughter rippled through the air.

"Oh crap!" Ricky exclaimed.

"Oh dear." Emily watched glasses roll off the table, crash into one another and wine splash everywhere.

"We'll get our drinks from him," the male said, pointing towards one of the roving waiters.

Ricky's face flushed. He grabbed a glass to stop it from rolling off the table, but in his haste knocked more glasses over.

The laughter grew louder.

"Let me help," Emily said. She set her handbag on the ground, righted a couple of glasses and risked a glance over towards her friends. Lisa was sniggering behind her hand while Marie and Andrea clutched each other, giggling.

"It seems like I'm putting on a good show for your friends," said Ricky. A cross between a smirk and a grin flickered across his lips.

Guilt expanded in Emily's chest. "It's just an accident. I'll help dry the tablecloth for you." She picked up a couple of serviettes.

"Don't bother. Despite your low opinion of me not being able to pronounce wine names, I can clear up my own mess." His voice bristled with scorn.

Emily shrank back. She twisted a serviette around her left hand.

Ricky snatched the serviette from her.

She drew her hand back and buried it in her dress. "I'm sorry. I didn't mean-"

"Everything okay here, Ricky?" One of the male waiters had returned.

"Just a bit of an accident." He picked up more serviettes and mopped up the remaining wine on the tablecloth.

"Can I get you a drink?" the waiter asked Emily.

"She's decided to get one from one of the other waiters," said Ricky, glaring at Emily.

"Oh, yes, sure." Her thirst had disappeared. She picked up her handbag and wandered back to her friends who were still giggling.

"You got yourself a real klutz there," said Lisa, swallowing the last of her wine.

"Did you see him try and tidy it up? The more he tried the worse he made it," Andrea said.

"And you still came back with no wine," Marie said.

Emily sat down on the couch.

"Did you at least get his phone number?" Marie asked.

"What do you think?" Emily snapped.

"Don't worry. He didn't look like your type."

Emily brushed back her hair. *My type. What is my type?* Josh, her ex-fiancé, who'd left after the accident? The men who didn't take things past the first date once they saw her disfigured hand?

She looked toward the drink gazebo. Ricky was setting up again, slowly placing glasses on a tray. This game had turned out badly. No phone number, but that wasn't what was bothering her. Lisa's game had gone too far this time. And she'd left Ricky not only mopping up a mess but licking his wounds from the public humiliation she had caused.

Chapter 2

Emily wiped a cotton ball dipped in skin toner over her face. Sunday morning, and she'd risen early to meet with Stan, the project manager of Gardenway Homes, to discuss progress on the house she was having built.

She looked in the mirror as she combed her short, straight black hair, smoothed moisturiser over her face and applied eyeliner on the rim of her eyelids, accentuating her deep-set violet eyes.

Scanning her wardrobe she finally settled on dark blue jeans and a crisp, white T-shirt. Casual but professional.

She tiptoed out of her room, down the hall and into the kitchen.

Marie was sitting at the breakfast bar. "Hey," she mumbled, her mouth full of toast.

"Morning." Emily reached up to take a bowl out of the cupboard. "The other two still in bed?"

"It's early Sunday morning. What do you expect?"

Emily smiled. Nothing much changed there. Lisa and Andrea were the night owls and Emily and Marie were the early birds.

"What are you up to today?" asked Emily.

"The hiking club is going to tackle Red Hill. It's a gentle two-hour hike. Would you like to come along?"

"Thanks for the invite, but I'm off to check on the house."

"It must be exciting to see it take shape."

"Yeah, but it's stressful, particularly when your family has lent you the money to get it started. Fortunately they're not charging me interest." The whole house building process was taking up heaps of time. She didn't know much about building a house, but she was learning fast.

Two years ago her older brother, David, and two older sisters, Bridget and Yvette, had joined with her in partnership so she could build her own house. They'd all pitched in and bought the land together. she had paid the first instalment to get the foundations poured. They had each paid $20,000 to start the next phase – the framing and the roof. Emily had taken out a bank loan for her $20,000. Her dream of owning a house, having her own space had been a welcome distraction after Josh had walked out.

"I think what you're doing is very brave," Marie said, as she buttered another piece of toast. "I'm going to wait for a sugar daddy to turn up before I commit to anything that money-hungry."

Emily poured the cereal and milk in her bowl then sliced some strawberries on top. She gazed out of the large window into the garden. The grass seemed beyond hope, all dried up from the summer heat. She was the only one who had tried to keep the lawn watered regularly. She'd planted flowers around the outside of the house but they kept dying. A combination of the wrong type of soil, lack of fertiliser and a puny irrigation system hadn't helped. She was already planning the garden at her new house. A cereal flake caught in her throat and she coughed. "Marie?"

"Hmm…"

"You know the waiter guy at the garden party yesterday?"

"The one who shouldn't have been there, the one who didn't know what he was doing?"

"The one we laughed at," Emily said.

"Yeeesss." Marie looked at Emily sideways. "You like him!"

"No, no, no. I just felt really uncomfortable afterwards at the way we treated him. It wasn't very nice."

"Oh, come on. We were only having a bit of fun," she said, as she popped the last bit of toast into her mouth.

"We embarrassed him and it's been bugging me." Emily chased half a strawberry around her bowl with a spoon.

"Hey, we play this game all the time. I bet what's annoying you is you didn't get his phone number."

"No. I just don't feel right about it."

"So, you've a conscience now?"

Emily shuffled in her seat. "I think I should apologise."

"And get his phone number."

"Will you stop going on about his phone number?" She stabbed the strawberry slice with her spoon splitting it in two.

Marie propped her elbows onto the breakfast bar. "I think that would be a chivalrous thing for you to do."

Emily threw the last strawberry slice at Marie.

"You could've at least aimed for my mouth." Marie brushed the slice off her arm and onto the bench.

"I'm trying to be serious."

"Go for it," Marie said. "How are you going to track him down?"

"Not sure. But it can't be too hard. It's a small town. Someone will know him."

"Good luck. I'd like to know where this goes. After seeing his reaction yesterday you might want to wear some armour." Marie looked at her watch. "I'd better get going." She grabbed her backpack and headed out the door.

***

Emily drove down Misty Springs' Main Street. She passed the town's most famous tourist drawcard – the sulphur thermal pools – where big steam plumes rose into the air. Backdropped by mountains and the Waiau River, the tiny town – population 840 – was a naturalist and adventurers paradise with activities ranging from jet boating and bungy jumping to mountain biking. Heading out towards Hillview, one of the new subdivisions that were sprouting up around the edges of town, she passed area covered with native bush. In the distance, a patchwork of fields all the way back to the rolling hills. She loved the big open spaces, the fresh clean air and the unhurried, casual way of life. She'd bought the land at the right time – just before prices had begun creeping steadily upwards. If she'd left it another year it would've definitely been out of her reach, even with financial help from her family.

Emily pulled down the visor so the early morning sun didn't hit her straight in the eye. The asphalt on Old Bridge Road ended and the road narrowed. She drove over the old wooden bridge and past the lavender bushes that blurred in a purple haze. Big pine trees rose up on either side. She pulled the car into the gravel driveway.

Stan hadn't arrived yet, but she got out of the car and walked onto the grass where survey pegs dotted the section. There was a port-a-loo in one corner, a rubbish pile in another and a Gardenway Homes sign out front. In the corner, stood a big willow tree that she insisted remain on the section. She had plans for the tree.

Emily looked at her phone. – 9.10. *Their meeting was at 9. Wasn't it?* She checked her calendar. Yes, 9.00 Sunday. *Where was Stan?*

She was about to give him a call when a black station wagon roared up.

"Hey, sorry I'm late," Stan yelled, as he got out of the car. "The kids were taking forever with breakfast and the wife is sick so it's been chaotic."

"No worries. I just got here."

Stan walked over to Emily straightening his T-shirt over a small pot belly. He looked like he'd just gotten out of bed with his stubbly cheeks and slightly greasy brown hair. "So, as you can see the concrete foundation has been poured. Come over and have a look.”

Emily walked over toward the concrete slab. Finally, her house was beginning to take shape. Concrete wasn’t anything to get excited about, but it was a start and she was getting closer to her goal.

“What happens next?” Emily asked.

“The framing crew will put in the sill plates, walls and then the roof structure.”

“I’d like that to start this week.”

“Yeah, sure.” Stan reached into his pocket and pulled out his phone. “Sorry, I just need to take this.”

Emily looked again at the huge concrete slab. Once the framing was up she’d be able to get a better idea of how the house would look. While Stan yacked on the phone, she grabbed the house blueprints out of her car so she could compare the blueprints with the foundation. *Having the plans round the right way would be a good start!* Emily turned the blueprints so they were directly facing the front of the slab. Or were they? She squinted at the blueprints. She had never been much good at reading plans and directions. She smiled. *What was that saying? Women can’t read maps?*

Stan was still on the phone. *Some help around about now would be good.* She turned the plan around again.

“Hey, sorry about that,” Stan said.

The guy seemed to be forever apologising.

"Can you help me? I'm not sure I've got the plan-."

"Look, sorry. I'm going to have to go. Family emergency." Stan pointed towards town. "We can have a proper catch-up next week after the framing's gone in. Something more exciting for you to look at, aye? I'll text you with a time."

Before Emily had a chance to respond Stan was in the car, backing down the drive then heading toward town. *Great. He hadn't been any help.* She sighed, scratching her head. There wasn't much to see anyway. Maybe after the framing was completed she'd have a better idea of how it was all going to come together.

Emily rolled up the blueprints and placed them in the back of her car. Her next mission was to do some digging around to find out how she could make amends with the garden party waiter. *What was his name again? Richard... Ricardo... Ritchie.* The name would come back to her she was sure. But until it did she had little to go on.

Chapter 3

Early Monday morning Emily stepped out of the bathroom with a towel wrapped around her.

Overall she enjoyed living with the girls, but the one thing she'd learnt was, if you weren't in the bathroom first, you'd never get to work on time. It definitely helped if you were also an early riser. Routines had been established. The larks, she and Marie, were typically in the bathroom first and then Lisa and Andrea fought it out for the next spot.

Emily passed Marie in the hall.

"Ouch! Ouch!" Marie exclaimed, clutching her calf.

"I thought you said it was going to be a gentle hike," Emily said.

"There are obviously different interpretations of gentle."

Emily smiled. "Oh, you poor thing."

"Any luck with the garden party guy?"

"I'm having trouble remembering his name so haven't gotten very far."

Marie pushed the bathroom door open. "I wonder if I can risk a long soak in the bath."

"Hey, can you keep it down?" Lisa yelled from her bedroom. "Some of us are trying to sleep."

"Hot water's almost out," Emily yelled back, winking at Marie.

"You don't really want to upset the boss first thing Monday morning," Marie said.

"It'll be your head on the block if you really do use up all the hot water."

"I'll take my chances." Marie closed the bathroom door.

Emily pulled on her bright red smock that scratched her skin. She had no idea why Lisa had chosen these smocks. Red had never been one of her favourite colours; it was too loud, too energetic, and too hot. None of the feelings she wanted or wanted her clients to have.

After breakfast she left the house and wandered down the main street. The beauty of living so close to work in a small town was that she didn't need to use her car.

The morning sun peeked through the mist surrounding the huge pine trees that lined the middle of the street. There hadn't been any rain for at least a week and the scent of dry pine needles hung heavy in the air.

The street was mainly empty. Because of the mist some camper vans were slowly driving by and a few locals were out walking their dogs.

Emily crossed the road, walked past the shops and cafes and turned left into the Serenity Day Spa.

Normally the first one in, she was keen to set the spa up in preparation for her first clients.

Scanning the computer, she noted a meeting at 9 and appointments at 10, 11.30, 2 and 4. A normal quiet Monday.

Although that could change. The spa was currently experiencing a higher number of walk-ins, mainly tourists. She tried to book them in between scheduled appointments. The more appointments, the more money she made. The girls operated on a profit/expense share system. On top of the weekly wage Lisa paid her, she, Marie and Andrea also got a monthly bonus depending on how many new clients each of them brought in and the overall profit for that month.

Emily turned the light on in her treatment room. She would have plenty of time to set up in preparation for her 10 am appointment.

It was a small internal room with no natural lighting. The enclosed area could be claustrophobic, but Emily had hung mirrors along one wall which opened up the room.

The walls were brown and accented by red ornaments, a red throw rug and cushion. *Ugh! The red thing again.* She had subtly dropped hints to Lisa about changing the furnishings but Lisa had insisted the room remain the same so the "décor flowed throughout the salon."

Running her hand over the crisp, white sheets she straightened them, switched the electric blanket on to low and dimmed the lights.

She double-checked the supply of towels in the linen cupboard, topped up the water cooler and set up clean glasses. Turning the CD player on, she popped in a sleep lullaby disc and then opened the small wooden box that contained her aromatherapy oils. The salon had oils that Lisa wanted the girls to use but Emily had insisted on using her preferred brand. They were expensive but high quality oils made by a local South Island provider. Reluctantly Lisa had given in.

Her 10 am would be Gabby, a regular, who liked a de-stressing aromatherapy massage. She pulled out the lavender, chamomile, white chamomile, marjoram and orange oils, mixed them up, and poured some of the mixture into a spray bottle.

Noises down the hall indicated that the others had arrived.

She checked her watch. Almost 9. Time for the team meeting.

Emily shut the door, grabbed a big glass of water from the kitchen and made her way into the meeting room.

Emily asked Marie, "How's your calf?"

"Better. The long soak helped, but Lisa's mad at me. I did use up all the hot water."

"Oh dear."

"Not good. She washed her hair in cold water and because she got up late, she didn't have time to blow dry it so she looks like a drowned puppy."

"Who's a drowned puppy?" Lisa asked, poking her head into the room.

"No one," Marie replied.

"I've just got to fix something up then I'll be back in a minute. A new box of natural moisturisers arrived. Would you like to have a look?" Lisa asked

"Sure," Emily replied. She took the box from Lisa and placed it on the table. This was one of the cool parts of the job – getting to try new products. "I feel like a kid in a lolly shop." She pulled out a couple of small purple bottles, opened one and sniffed. "Quite strong." She turned the bottle around to look at the back of it. She scanned through the ingredients. Propylene Glyrol, Triethanolomine, DMDM, Hyantoin, Petrolatum, Methylparaben, Propylparaben, Carbomer. *Natural? No way.*

Lisa popped her head back in. "Sorry, Emily. I didn't think Andrea would make it into work today. She's still hungover from last night. And she obviously forgot the team meeting at 9. She's booked a client in. You'll have to do it."

"I've an appointment at 10," Emily said. "That's cutting it too fine."

"I'll do it," offered Marie. "My first isn't until 11."

"I'd like Emily to do it," Lisa replied. "We'll cancel today's team meeting. You can help me with getting a window display set up with these new products." She turned to Emily. "I've put the client in your room. His health history form is at reception."

"Right," Emily said. "I'd better get started."

She picked up the client form from the desk and read the general medical history. He'd ticked back pain, neck pain and bursitis. He'd had no surgery... didn't wear contacts... no prescription medications…. no allergies… and there was nothing in 'other'. He'd signed the consent form in an illegible scrawl. She turned back over to the front page. No phone numbers, no address, Hmm… a mystery guy. What was the guy's name? Ricky. The name rang a bell.

Time to find out more. She knocked on the door of the treatment room, waited, then stepped inside.

The guy was sitting on the chair, his leg jiggling up and down.

She stopped dead in her tracks. It was the garden party guy. Ricky. "Oh. It's… You."

Ricky stared at her. "I don't believe it. You."

"Oh… I… Um…" *God, how embarrassing was this?* A wave of heat travelled across her chest and she wanted to itch the place where her ring and index finger should've been.

"Disadvantage of a small town," Ricky said.

Emily stared at the ceiling. *How would she play this?* She could apologise for her thoughtlessness from Saturday. Or maybe she'd just be professional and not mention it.

Ricky's leg stopped jiggling.

She'd play the professional card, referring to his health form. "So you were booked in for a massage with Andrea. Andrea's sick today so I've taken over her appointment. Unless you'd like to rebook or have someone else do it?"

Ricky smiled. "No. You'll do. Emily, is it?" His eyes averted to her chest where her name tag was pinned.

How was this for de je vu? "Yes, well, you're here for a deep tissue massage, is that right?"

"Yip."

"Have you had one before?"

"Nope."

A one-word guy. Great. "What do you do for an occupation? I see you've left 'occupation' blank."

"I'm a builder."

"Oh, I thought you were a waiter."

"Just casual work."

"Right. Shouldn't you be at work then?"

"Boss lady, Christine, sends all her builders for massages once a week. This is my day off."

"That's a nice thing for Christine to do." Christine ran one of the local building companies in Misty Springs. She'd seen her in Red Hill Bar with her builders on Friday and Saturday nights.

"I'm not really into this massage thing. A bit girly for me."

"You might be surprised how helpful massage can be for you. I see you've put a tick beside back and neck pain. Tell me about that."

"Nothing major." Ricky rubbed his lower back. "Just gets a bit sore at the end of the day from all the lifting and climbing."

"OK. I'll see what's going on then. Any questions before we get started?"

"Nope. I'm actually looking forward to this now."

I bet you are. How was she going to say the next thing without blushing? *Stay in control.* But the words came rushing out. "If you could just take off your clothes. Leave your underwear on and get under the first towel." She patted the bed with her right hand but didn't dare look at him. "Face down with the head in the hole and I'll be right back." She bolted from the room bumping into Marie in the hall. "You won't believe this," she whispered.

"What?"

"The guy in there." She pointed to the room. "Ricky."

Marie's face was blank.

"The garden party guy."

"Nooo."

"Yes."

"How bizarre."

"My thoughts precisely. There must be some kind of bad karma going around today."

Marie laughed. "This is perfect. You wanted to apologise. Here's your chance. And you can get his phone number too."

"You're no help."

"I can't wait to see how this turns out."

Emily looked at her watch. "Do you think that's enough time? I'd hate to walk in on him, you know... He's trying to make things difficult for me."

"Like we made things difficult for him?"

"Yeah, and now *I'm* the one paying for it."

Marie sniggered. "Get in there and get it over with."

Emily knocked on the door, waited a second and then entered. Thank God. Ricky was lying face down on the table, the towel over his back and mid-section.

"OK. I'm just going to mix up some oils for you and we'll begin. You all right there?"

Ricky grunted.

She presumed that was a yes. Studying the oils in the box and settling on lavender, lemongrass and bergamot, she mixed them together and poured them into a spray bottle.

"Okay," Emily said, lowering her voice and moving around to the bottom of the table. "I'm just going to align you straighter on the table." She moved Ricky's feet so that his body was aligned properly. Stepping back to the head of the table, she placed both hands on his shoulders, gave them a slight squeeze then ran her hands down his back. She took a deep breath, pulled the towel all the way down and tucked it into his underwear. *Focus. Focus.* She concentrated on his tanned skin – hairless back and head. He obviously worked with his shirt off.

She squirted the warm oil onto her hands and spread it over his back running her forearm up his back and then down avoiding pushing on the spine. With the physiotherapy she'd received over the last few years she'd been able to improvise her massage technique using the thumb of her left hand for some of the basic strokes. She moved down to Ricky's lower back and used her fingertips and thumbs to probe the muscles in his lower back. They were as tight as guitar strings.

"There's quite a bit of tension here," Emily said, her voice still lowered.

Ricky moaned.

"How's the pressure?"

"Good." His voice was muffled by the hole in the table.

She applied more pressure.

Ricky moaned again.

"Okay?"

"Yeah."

The moan didn't sound like it was one of pain. More from relief.

"You're holding your muscles stiffly. Just relax." Emily immediately felt the muscle release. "Good."

She was starting to get into her stride, finding momentum and rhythm. His muscles were well defined and strong, his shoulders broad and his backbone fleshy. Her hands slid easily over the contours, dips and rises.

Shaking away the lightheadedness, she concentrated on his lower back, working on the knots, sinking her finger tips into the tense muscles.

"Ouch!"

"Sorry." She eased off on the pressure and applied more oil onto her hands. With a variety of movements – stroking, smoothing, and gliding – she worked diligently at loosening his muscles.

She glanced at the clock. Five minutes to go. "Ricky. We've almost finished. How's your back feeling?"

Silence.

"Ricky?"

A wee snort erupted from his nose; he'd fallen asleep.

She grinned. The best compliment a massage therapist could have. Now she had to wake him up. "Ricky. We're done," she whispered. She put her hand on his shoulder and gently squeezed.

"Huh?"

"The hour's up. How are you feeling?"

Another grunt.

"I'm just going to leave the room now. When you're ready, get dressed and I'll pop back with a glass of water."

Emily left the room. She welcomed the cooler air in the reception area where Gabby was waiting for her. "Hi, Gabby. I'm just finishing with a client. I won't be long."

Emily looked at the clock. She'd give him another couple of minutes. She filled up a glass with cold water, knocked on the door and entered the room.

Ricky was dressed and sitting on the table. She handed him the glass of water.

"How's the back?"

"Mmm." He took a big gulp.

She watched him. He had that dreamy, out-of-this-world look the majority of her clients had when they'd had a treatment.

He drained the glass and handed it back to her.

"So you're not working today?" she asked.

"No. Why?" He looked at her suspiciously, with his brown eyes.

Does he think I'm being nosey? "You need to let the muscles settle. It would be a good idea to take it easy today. Drink lots of water. It'll help flush out the toxins.

"You might need to drink some water too."

"Oh," she said. "Why's that?"

"You look flustered. And a little hot."

The cheek! She played with the towel on the bed. "Would you like to make another appointment?" she stammered. "With Andrea. I'm asking this because that's what we ask all our clients. It's not personal."

"Let me think about it. As I said I'm not really into massage. I'm only here because Christine thinks it's a good healthy thing to do."

"Okay, that's fine," Emily said, lowering her head. "About the other day-"

"I'd better go," Ricky said.

"Sure. We can fix up payment on the way out."

Emily held the door open and escorted him to the reception area. "Looks like this is already been paid for by

Christine. Not too many bosses would pay for massages for their employees."

"Yeah. I guess so but like I said-"

"You're not into massages."

"Right."

"Okay then. I'll let you go. Have a nice day," she said to his retreating back.

"You too," he said.

Ricky walked slowly down the path. When he got to the gate he turned, looked at her card then her, holding her gaze with his dreamy eyes.

Her heart beat a little faster.

Chapter 4

The week flew by. The girls were run ragged with 12-hour days and back-to-back appointments at the salon.

They left work in the evenings walking back together to the house. Too tired to cook they ordered takeaways and drank wine.

After her final appointment on Friday, Emily breathed a sigh of relief. She cleaned the room and set it up for Monday.

She checked her phone and sighed. Stan still hadn't returned her phone call and she made a note to ring him.

Two things left to do. She checked out the window display that Lisa and Marie had created with the new Nature's One products. She picked up one of the bottles, opened it and inhaled. The strong, chemical scent came back to her. There were a heap of chemicals in these products.

Emily stood back and looked at the display. Lisa and Marie had stacked the body creams and moisturisers on top of each other to form a pyramid. Along with the company's promotional material, they'd designed some additional flyers. There was one word that stood out – natural. *These products weren't at all natural. Had Lisa not read the ingredients? That would be typical of Lisa. Rushing into everything.*

"Are you coming with us to the bar tonight?" Marie asked, after she saw her last client out.

"I could really do with a night in and a healthy meal," Emily said, stretching her back.

"I need to blow off some steam. Lisa and Andrea are keen. Come on, one drink and then you can be a party pooper."

"Okay. I don't think I need too much convincing. I might even stay for a meal. What do you think of these Nature's One products?" she asked, changing the subject.

"Have you tried them? I've been trying them out on myself. They're quite rich and the smell is intense," Marie said, screwing up her nose.

Emily frowned. "I don't think they're as natural as they claim to be."

"I'm sure Lisa's checked it all out. I bet your creations will be much better."

"Speaking of which I'd better just check on them." Emily wandered into the back room-cum-kitchen-cum spare room.

She'd been experimenting with making her own cosmetics over the last few weeks. This was something she'd always wanted to try. She had not yet fully defined her vision, but the idea of being able to make her own cosmetics to use in the salon was definitely a part of it.

Her latest creation was lavender and magnesium body butter. She'd always been interested in the sleep-assisted powers of lavender. Combined with the magnesium, a body butter applied to the skin just before bedtime could calm the body further, helping provide a better night's sleep. Last week she'd made a large batch totalling ten containers and had left them out on the bench. She unscrewed the lid of one jar and on top were little mould spores.

"Oh no." She undid the next lid. Same. More mould. She quickly undid the lids of the remaining containers. "No. No." All the mixtures had greeny-blue mould patches on them. Totally ruined and unusable. She scratched her head. *What have I done wrong?* Using rubber gloves, she furiously scooped out the containers dumping the offensive mixture into the trash can then washing away any remaining goop in the containers. She sighed. She'd have to start all over again.

***

The girls ran back and forth between the bathroom and their bedrooms getting ready for their night out.

Emily pulled on a floral maxi dress with a halter neck. She massaged a natural tan moisturiser onto her arms and legs, spritzed *Beautiful* perfume in the hollow of her neck and carefully applied a pink lipstick. There were slight dark circles under her eyes. All she really wanted to do was to chill out at home and figure out what had gone wrong with the body butter.

She and Marie waited in the lounge while Lisa and Andrea finished.

"Come on. We're hungry," yelled Marie.

"Coming. Coming," Lisa said as she joined the girls in the lounge, followed by Andrea.

Lisa's short black skirt emphasised her long, tanned legs. Her low, red singlet top and short black mini skirt screamed, 'look at me'. Subtlety wasn't one of her strong points. "All right. Let's go."

They walked down the footpath; Lisa and Andrea behind Emily and Marie.

The sun, which had been streaming brightly all day, began its slow descent behind Red Hill. The pine trees threw long shadows across the street. Passing the steamy hot pools complex, laughter, splashing and shouts rang out as families went for a dip, making the most of the summer evening.

"Hey, Emily. How did your 9 am appointment go?" Lisa asked.

"Fine. Why?"

"Wasn't that the waiter want-to-be from the garden party?"

Did Lisa set me up? "Yes it was."

"He must've needed a de-stressing massage after Saturday's performance."

"He came in for a deep tissue massage. He's a builder. And he

was very nice."

"I hope he's a lot more co-ordinated on a building site," Lisa said.

"Why didn't you book him in with Marie?" Emily asked.

"And miss the fireworks. No way." Lisa and Andrea laughed.

So it had been a set up. But it was Lisa's game through and through. Stirring the pot. She sighed.

"You still haven't got his phone number," Lisa persisted.

Would she ever give up? "If we're playing the game tonight, leave me out of it. I'm bushed," Emily said.

Reaching Red Hill Bar, Emily pushed open the door and headed toward their usual spot, a booth overlooking the street with a view to the bush-clad Red Hill.

Country music played loudly and the Friday night work crowd was steadily filing in through the front door; the usual mix of office workers, retailers, and tourists.

"First round of drinks is on me," Lisa said.

"Yay," Andrea said. "Usual for me."

"Rum and coke," added Marie.

"OJ," said Emily.

"What are your weekend plans?" asked Andrea.

"No hiking for me. I'm still recovering from last week," Marie said. "Emily?"

"I need to chase up Stan, and I'll be making a new batch of body butter. The last one's grown mould."

"Eww!" Andrea exclaimed.

"I know. I can't use it or sell it like that."

"Where are our drinks?" Marie asked.

The girls turned towards the bar. Lisa was propped up on a stool drinking a glass of wine and chatting with a guy.

"God. She never stops and she seems to have forgotten our drinks," said Andrea, as she rolled her eyes.

The next sentence was drowned out by several voices as a bunch of guys crowded into the booth behind them.

"Where's a menu?"

"Who wants drinks first?"

"Have to take this call."

"I'm up for a drink."

Emily, Marie and Andrea turned around to watch the commotion. There seemed to be five of them but Emily couldn't tell for sure in the blur of heads and T-shirts. A combination of manly sweat and aftershave hung in the air.

"I think there're the new building crew," said Andrea. "There's been more men move in since the new subdivision started up."

"How do you know?" asked Marie. "They don't look like builders."

"I know," said Andrea. "I have experience in this area."

Emily turned back around. Builders. *Please don't let Ricky be here*. She couldn't face any more humiliation. Not until she figured out her next approach.

The music pumped out louder. The light from the window vanished as it grew darker and the sun completely disappeared. The noise had reached crescendo. Glasses clinked, plates came out with food for the early evening diners and laughter roared out from the bar.

"We could be waiting a while for our drinks," Marie said.

"I'll get them," replied Andrea, as she wriggled her way past Marie.

"And get some menus," Marie said.

Andrea arrived with the drinks and the menus. "I think we've seen the last of Lisa for the night."

"Is that the same guy from last Saturday night?" Emily asked.

"No. I think that's the guy from the previous weekend." Marie peered over towards the bar. "Anyway, I think we're on our own."

The girls ordered their meals. Emily settled on the mushroom risotto.

By 9 pm she'd had enough of the noise. "Hey guys. I think I'll head back."

"What? The night's still young. Look at all the men here. We're outnumbered," Marie said.

Before Emily had a chance to respond, Lisa joined them.

"I think we're back on," Lisa said, pointing her head towards the bar.

"Who?"

"Hunter."

"I didn't think you and Hunter were ever 'not' on."

"I'm sure I'm about to get lucky tonight," said Lisa. "Anyway, whose turn is it for drinks?"

"I'm just leaving," said Emily, gathering up her bag.

"Oh, come on. Stay."

"That's what I said," said Marie.

"I promise I'll behave," said Lisa, winking at Emily.

"Okay. Okay" Emily sighed. She really didn't want to be a party pooper or get on the wrong side of Lisa. "One more round and then I'm off." She made her way over to the bar, waited for her turn, then ordered the four drinks.

Now she had to get the drinks back to the girls, through the crowd. She manoeuvred the four glasses together and wrapped her right hand round the sides of her left hand fingers; forming a 'V' and supported the glasses with her thumbs. She'd never let her disfigured hand get in the way of achieving what she needed to do in both her work and social activities, but sometimes she over estimated what she was really capable of doing. *Maybe I should've asked for help.* She looked over at the girls who were laughing, but they weren't looking her way and the guys in the front booth were doing much the same – eating, laughing and drinking. She had a better view of all the guys now. One profile stood out from the others – bald head, goatee. Ricky. *Bother. Can I get past without him seeing me?* She'd have to.

She breathed in deeply, secured her fingers tighter around the glasses and lifted her hands up. The glasses were heavy and slippery.

As she moved carefully through the crowd, people stepped aside to make a clear path for her. *Careful. Careful. Steady. Keep your eye on the drinks.* She was almost at the guys' table.

"Hey Ricky. Isn't that the chick that gave you a massage?" one of the guys jeered.

"I wonder if she offers any other kind of massage," someone else responded.

Deep male laughter

Keep going. Ignore them. She inched past the booth.

"I've got a sore leg, ma'am. It's in need of some rubbing."

"I've got something else that needs rubbing." More laughter.

Heat rose in Emily's cheeks. The glasses were slipping. She adjusted her right hand but it was putting too much weight against her left hand.

"Do you make house visits?"

The glasses were slipping further; she gripped harder.

"Lay off guys." Ricky's voice was low, but the meaning was clear.

She was almost there, but a slight shift in weight unbalanced the glasses and they dropped to the floor with a loud crash. Wine, OJ and lemonade splashed up over her dress.

The whole bar went quiet. Then, loud laughing and clapping as faces turned to stare at Emily.

"Oh. Oops," one of the guys said. "Look what you made her do." He jabbed an elbow into his mate's ribs.

"Let's clean up the mess," said Marie. "I'll get a brush and shovel."

A roaring started in Emily's ears and tears pricked her eyes. The drinks, tiredness and stress of the week had finally gotten to her, and the air in the bar was suffocating.

She wiped a hand across her forehead. *I have to get out of here.* "I'm sorry…," she muttered, and scurried towards the door.

Outside she gulped in the cool night air. She walked across the road, her sandals flapping quickly on the concrete. Home. She just wanted to get home.

"Emily. Wait up." A voice came from behind.

It was Ricky's. She walked faster.

"Hey, wait up."

She had no intention of waiting up. She wanted to be as far away from the bar as possible.

His thudding footsteps grew closer. A hand grabbed her shoulder.

"Stop."

Emily whirled around. "Why? So you can rub it further in my face?"

Ricky's face clouded over. "Why would I want to do that?"

"Well, I suppose you're going to gloat now and say I deserved it. That I've had a taste of my own medicine and how does it feel?"

"Do you think I was that concerned about your little show at the garden party? Yip, it was embarrassing, but I'm over it. I've got a relatively thick skin. But I don't like to see others humiliated in public."

Emily gulped. "Great mates you have. Are they always like that?"

"Yip. They're guys. What do you expect?"

Emily shivered and wrapped her arms around her. She pulled her left fingers into a fist.

Ricky's eyes studied her left hand. "You've had an injury to your hand?"

So he'd noticed. She clenched her fist tighter. "It's nothing," she said quietly. "I shouldn't have tried to carry so many glasses at once. I sometimes overestimate what I can do."

"It doesn't seem to affect the way you massage."

"Is that supposed to be a smart comment?"

"No. Not at all. You're very defensive."

"I'm not."

A slow smile curled at the edges of Ricky's mouth. "I think your massage techniques are great. Although I've nothing to compare it to. My back is feeling much better."

"You don't have to lie."

"I'm not lying. Why can't you just accept a compliment?" Ricky's white T-shirt stuck out under the street lamps emphasising the muscles in his biceps.

Her heart skipped a beat. She looked away. "Thank you," she whispered.

She wanted to be as far away from Ricky as possible but she could use this opportunity to do what she had wanted to do since the garden party. "Look, I'm sorry for what I did the other day. It was petty and stupid and immature." She breathed out, glad that that was over and done with.

"Apology accepted." Ricky looked at her "You know, I think we got off on the wrong foot. Let's start over. I'm Ricky." He held out his hand.

"Emily." She shook his hand, his grip was strong yet gentle and caring.

"Where were you going?" Ricky asked.

"Home. I live just down the road."

"I'm going that way too. Mind some company?"

Emily hesitated for a moment "Okay."

They walked down the footpath in silence. The tops of the trees stirred with the gentle shift of wind. Five minutes later they'd reached Emily's house.

"I live here," she said, gesturing towards the house.

Emily shivered again.

"You're cold. We could stand outside chatting while you shiver away or you could invite me in."

"That's bold."

"We're just getting to know each other. But I bet we could do it some place warmer."

"Okay." She held open the wooden gate and he stepped through. "Would you like some coffee?" she asked, as she opened the front door and switched on the lights.

"Sure."

"Make yourself comfortable in the lounge. How do you like your coffee?"

"Black."

She made a cup of coffee for Ricky and a lemon and ginger tea for herself then sat opposite him in the lounge after handing him the mug.

"Do you live by yourself?"

"No with Lisa, Marie and Andrea. The girls I was with tonight. I work with them as well."

"Their bad influence is rubbing off on you."

"To be honest, I'm not all that keen on those games we play."

"Scored any men?"

"Let's just say I've had limited success. What about you?"

"Single at the moment. I've been moving round a bit so it's hard to have a relationship."

"Nice place, "said Ricky. His builder's eyes travelled along the wooden beams.

"I'm only flatting here. I'm having a place built out at Hillview."

"Who's doing the building?"

"Gardenway Homes."

"Oh?" Ricky raised his eyebrows.

"There's supposed to be a framing crew working on my house at the moment but I haven't heard anything from Stan, the project manager. Is there a problem?"

"I'd heard that they'd finished all the framing around here and had gone back to the city. They won't be back for another month. But that might just be a rumour."

"I should follow their progress up tomorrow. Whereabouts are you working?"

"Morningside," he said, referring to another sub-division on the other side of town.

"Have you always been a builder?"

"Pretty much," said Ricky, draining his mug.

"What's with the bar tending?"

"You gotta do what you gotta do." Ricky looked at his watch. "I really need to go." He stood up.

"Oh," said Emily, startled by the abrupt end to the conversation as she stood up as well. "I'm glad that we've managed to clear the air. I hope you don't think I'm shallow."

"Umm..." Ricky winked at her sending tingles up her spine.

"Oh, come on." Emily placed her hand on his arm. He'd seen her left hand now and it hadn't seemed to have bothered him.

"I accept your apology but it doesn't mean I've forgiven you," said Ricky.

"What do you mean by that?"

"Would you like to come out with me on Sunday?"

"Oh," Emily said. "Like on a date?"

"I'm not sure that I'd define it that way."

"Oh," she said again.

"How about coming with me to the Rahu A and P Show. I'm competing in the wood chopping."

"Wood chopping?"

"Yes. You've heard of such a thing?"

"Yes, but I've never seen a wood chopping competition."

"Great. It'll be a new experience for you."

"Uh, okay."

"There's a catch though."

Emily cocked her head.

"Seen as I haven't completely forgiven you, you'll have to drive us there."

"Drive you?"

"Yes."

"Don't you have a car?"

"Not at the moment."

"Seems unusual for a guy not to have a car."

Ricky didn't reply.

"How do you know I have a car?"

"I've seen you driving around in your hatchback."

"Spying on me now?"

"It's a small town."

Emily considered his proposal. "Okay. I'll take you. But then we're even."

"Then we're even."

"What's your phone number and I'll put your details in my phone. We can make further arrangements later?"

"How about I pop round and see you tomorrow?"

"That's convenient now that you know where I live." She opened the front door and they walked down the path.

"When would be a good time?"

"How about tomorrow mid-morning?"

"Good for me."

They'd reached the gate.

"So where do you live?" Emily asked.

"Just down there." He pointed vaguely down the road towards the south end of town.

"Out in the valley?"

"Kind of. Anyway, see you tomorrow."

And he was off, disappearing into the night.

Well, I did apologise. Now she was intrigued by Ricky. No, more than intrigued. He was a complete mystery. He'd refused to give her his phone number, had no car, gave a vague indication of where he lived and offered no details about his Morningside job. And what did he mean by 'you gotta do what you gotta do'? But was it the unanswered questions that intrigued her or was it the fire that stirred within her whenever he was near?

Chapter 5

Emily woke early on Saturday morning. She didn't work weekends – she needed the time to devote to the new house.

Marie was in the kitchen pouring coffee.

"Full day of clients?" Emily asked.

Marie nodded. "Two spots free but I'm sure they'll get filled up quickly with walk-ins."

"I'll walk down with you. I need to start a new batch of body butter.

"Great. I'll be ready in two ticks."

Emily finished her cereal and fruit, and wandered into the lounge.

On top of the bookcase were bunches of lavender she had picked up from Nana Rose a few weekends ago. She'd been meaning to dry them properly, but the insane work schedule and tending to the new house and had left her with little time.

Nana Rose, Emily's only living grandparent, lived 150 kms from Misty Springs on a small lifestyle block. The days had gone when Nana Rose and Grandpa Tom had raised sheep. When Grandpa died, Nana sold the sheep but still took in orphan lambs from neighbouring farms. Apart from the odd lamb that stayed on, there were now only two goats. Nana Rose grew lavender which she sold to a pillow making company. This brought in an income that allowed her to stay in her home.

Emily had visited Nana Rose a couple of weeks ago. She'd asked if she could have some lavender to use in her cosmetics. Nana Rose had cut big bunches of longer stems, tied a pink ribbon around each bunch and presented them to her granddaughter.

Emily removed the ribbons and replaced them with a rubber band because the lavender would shrink further as it dried. She tied a piece of string around each bunch and hung them upside down along the curtain rail in her bedroom. She brought one of the bunches up to her nose, inhaling in the soothing scent.

There was a knock on her bedroom door.

"I'm ready," Marie said.

They walked down the footpath. Even at this early time of the day the sky was a clear blue. The tall pine trees stood still, reaching up towards the sky. In the distance, pockets of mist hugged Red Hill. The mist that always calmed her.

"How are you feeling about what happened at the bar?" Marie asked.

Emily shifted her bag to her right shoulder. "Embarrassed. Thanks for cleaning up. I should've stayed, but all I could feel was those guys' staring at me. But what made it worse was that Ricky was there too." *Why do my cheeks burn and my insides flip when I say his name?*

"What happened? I saw him run out after you."

"He was quite gentlemanly actually. We both acknowledged we'd got off on the wrong foot so we both – well,

I – apologised. He stayed for coffee and then, the cheek of it, he's somehow managed to wrangle me into driving him to the Rahu A and P Show tomorrow. He's competing in the wood chopping."

Marie scratched her arm. "Well, you're more than making up for your guilt."

"I could've said no…"

"You're blushing! Ah, so you like him," Marie said, scratching her other arm.

Emily turned her head the other way as they crossed the road. "He does have a very good body."

"Mmm. Maybe I'll have to get in on the act as well." Marie laughed.

"Remember, he's Andrea's client. We'll have to steal him away from her first. Above the neck, he's not the kind of guy I'd go for. No hair, goatee. I think it's his eyes. Sometimes I feel like they're boring into me with such intensity, trying to read my secrets."

"Have you told him about what happened to your hand, and Josh?"

"Too soon for that. I don't want to scare him away. But I think he's got a few secrets of his own."

"Why is my skin so itchy?" Marie raked her nails back and forth across her arm.

They'd arrived at the salon.

"Here, let me have a look at that," Emily said, turning Marie's arm toward the light.

Little bumps ran across the skin on both arms, red and raw from Marie's scratching.

"Something must've bitten me last night," Marie said, as she scratched her arm again.

"I've got some aloe vera cream in my room."

"That'd be great. It wouldn't be a good look for my clients if I'm scratching all day."

After Emily gave Marie the aloe vera cream she walked down to the kitchen.

First, she needed to make an infusion for the rosemary and lavender soap she was experimenting with. She boiled the water, then poured it over some lavender flowers and rosemary leaves, leaving the mixture to steep for ten minutes.

She gathered the ingredients to make a new batch of body butter. Combining the shea butter, avocado oil and emulsifying wax in a jar and heated the mixture thoroughly while stirring. Once the mixture was cool, she then poured it into a bowl then stirred it using an immersion blender while adding the magnesium oil.

She placed the bowl in the fridge for 20 minutes then removed it. The mixture now looked like butter. The shea butter, lavender and rosemary combined to create what Emily could only describe as a heavenly, inviting scent. She whipped the butter a final time then scooped it into sterilised jars.

Emily stood back and surveyed the jars. *Cross fingers that this time it will work.* She breathed out lightly. She was sure she hadn't made any mistakes in either the ingredient quantities or the process.

After she walked back to the house, she changed her clothes and then drove out to the sub-division.

Getting out of the car, she groaned. The site looked the same as it had last Saturday.

She walked over to the concrete foundations. No framing had gone up. She put her hands on her hips. *What had Ricky said yesterday?* That the framing crews had left Misty Springs? But her framing still needed to go up. And where was the timber for the framing? It was no longer where it had been last week. Had it been stolen? By the framing crew?

She pulled her phone out of her bag and dialled Stan's number.

A female voice started speaking. "The number you have called is no longer in operation. Please try again."

What? This was a number in her contacts. She had dialled it many times. She tried again but got the same response.

Confused she stared at her phone. A flicker of apprehension twitched inside her. All sorts of scenarios played through her mind: network outage, or Stan had changed cell phone numbers. There was probably not much she could do about it until Monday but she'd have another chat to Ricky. See if he'd heard anything more.

She drove back to the house and pulled into the drive. There was Ricky sitting on the porch.

"Hi," Emily said, getting out of the car. "Have you been waiting for me?"

"Hmm mmm," Ricky said, getting up.

"What have you been doing?"

"Just watching the world go by. I don't often get much time to myself. It's been quite relaxing. What have you been doing?"

"I went out to my house to see what's been going on."

"And?"

Emily's chest tightened. "Nothing. The framing crew hasn't started, the timber is gone and the weird thing is, I keep getting a disconnect message from Stan's number."

"Sounds dodgy."

"You don't know anything more, do you?"

"No. Nothing new since last night. I'm sure it's nothing but I'd definitely check it out on Monday."

"That's what I thought." Her stomach growled. "I was going to grab some lunch at Café Steam. Would you like to join me?"

"Thanks but I've got to get going."

Emily's shoulders slumped.

"About tomorrow..." Ricky said.

"You're still wanting a lift?"

"If that's okay."

"It seems I haven't got much choice if I'm going to keep my end of the bargain."

"Hey, if it's a hassle don't worry. I'll hitch a ride somehow."

"No. I'm staying true to my word."

Ricky smiled. "Good. For a moment there I thought you were a promise-breaker as well as a public humiliator."

"Hey, ease up there with the name calling," Emily teased. "What time then?"

"How about seven?"

"Seven!"

"We start at 10 and I'll need to prep beforehand. It takes one and a half hours to get there. Well, maybe two in your wee shopping trolley."

"Don't knock your chariot."

"Seven then?"

"Okay, seven. I'm, dying for a sleep–in."

"After tomorrow you'll be done with your commitments to me and you can sleep as long as you like."

She pressed her lips tight. She wanted to see Ricky again – she liked him. He'd impressed her by running after her last night to make sure she was okay and had waited an hour for her this morning.

When was the last time a guy had paid that much attention to me?

***

Emily rose at six on Sunday morning, blurry eyed and hazy. She had a quick shower to wash away the nights' sleep and wake up.

A pair of khaki pants, a pink T-shirt and some sneakers would do. Oh, and a sweatshirt in case the weather turned later in the day.

The house was silent. Slight snoring noises came from Marie's room. Andrea had had Vinnie stay over, based on the sounds coming from the bedroom next to Emily's during the night. One of the disadvantages of sharing a house. Lisa's door was open; she'd obviously overnighted somewhere else. She tiptoed into the kitchen.

In between mouthfuls of cereal and OJ she filled up a water bottle, made some sandwiches, poured some almonds into a container, grabbed the suntan lotion, and juggling everything expertly between two hands, popped everything into her backpack.

She quickly pulled the front door closed behind her and backed her car out onto the road. Thank goodness for automatics. She seldom let her hand deformity get to her but this made it much easier for her to drive without having to manipulate gear-changing with her left hand.

Looking in the rear vision mirror, she could just make out a solitary figure walking down the footpath. The stocky build told her it was Ricky as she got out of the car.

"Morning," Ricky said, as he approached Emily.

"I'm slowly waking up. Morning," Emily replied. "You're ready then?"

"Yes."

"Um, don't you have any like, axes you should've brought with you?"

"I'm borrowing them."

"Right." More mystery. *Why didn't he have his own?*

"Besides," he said. "They'd be too heavy to carry this far."

"I could've picked you up. It wouldn't have been a problem."

"No worries. I appreciate you taking me."

She grinned. "I was coerced."

"It didn't take much coercion. Shall we go?" he asked, returning the grin.

"Jump in."

Within five minutes they'd left Misty Springs behind. It was going to be another clear, sunny day. White fluffy clouds dotted the sky. She drove alongside the river past the turn-off to Hillview subdivision. Five kilometres out of town, Red Hill receded into the background. Now both sides of the road were surrounded by fields of cows, sheep, or corn. On a slight rise, just beside the railway line, stood an old wooden house. Every time Emily drove past the house it amazed her that it was still standing. It looked ready to collapse at any moment. The paint had completely worn off exposing the wooden slats, and the place was bound to be full of borer. A car was never parked in the drive, or any washing on the old rusty clothesline and the gate was always closed. The lawns needed a good mow too. She shivered. "That house we just passed. It really should be bulldozed down. It's an eye-sore and must be freezing cold in the winter."

Ricky stared straight ahead. "I suppose so," he muttered.

Emily looked at him. His eyes dropped down to study his lap and he fidgeted in his seat.

With one and a half hour's journey ahead of them this was Emily's chance to find out more about Ricky. "How did you get into wood chopping?"

"My old man used to woodchop. I come from a farming background. I remember going with my dad to A and P shows when I was a kid and watching him compete. Granddad used to as well. In fact, both of them competed at wood chopping comps overseas and did quite well. We're good at the underhand chop, which is what I'm doing today."

"Have you got to championship level?"

"No way. I'm not training enough. And it's expensive. One axe can set you back $700."

"Wow. Now I see why borrowing one is cheaper. What is it that you like about wood chopping?"

"It's a chance to show off my biceps and strength to the ladies."

They both laughed.

"I'm sure it attracts a few goggle eyed women," Emily said.

"Seriously. It's the adrenaline rush of powering down on a block of wood and trying to beat all the other guys. It's all very Neanderthal."

"Do women do it?"

"Yip. Our club has some up and coming women woodchoppers."

They spent the rest of the trip finding out more about each other. But every time Emily asked a question about his family, where he used to work before moving to Misty Springs, or where he lived, Ricky would quickly change the subject. By the time they arrived at Rahu, he had been so elusive she had convinced herself that he had to be a fugitive. But she had found out he liked Nickelback, Puddle of Mudd, Hinder, Lifehouse, potatoes and hated Brussel sprouts (she wholeheartedly agreed). His favourite movies were *The Fast and the Furious* and anything with Matt Damon in it. He loved to watch rugby, particularly the All Blacks. He liked meat lovers pizza and orange chocolate chip ice-cream.

"The showground's coming up here on the left," Ricky said.

Emily reduced her speed as they entered an 80 km area.

"See the big sign." Ricky pointed up ahead to the Rahu A and P Show.

Emily slowed down, turned left into the driveway and joined the cars queuing to get in. She stopped at the entrance and wound down the window.

A guy with *Rahu A & P Show* printed on his T-shirt bent down.

"Two adults? Ten dollars each."

"I'm competing in the wood chopping," Ricky said and showed him a plastic ID card.

"Okay. That'll be just ten dollars for the lady."

Emily handed over the cash.

"Park anywhere over in that paddock there," said the man.

Emily followed the car in front and parked. She got out, stretching her legs and back.

The stench of cow poo lingered in the air. Music from the entertainment area where the Ferris wheel, octopus, and ghost train drifted their way.

"I need to find where the wood chopping area is. We should do a quick tour around," Ricky said.

Emily pulled both backpacks from the boot and handed Ricky his as they wandered into the grounds. Steam engines rumbled on one side of the main dirt road and a display of tractors for all types of farm work stood gleaming on the other.

"Here we are," said Ricky. "That wasn't too hard to find."

A ring was set up with various types of wood on both vertical and horizontal blocks, the latter obviously to be used for the underhand events. Some guys were wandering around inside the ring stopping to inspect the wood and chatting.

"I'd better go and get myself organised. The first underhand heats kick off at ten," Ricky said. "I need to find Lenny; he's lending me his axes."

Emily had half an hour to fill in. "I think I'll just sit up on the benches. If I wander too far away I might miss the big show."

Ricky grinned. "I hope I don't get performance anxiety."

"I'm sure you'll do well. Good luck."

She headed to the top of the tiered benches settling onto a seat. From there she had a good view of the show. A couple of paddocks down, the equestrian events were underway with the show jumping. A line of cows were being paraded and judges were inspecting them, rapping a rump or moving a leg into another position. Sheep were baaing in a big truck. No doubt they would be shorn later in the sheep shearing competitions.

Her attention focused back towards the wood chopping as more contestants milled around. Ricky wasn't hard to spot. He easily stuck out with his bald head and goatee. All contestants were wearing the regulation white trousers and singlets advertising their club and sponsors.

"Okay guys. We'll be ready to roll for the first underhand chop heat in fifteen minutes," the commentator said over the PA system.

Ricky had moved over to a block. He squatted down and drew markings on the wood. Using his axe, he carefully cut narrow flecks into the stand for footholds. He then drove slab nails into the sides of the block. Ricky had explained to Emily some of the preparation they had to do before the heat began. The slab nails held the wood in place and prevented it from splitting along growth rings.

"We'll be ready to run this heat in five minutes. If we can have just the competitors in the ring, everyone else out please."

People had begun filling up the seats eager to get a good view. Some couples but mainly families made up the audience with kids dressed up for a day in the country – shorts, T-shirts, hat, and mum fussing with the sunscreen and drink bottles.

Emily straightened up; her stomach wavered with butterflies.

"This is a handicap race. Front markers will start on the count of three and we'll go up to fifteen for young Paul down the back," the commentator continued.

'Young' Paul, who looked fifty, gave the crowd an embarrassed smile and a wave.

"Next to Paul we've got Mike, top woodchopper from last season, then there's Lenny and Wiremu visiting from Culverden. Been around these guys but they're a treat to watch. Then we've got Ricky Coles just starting out this season after taking some time out. "Axemen, stand to your blocks."

Ricky took his position on his block. His stance was narrow as he bent over and raised his axe directly above his head, anticipating the commentator's countdown. The distance between each foot looked to be about 15 centimetres.

"Three… 4… 5…"

Two woodchoppers let their axes fall.

"Six… 7…"

Ricky began his first drive with his left hand on the bottom of the axe. The first blow landed near his right foot. He continued driving down, lifting the axe, powering through as he chopped, his rhythm quickly established.

The crowd yelled out encouragement.

"Go Paul," someone shouted.

Axes flew, woodchips flew. The crowd shouted louder. A couple of people whistled.

Mike turned first to the other side, then Wiremu, then Lenny. Ricky turned last. The choppers grunted with exertion, sweat flew and the axes whooshed through the air.

Emily sat on the edge of her seat mesmerised by the rise and fall of Ricky's axe. Each time the axe landed accurately in the tiny space between Ricky's legs. *And all those choppers wore were sneakers. One false move…* She shuddered and rubbed the stumps of her left hand. *What if he missed? He could cut off his foot. Any of them could cut off their foot.* Perspiration broke out on her forehead. Fear rumbled through her stomach in icy sheets. From her memory, a doctor's voice, telling her they would have to amputate two of her fingers. Pain…

The commentator's voice brought her back to the present. She had barely registered that the heat had finished. Paul was declared the winner and she had no idea where Ricky had placed.

The crowd clapped and cheered. Emily joined in but her mind was still in a haze.

Ricky glanced up at the stand searching for her. She put one hand up in acknowledgement and he grinned back. But she couldn't watch anymore as she made her way down the stand her legs wobbly. She fumbled in her backpack and sucked on her water bottle drawing in the cool liquid.

What she needed was to be as far away from the wood chopping ring as she could get; far away from anything that could cause injury.

She wandered around the grounds stopping off at the sheep shearing, but didn't stay long. The whirring of the blades and the small amount of blood coming from one of the sheep as a shearer nicked its skin raced around in her mind combining with axes and a foot potentially being in the wrong place. As she weaved her way through the crowd, she caught the back of someone who looked like Stan. Perfect. She'd be able to find out now what the story was with his cell phone and more importantly what had happened to the framing. She ducked her head to the left but someone taller than her blocked her view.

She ducked back the other way and almost collided with a couple pushing a stroller.

"Sorry," she said. She shot back to the left side, stood on tiptoes searching for the brown head but it was too late – she couldn't locate whoever she'd seen. *Bother. I'm sure it was him.*

Making her way across to the entertainment area, screams spiralled overhead as people hurled by on the whizzer. The crowd grew bigger – a mixture of city and country folk, easily distinguished by the farmers' shirts, jeans and cowboy hats. People started to queue up outside the food caravans set up around the perimeter. She caught a whiff of chips, hot dogs and tomato sauce. Children lingered around the stand that was doing a sausage sizzle to raise funds for the local school.

Emily spied a hay bale where she could eat her sandwiches. The last time she was at an A and P show was as a child. All the grandchildren had spent summer holidays with Nana Rose and Grandpa Tom. They had taken her to one of the shows. She'd had a ride on the chair-o-plane and thrown up her vanilla sundae afterwards. Then Grandpa had bought her a shiny fairy that spun around on a stick in the wind. She'd felt much better after that.

Two girls walked by with candy floss. Ahh! That was probably the last time she'd had candy floss too. What was a day out at the country fair without candy floss? She wiped the crumbs off her hands and joined a queue to buy a bag of candy floss. Ripping the bag open, she twirled a finger around inside and popped the pink sugar into her mouth holding the mixture against her tongue savouring the flavour as the floss melted away. Oh, the memories food contained - Grandpa buying Emily candy floss and Nana Rose tut-tuttering saying she'd spoil her dinner, and after she'd just thrown up too. She put more of the feathery floss into her mouth, licked her sticky fingers and closed the wrapping over the opening. Too more-ish. If she didn't stop now she'd eat the whole thing.

Emily wandered down the far side of the grounds coming across the dog trials. She clambered up onto the seats and spent a pleasant hour watching the skill of the dogs in a battle of wits against the wiry and stubborn sheep. She wasn't sure at the end of each trial who'd actually won – the sheep, the dog or neither.

Occasionally the commentator's voice from the wood chopping ring drifted over her way. She supposed she'd better go back and see how Ricky was doing. *Can I continue to watch him with fear coursing through me?* No. One heat was enough. She'd hang around down here for as long as she could.

Eventually as the afternoon sun dipped low in the sky, she wandered back to the wood chopping area.

There was a results board at the entrance. All of the heats had been held and the underhand final had also taken place. Ricky's name wasn't among those who had placed.

The last event of the day, the jigger board, was underway. In this event, the chopper stood on the board stuck into the side of a tree which he then chopped a log from. Emily could see the immense balance and co-ordination required to stay on the board while chopping. *What if he fell? What if he fell and landed on the axe? For goodness sake! Now I'm getting paranoid.*

The crowd cheered and whistled as the first block fell.

"There you go ladies and gents," said the commentator. "I hope you've enjoyed today's events. We've got an awesome amount of talent amongst these men – and women – so please put your hands together for today's display of strength and athleticism."

Everyone clapped, and people started to leave the spectators area, and drift away.

Emily stayed seated. It was probably the best way for Ricky to find her.

"Hey," Ricky said.

"Hey." Emily climbed down off the stand.

Ricky was rubbing his shoulder. "Man, what a workout I've had today."

Ricky grimaced. "Owf"

"You might need a spot of massaging. Not that you really like that kind of thing."

"I don't think I'm going to need much convincing about the benefits of a massage."

"You look like you've got sunburnt too." Emily glanced at the reddened skin across Ricky's broad shoulders. "I could give you something for that."

"As long as I don't end up smelling like a girl."

"You won't smell like a girl," Emily reassured.

"I saw you watching my first heat but I didn't see you after that." Ricky peered at her.

"If you're ready we should probably get a head start on traffic." Emily turned away. *So Ricky had noticed I hadn't seen all of his events.* She wasn't sure what to say so she walked down the dirt road towards where the car was parked.

She didn't have to worry about having to explain why she hadn't stayed at the wood chopping. Ricky was like the energiser bunny high on adrenaline and jabbering away.

She caught the odd word. "Drive… whacked… best event… handicap of 25!… next competition… good to catch up with the guys."

The day in the country air had made her tired. She stifled yawn after yawn. A long soak in the bath… A book… glass of wine and then sleep.

"Emily?"

"Sorry, pardon."

"Do you think you'd like to come along to the next comp – probably in a months' time?"

"I don't know. I've a pretty full schedule at the moment. And remember this was only to settle a score." She risked a glance his way.

For the first time since they left the show, Ricky was silent.

They were only ten minutes out from Misty Springs.

"Where should I drop you off? You live out this way somewhere, don't you?"

"If you could drop me off back at your place. I've got a couple of things to do in town before I head home."

"You sure? It's not a problem."

"No. It's fine, really."

"Okay."

Emily pulled up outside the house and Ricky collected his bag from the boot.

"Thanks for today," he said. "It was nice to have some company."

"I enjoyed the day too."

"I'll see you around then."

"I'm sure."

Ricky turned and headed up the footpath.

She watched, admiring his back view - shorts covering a cute butt. *Why hadn't he suggested they get together?* Despite the circumstances they'd met under and even though he wasn't really her type, his warm and caring manner was slowly winning her over. Not to mention the cloud of mystery that surrounded him and kept growing.

Chapter 6

In Cache, her favourite store, Emily picked up the dark purple chenille blanket and ran her hand over the soft fabric. This would be a perfect accessory for her therapy room. She put the blanket back down. Lisa wouldn't allow it. It certainly didn't fit the current overly red colour scheme.

Every week she was in Cache browsing through well, just about everything. It was a lifestyle store almost modelled on the old country grocery stores of the past. She flicked through the scarves and stopped to look at some of the new kitchen utensils, which had just arrived. In the cosmetics section, she picked up a body cream, opened the tester container and sniffed. Vanilla. Nice. If she could just get her formula right maybe she'd be able to make some additional money by selling her cosmetics in Cache.

The store started to fill up with Sunday morning tourists. She exited, stopping to examine the incense sticks on the wooden containers stacked outside.

A dog barked. Emily looked down at a black border collie staring up at her. His leash was tied around the sign that said, 'Dog resting area'. The collie licked water out of a bowl that had been left beside the sign.

She bent down to pat the dog and was greeted with a happy bark. "I'm sure you won't be by yourself for long."

She continued walking down Main Street, past the shops and the local laundromat.

The door opened and out stepped Ricky.

"Oh!" she said.

"Emily, hi," Ricky said. "I've just been catching up on the laundry. Boring task for a Sunday."

Emily eyed the large canvas bag he placed on the ground. Wherever he lived didn't have a washing machine. "Only clean people have dirty washing."

Ricky laughed.

Should I try again to ask Ricky if he'd like to have a coffee with me? She'd been certain she was getting positive vibes from him. She swallowed. "Do you…"

"Would you…"

They both began at the same time.

"You go," Emily said.

"Would you like to grab a coffee?"

"Yes. I'd like that."

"There's something I'd like to ask you."

"Oh." She raised her eyebrows. Was he going to press her for a commitment to go to the next wood chopping competition? She'd have to work on an excuse. She didn't think she could handle axes, feet, injury…

"Come on," he said, picking up his bag.

They crossed the road and headed towards Café Steam, a local favourite with fresh homemade baking and good coffee.

"Hi, Linda," Emily said, as she peered into the cabinet.

"The usual, love?"

"Yes, plus a medium latte. Busy morning?"

"Hectic. I'm making hay while the sun shines. We've been selling out of everything by the end of the day. No food left over, which is great. This fine weather is making the holiday makers and the locals hungry."

"I'm glad business is going well."

"How are you girls doing?"

"Great." Emily swiped her card through the machine. "Like you, the salon is steady and we're just about turning people away."

"Long may it last. Okay, what would you like?" she asked Ricky.

"Black coffee, and a steak and cheese pie."

"Exactly what I'd order on a Sunday morning too." Linda laughed. "The usual male order is coming right up." She used the tongs to put the pie on the plate and passed the drinks order to the barista. "Nine dollars, fifty."

Ricky put his hand in his pocket and fumbled around searching for something then fumbled around in his other pocket. "Strange," he muttered.

Linda threw Emily a puzzled look.

Ricky popped his hand in the left pocket again. "I know I've got $10 here."

The man next to Ricky blew out an exasperated sigh. The queue was growing larger.

Ricky patted his back pockets. A red tinge crept over his face. "I don't understand..."

"I'll get this," Emily said.

Ricky was getting more embarrassed by the minute and people were straining their heads to the front to see what the hold-up was.

She handed over her card again and Linda swiped the transaction through. "Take a seat and I'll bring the drinks over." She handed Emily the receipt.

Ricky had already found a table by the window in the corner, the furthest away from everyone.

Emily picked up her plate with her ham roll on it and the other with the pie. Now she needed cutlery and some serviettes. No, that wasn't going to work. She didn't have enough hands – or fingers. She would have to make two trips. *Why can't I just be like everyone else?*

She looked towards Ricky who was staring at her. She nodded down at the plates and towards the table with the cutlery and serviettes.

He jumped up. "So sorry. I should've thought."

"It's OK. I wasn't going to risk dropping things again."

Ricky took one plate from her and grabbed the other bits on the way back to their table. "It must be awkward for you."

Emily sat on her left hand. Some days she was more subconscious than others. "I do the best I can. It takes your independence away but I've got used to it." *Please don't ask me what happened, how my life came apart.* She wasn't ready for that.

"I'll pay you back for the food. I'm sure I had a ten dollar note." Ricky's brow furrowed in a worried frown.

"No. Don't be silly. My shout." Emily bit into her roll. "How's your shoulder?"

"Not as bad. That was one of the things I wanted to talk to you about."

Emily put her roll down.

"I know I gave you a rough time on this whole massage thing but I admit it does have benefits."

"That didn't take long. Converted already."

"It must be your magic hands. I wondered whether you would be my therapist?"

Emily choked on a piece of ham. The other day was just temporary. She didn't think she'd be ever massaging Ricky again. Her finger tingled and heat rose in her chest.

"You look a little flustered there. You okay?"

Emily coughed. "Fine. Just something caught in my throat. But unfortunately I'm not sure I can. You were Andrea's client to start with and she might not like me stealing you."

"Could you do a swap?"

"Maybe. It's not quite as simple as that. On top of our wages we get a commission, which is based on our clients. How many times have you seen Andrea?"

"Only once. She can sure talk a lot." Ricky forked the last bit of pie into his mouth.

"Yes. That's Andrea. If you've only seen her once it might not be a problem. I'll ask her and let you know." She sipped on her latte. "You were going to ask me something else?"

"Would you like to go out with me on Wednesday night?"

Emily smiled. "Like on a date?"

"This time, like, on a date."

"This isn't a trick?"

"Absolutely not. 100 per cent straight up."

"I'd like that."

Someone scraped their chair over the wooden floor.

"Good. How about the place next door? Strawberry Desert. What's up with the name by the way?"

Emily stirred her latte. "That's a bit of joke around town. The sign writer made a mistake when painting it. Obviously it's supposed to be Strawberry Dessert. The owner kind of liked it and so it's stayed."

"Well, if I was stuck in a desert, strawberries would be okay with me."

"You'd have to have ice-cream with the strawberries but maybe not so great in the desert."

"How about I meet you outside the restaurant, say six-thirty?"

"Sounds good."

"Anyway I'd better get going. I've got more domestic stuff to do before work tomorrow."

"It was nice chatting," said Emily, screwing her serviette up into a ball.

"Thanks for the food again. Sorry about the, you know."

"Don't worry."

"See you Wednesday."

"See you Wednesday."

She smiled. *At long last. A real date with Ricky.*

***

Monday and Tuesday dragged. The number of clients Emily had had dropped a fraction but this was expected. The beginning of February marked the start of the new school year and Misty Springs had virtually emptied out yesterday as the last of the holiday makers packed up and headed back to the city.

Wednesday finally arrived.

"A date with Ricky," said Marie, as she pulled a bunch of towels out of the salon dryer.

"I'm really looking forward to it. At last something that feels like a genuine date and not one where I gained a phone number as part of some silly dare." Emily picked up a towel and folded it.

"He likes you. See, I knew there was something going on there."

"You did not. You're just trying to match make."

"Nothing wrong with that."

And he didn't seem phased by her disfigured hand. He'd seen her struggle twice now and, if anything, he was more than willing to help her when she needed it.

Marie handed Emily another towel. As she took the towel from her the sleeve on her top pulled up exposing her arm.

"How's your skin?" Emily asked. "It's still looks red and sore."

"It is." Marie pulled the sleeve up so Emily could see it further. "It's itchy like mad but that aloe vera cream you gave me has been a life-saver. I think if it's not better by the end of the week I'll go to the doctor. Maybe I've developed an allergy or something."

"That's a good idea."

Emily's last appointment was at 4 pm and after tidying up the room and preparing it for the next day's first appointment she raced home. She had a quick shower and with the towel still wrapped around her, she flicked through her wardrobe pushing aside garments. "No... No... No... He saw me in that at the garden party..." She slid hangers to the left. "I have nothing to wear." She groaned, then sank onto her bed.

The front door of the house slammed shut and Andrea walked past Emily's bedroom. "What's wrong?" she asked.

"I've nothing to wear."

"The big date with Ricky."

"How do you know?" The only person she'd told was Marie.

"You know Marie. She can't keep a secret for long."

"I have a wardrobe of stuff and nothing to wear," Emily moaned.

"You and I are about the same size." Andrea grabbed Emily's hand and pulled her into her bedroom. "Now you want something sexy but not in your face." She slid the hangars across. "Now where is it… Ah, here we are." She pulled out a one-color, long tangerine dress with spaghetti straps and a blue contrasting belt. "This will be perfect for you. It doesn't show too much cleavage."

Emily brushed a hand across her chest.

Andrea held the dress up against Emily's face. "It shows off your gorgeous peaches and cream skin and here," Andrea rummaged around, "are the perfect shoes." She held up a pair of black heels. "And this," Andrea handed Emily a black lightweight knit cardy, "is perfect for covering you up when the temperature drops."

"Thanks, Andrea. You're a lifesaver."

"No problem. Now get dressed. He'll be begging for sex when he sees you in this."

"Andrea!"

She ducked out of the way as Emily lightly slapped her friend on the arm.

But Andrea was right. Emily looked at herself in the mirror. The empire line of the dress hugged her curves and draped beautifully downwards. She blow-dried her hair and added a small silver clip. She put on foundation, eye liner and mascara and applied apricot lipstick. Digging around amongst her perfume bottles she chose a citrusy perfume, *Happy*.

She checked her watch – 6.15. She should start to walk down to the restaurant. Picking up her clutch bag and the black cardy, she walked down the hall.

Lisa, Andrea and Marie were in the kitchen cooking dinner.

"Wow! Look at you."

Lisa wolf whistled, Andrea clapped and Marie pumped her hands in the air.

"Stop it guys. You're embarrassing me." Emily gave a wave as she opened the front door.

"You go get him."

"Have you got condoms?"

"Andrea! Don't be so rude," scolded Marie.

Emily smiled as she closed the front door. She didn't really mind them making fun of her. She was in too good of a mood to let any of their teasing get to her. The short walk down the main street settled the butterflies in her stomach. The sun was still throwing out heat after a warm day and it would only get hotter at nights as they entered the last month of summer. Strawberry Desert was just across the road from the Serenity Day Spa. It was a cute wooden building painted strawberry red with the roof painted leaf-green.

Ricky was already waiting outside for her. He looked smart in his freshly-laundered dark blue jeans and pale blue shirt. She felt a small pull towards him.

"Hi," said Ricky.

"Hi."

"You look pretty."

"Thank you."

"Here, let me get the door for you." Ricky held the door open for her and they made their way to the front desk. "I've a booking for two. Coles."

"Yes, sir," the waitress said. "We've a table for you over here." She gestured towards the back. "I'll bring you some menus. Would like to order a drink now?"

"I'll have a coke," said Ricky.

"Lemonade for me, thanks"

Ricky pulled out her chair for her. "Have you eaten here before?"

"No." She tucked her hand under her leg and looked around. "It's ridiculous really given the salon is so close, but it's extremely popular and you can't get in without a booking."

She glanced around. There were lots of knick-knacks on shelves and a big strawberry wreath hung over the door. Photos of strawberries decorated the walls and red and green checked tablecloths covered the tables. Curtains lined the windows giving the restaurant a cosy, cottage feel.

The waitress brought over their drinks and menus and lit the tea candle.

Emily sucked the lemonade up through the straw and opened her menu. The selection was mainly salads; everything from chicken, avocado and strawberry salad, strawberry and radish salad to strawberry and blue cheese salad.

The front door opened and a noisy party of six crowded in.

"Mmm," Ricky said. "We'd better order soon judging by the look of that hungry group. I've heard the service can be slow." He signalled the waitress.

"Ready to order?" she asked, pushing some buttons on a tablet screen with a stylo pen.

"Emily?"

"I'll have the chicken, avocado and strawberry salad."

"And I'll have the steak, chips and salad."

"Sure. Any more drinks?" the waitress asked.

"Water would be good," Emily said.

The waitress picked up the menus and left.

Emily asked, "You're not having anything strawberry to start off with?"

"Nah. I think I'll leave that for dessert." His brown eyes twinkled in the candlelight. "Tell me about your work. What made you become a massage therapist?"

"I guess I was the typical girl when I was younger. I loved making homemade cosmetics or much to my mum's disgust, trying to add new ingredients to her face creams. She didn't really appreciate my attempts to add pulped nectarine to her $90 face cream."

Ricky laughed.

"From there I wanted to be able to help people feel better about themselves, help them relieve stress through the power of touch. I studied massage and aromatherapy and gained quals in therapeutic and relaxation massage. I really enjoy my job. Especially when people like you fall asleep during a treatment."

Ricky ducked his head. "Does that happen often?"

"Surprisingly, yes. There must be a whole lot of really stressed people out there."

Their conversation was interrupted when the waitress brought out their meals.

Emily's salad looked tiny compared to Ricky's meal.

"Heavens," Emily said. "That's a man meal."

"I use up a lot of energy each day working so I eat a lot of food."

Emily made a number of attempts while they ate to find out more about Ricky but he somehow managed to steer the discussion back to wood chopping. She wasn't sure what was going on but she was happy for now to go with it. For her, only two topics were off limits: her hand and whether she'd go with him to the next wood chopping event.

Ricky ate like it was the last supper and let out a satisfied groan when his plate was clean.

"Do you eat special food when you're training?" she asked.

"Just lots of protein for the muscles and I carb load during events. A good breakfast to have before a comp is bananas and strawberries. What about you? Do you have to eat special food for your job?"

Emily grinned. "I just try to eat healthily."

The waitress returned to clear their plates and hand them the dessert menu which detailed strawberry and chocolate pancakes, waffles, cheesecake, cupcakes, shortcake, strawberry pie and sundaes.

She didn't know where to start but finally settled on the chocolate and strawberry pancakes and Ricky chose the strawberry cheesecake.

There was a wait for the desserts as the restaurant began filling up.

Emily sucked on an ice cube in her drink.

"How did you get on with, is it Stan, regarding your house?" Ricky asked.

"I keep meaning to give him a ring but I keep forgetting. I must do that tomorrow."

"I asked around for you this morning. Word is the framing crew have definitely gone back to the city. There's no work scheduled for them for at least a month when the next lot of foundations are done."

Emily frowned. "That's strange. Now I'm getting worried." A niggling feeling that something wasn't quite right was growing stronger. "I'll definitely try and hunt Stan down tomorrow." She punched a reminder into her phone.

The desserts arrived. Ricky's eyes boggled. "This must be the largest piece of cheesecake ever. Is there anything left for others?"

"There's more than enough for everyone," the waitress reassured. "In fact, you could have another piece if you like."

"Ah, no thanks. This will be more than enough."

They ate in a comfortable silence and upon finishing, the waitress confirmed they'd finished ordering, she ran up the bill and placed it in a black folder on the table.

Emily reached for it.

"No," Ricky said, picking up the folder. "I'll pay."

"I'm happy to go halves."

"You might have to. $3,000..." Ricky peered up at her over the folder, a mischievous glint in his eyes.

"Must have been your cheesecake."

"You ready to go?"

"Yes."

They made their way over to the counter.

"That's eighty-five dollars please," the waitress said.

Ricky handed over his card.

"Did you enjoy your meal?"

"Lovely, thanks."

Emily nodded.

The waitress peered at the screen. "Oh, your card's declined."

Ricky froze.

"I'm sure it's nothing," the waitress said. "I'll try again."

Ricky re-swiped his card.

Emily stared out the window. The silence was heavy.

The waitress looked at the screen again. "Um... it didn't go through. Maybe it's this end. Shall we have another try?"

Ricky repeated the process tapping his card on the counter.

"Sorry. It's saying it's declined. Do you have another card?"

Ricky bowed his head and muttered something.

Emily looked at Ricky. *This was getting to be a habit.* She'd have to pay if there wasn't going to be a repeat of Saturday's incident at the café.

"Here try this," said Emily, handing over her card.

The waitress processed the transaction. "All good." She handed Emily the receipt. "You folks have a good night."

Ricky hot trotted it out of the restaurant in front of Emily. He turned and faced her. "I'm so sorry – again. I'm just.. It's just that..."

Emily squirmed. He was obviously embarrassed.

"I'm sure it was just as the waitress said. A problem at their end. Or maybe it was a problem with your card." Emily clutched at straws to lessen Ricky's discomfort.

Ricky was staring down the street at a loss of words.

"Do you want to walk me home?" Emily suggested.

"Ah, yeah."

They crossed the road and down the path, walking side-by-side in silence, the awkwardness falling between them.

Emily stared up at the trees. *What was going on with him? Will we ever stop being in situations where embarrassment rears its head like a lead balloon?*

Ricky's hand brushed against hers. She entwined a finger around his and squeezed. He squeezed back. His coarse and roughened fingers glided over the stumps, lingering for a moment. But he didn't seem repulsed. He rubbed his finger gently back and forth exploring the gap. The sensation was weird after so many years. Ricky was the first man since Josh to touch her hand in this way. And she was okay about it.

They had reached the house.

Ricky dropped his hand, breaking the connection. The wind skipped through her fingers and the sudden coolness made her gasp.

"I'm sorry," Ricky said again. "I'll pay you back."

I hope so. I can't afford to keep bailing him out. "Would you like to come in?" she asked.

"Thanks but I'm going into Red Hill Bar and see if I can wrangle a ride home."

"Sure. Thanks for tonight. I had fun."

"Me too." Ricky leaned towards Emily and gave her a peck on the cheek. "I'll call you." He turned and walked back into town.

He wants to see me again. She smiled as she walked up the path. And hopefully the next time his 'financial issues' would be solved.

Chapter 7

The next day Emily didn't have any clients until 10 am making it the perfect opportunity to do her once-a-week walk up Red Hill.

It was a half-hour, steady switchback walk up through the forest.

When she arrived at the top of the hill, she paused to take a drink from her water bottle.

The sun burned brightly and the air was filled with the Christmas tree scent of dried pine needles. Down below over the tops of cypress and cedar, Misty Springs township was awakening. Little dots of red moved down the streets - the Misty Springs Primary School uniform – the wearers attending their first day of school for the new year. A tractor started up in the distance. Further down the valley the lushness of the trees marked their way through Flaxmere River.

Emily peered up at the blue sky breathing in again the forest and reflecting on last night's dinner. She'd enjoyed her date with Ricky and she wanted to see him again. But something wasn't quite right. Twice now he'd had an issue with money – he'd either lost it or his card wasn't working. Or so he claimed.

She put her leg up on the bench and gave it a good stretch as she peered out over the valley. One day she'd make it up here much earlier in the day to capture the sunrise. She'd seen the magnificent sunsets from the town with Red Hill silhouetted in the background against a sky on fire. The locals said that the sunrises were pretty spectacular too but it would mean she'd have to sacrifice one of her sleep-ins.

Swapping over to her other leg, she gave it a quick stretch and walked back down the Red Hill track.

***

After her morning's appointments she caught up with Marie in the lunchroom and filled her in on her date but leaving out what happened when Ricky went to pay.

"So what do you want to happen next?" Marie asked.

"I'd really like to see him again." Emily nodded, confirming what she'd been thinking since last night.

"Are you going to ask him out?"

"I'm not sure. Maybe. Or maybe I'll just play it by ear."

"I'm sure he'd be flattered if you'd ask him to. We shouldn't leave it for the guys to make the first move all the time."

"I don't know. What if he says no?"

"Not likely," Marie said, as she scratched her arm. "He obviously likes you or he wouldn't have asked you out last night."

"Well, mystery man isn't making things very easy. I don't know where he lives and he has no phone."

"Ahh, but you do know where he works."

True. *Could I be brave enough to go down to Morningside subdivision and talk to him in front of all his building mates?* No.

96

She'd take her chances and wait. She was bound to bump into him soon. They'd been good at doing that.

"You still scratching?" Emily asked.

"It's driving me nuts." Marie drew up the sleeve on the top. Her skin was fire-engine red and bumpy.

"I'm making an appointment to see the doctor tomorrow. I can't stand it anymore."

"Have you been using any new products?"

Marie tilted her head. "No. I don't think so. Just my normal body wash and cleanser. Actually, wait a minute. I have been slathering on that Nature's One moisturiser, the new products Lisa brought in and wants us to use. She gave me a trial tube to try out."

"I wonder if that's it."

"You may be right."

"The best way to know is to stop using it."

"I'll do that. That would certainly save me a doctor's fee." Marie glanced at her watch. "Mmm. Better go. I've got a Brazilian to do in ten minutes." She jammed the last of her sandwich in her mouth and bolted out the door.

Emily had ten minutes before her next appointment. Perfect time to try and get hold of the illusive Stan.

She dialled Stan's number again, but still got the disconnect tone. *Enough of this.* She pulled the folder with all her house building notes out of her bag. She located a letter that had the office landline number on it and dialled it. After two rings it clicked over to a message service telling her the number had been disconnected. *No. How could that be?* Panic coursed through her veins. Both Stan's and the office number disconnected? It seemed too much of a coincidence. What about the website? She typed the website into her phone and waited. The blue circle spun round and round. It finally stopped. 'Problem loading page'. She double-checked the website address, retyped it and waited. The blue circle repeated its cycle: 'Problem loading page'. Okay. Something was definitely wrong. She scratched her head. What now? How was she supposed to find out what was going on?

Ricky with no phone and not being able to contact Gardenway Homes. Had the whole world suddenly gone in communicado? Who could she talk to? Christine, Ricky's boss, was coming in tomorrow at 4 pm for her weekly massage. Maybe she could talk to her. Get some advice from her. Failing that and without making a trip to the city offices, she didn't know what else to do.

***

The first task on her list the next day was to check on the batch of body butter she'd made last week.

She drew in a breath and slowly unscrewed the lid from the first jar. The damp, off smell gave it away immediately. Mould. She took the lid off completely. *No. Not again.* Blue and green spores littered the top of the butter. She plonked the jar and lid on the bench and hurriedly unscrewed the next lid. And the next. And the next. Mould. Mould. And more mould.

"Arrgh!" Emily said.

Another batch ruined. *What I am I doing wrong?* She flung the lids into the sink.

Okay. Maybe we'll leave the body butter for a while. She pulled her plastic recipe book down off the shelf and flicked through the pages. Her hand stopped at a Citrus Lavender Lip Balm. She'd have a go at this one, confident this would work.

Emily covered the work bench with gladwrap and lined up five lip balm tubes. She measured beeswax granules, honey, lavender and lemon essential oil into the double boiler. She warmed the mixture slowly, stirring it gently with a rubber spatula. When the lip balm was completely melted she carefully poured it into a glass measuring bowl and then into the tubes. The mixture needed to be left overnight to harden.

Emily stepped back and surveyed her work. Cross fingers that this would work.

"That smells nice."

Emily turned around.

"You can smell it all the way down the hall," Andrea said.

The room lingered with the scent of lemon and lavender. Andrea put out her tongue and wiggled it.

Emily laughed. "What are you trying to do? Eat the air?"

"It smells good enough to eat. We need to find a way to bottle the fragrance. It's heavenly." Andrea rolled her eyes.

"I hope this experiment works better than the body butter. I'm not having much luck there. I've had to get rid of Potion No. 2."

"Are you ready for our meeting?"

"Meeting?"

"You know, the extra one Lisa wanted to have."

"Oh whoops! I'd forgotten. I wondered why I hadn't booked my first appointment until ten." She quickly tidied up the bench, grabbed her notebook and joined Andrea, Marie and Lisa in the meeting room.

"Just a quick meeting," Lisa said. "I just wanted to know how the sales of the Nature's One products were going, and if you have any feedback"

Andrea spoke first. "I've sold a few of the body creams and the response from when I used it for a massage was positive but-"

"Good. Good," Lisa said. "We really need to promote this product to our clients and use it as much as possible."

"-but," Andrea continued, "I did have one lady return it. She said it gave her a rash."

Marie caught Emily's eye.

Emily straightened up in her chair. "What was the problem?" Lisa asked.

"Her skin was really red and sore and she had these little raised bumps on them."

"I'm sure it's nothing," Lisa replied, dismissing the comment. "She could've been using something else. Also I've had a lot of clients complaining of allergies lately."

"Marie's been using it too," Emily said. "Her skin's not looking all that great."

Marie pulled up her sleeve and showed Lisa.

Lisa's face barely moved. In fact, she didn't even seem surprised.

"It's been driving me nuts and I've been trying to work out what's causing it. I think Emily has worked it out," Marie said.

Lisa threw Emily a murderous glance.

"I'm sure it's the Nature Own's moisturiser," Emily said. "Marie's itchiness only started after she began using it."

"You can't be sure of that," Lisa said, crossing her arms. "It could be anything."

It was time to stand up to Lisa. "Well, I wonder about the claims the manufacturer makes." She picked up one of the tubes off the table and read out the ingredients. "These aren't natural products. We can't sell these as natural. It's false advertising."

"It'll be fine." Lisa waved a hand dismissively.

"I'm not sure-"

"They say they've been tested and they're 100 percent allergy proof."

"Well, clearly they're not," Emily said.

"We have no proof that either Andrea's client or Marie's rash are linked to Nature's One." Lisa raised her voice. "We'll keep using and selling the products until we have proper, substantiated proof. None of my clients have had any problems. Now I expect all of you to promote these products and I want to see an increase in sales by next week."

Andrea shuffled in her chair. Marie itched her arm again just to prove a point. Emily looked at the painting on the wall.

"Andrea? Marie?" Lisa prompted.

They both nodded.

"Emily?"

What choice do I have? Lisa was the boss. But it didn't make it right.

"Emily!"

Emily's skin prickled at the harshness of Lisa's tone. She nodded.

"Anything else we need to discuss."

Emily cleared her throat. "I just wanted to ask Andrea whether she'd mind doing a client swap."

"Who did you want to swap?" Andrea asked.

"Ricky Coles."

Andrea laughed. "You must've really impressed him with your massage the other day."

Lisa smirked. "So things moving to another level between you two?"

Emily refused to be baited by Lisa. She wasn't going to tell her any more than she needed to know, besides it was none of her business.

"That's not what this is about. He's done the decent thing by asking me first. He could've just easily made his next appointment with me."

"A man with scruples. Nice. How did the date go the other night?"

Emily ignored the question. "If it's a problem just say so. I'll tell Ricky, but we may lose him altogether."

"Maybe Emily and I can get together and sort out some arrangement," Andrea suggested.

"I think it's simpler than that. How about if Emily has any free spaces any walk-ins Andrea gets first pick?" suggested Lisa.

"That's hardly fair. Walk-ins could turn into permanent clients," Emily protested.

"What's the deal? I think it's a good compromise. You already have Christine and now Ricky. You may end up with all of Christine's builders if she keeps her promise of sending all of them here for weekly massages."

Lisa had a point. She was sure though that her and Andrea could've come to a better arrangement. Maybe she should've talked to Andrea first rather than bringing it up at a meeting. "That's fine," Emily replied.

"And now you'll get to rub your hands over Ricky's body day and night," Lisa joked.

Somehow the joke fell flat. Andrea and Marie barely smiled and to Emily it just sounded sleazy.

***

Emily hadn't seen or heard from Ricky in the last two days. For someone she'd kept bumping into, suddenly Ricky had turned into the disappearing man. *Was he having second thoughts about me? Have I done or said something to turn him off?* It had to be the hand. She'd done her best to hide it so he didn't have to look at it, the disfigurement. But he'd held her hand, rubbed it gently. She closed her eyes bringing back the memory.

She opened her eyes and focused on the lip balm tubes in front of her and took in a deep breath. She took the top off the tubes. Emily inhaled the sweet scent. It had set nicely. She wound the tube up slowly and ran it over her lips tasting the citrusy gloss. Perfect texture. *Yes! Yes! Yes!* Finally, something that worked. Did this mean the Lemon Lavender Lip Balm could be the first product in her body care range? She'd still have to work on the body butter, but this had now given her the confidence to try other mixtures. She could use the infusion she'd made the other day for her Rosemary and Lavender Soap and make a sugar scrub. That was one recipe which never failed. She also wanted to try a lavender body cream, which had a different formula to the body butter. Her mind buzzed with ideas. She could make a business out of this, but she'd have to draw up a business plan, maybe apply to the bank for a loan.

She would need to get more supplies of containers and a name for her range of products. And what about label design? Perhaps Marie could help here. Emily had seen her simple pencil sketches, which she was always doodling. Unable to sit with her sudden extra energy, she stood up as Andrea popped her head around the kitchen door. "Ooh! I can smell lemonade."

"It's the Lemon Lavender Lip Balm. Here, have a couple of tubes. One for yourself, seen as you like it so much, and a couple to give away to your clients."

"Thank you. I'll be licking my lips all day. By the way, Christine's here."

"Thanks, Andrea." Emily gathered up the tubes and put them in her bag.

Emily walked into her treatment room. "Hi, Christine."

"Emily. How are you?"

"Good, thanks. What're we going to do for you today?"

"I've been helping out on the building sites. We're a couple of guys down. I think I've overdone it. My shoulders are quite sore," she said, rolling her shoulder.

"How about we do your normal massage, but I'll concentrate more on the shoulders?"

"Sounds good."

"Okay. Just give me a minute to make up a blend for you and then you can get changed." Emily opened her aromatherapy boxes. She chose a camomile, peppermint and rosemary oil, mixed these up and poured them into her spray bottle. She left the room while Christine got changed. When she returned she dimmed the lights and set the CD player. She sprayed some oil on her hands and rubbed them together releasing a mild scent of apples and herbs.

For the next hour Emily worked on Christine concentrating on the shoulders. She gently pushed down on the shoulders using gentle releases as she worked her way towards the middle of her chest. She used a variation of strokes and kneading techniques on the upper arms.

"Christine," Emily whispered. "We've come to the end."

"Mmm," came Christine's drowsy, muffled voice. "So soon."

"In your own time, get dressed and I'll get you a glass of water."

After five minutes Emily returned. "How do you feel now?"

Christine rolled her eyes skywards. "Much better. You're a wonder. Ricky raves about you. And that's saying something from someone who was very reluctant to get a massage."

Raved about her. Emily smiled. "If you're muscles are feeling better that's great." She handed Christine the glass of water.

"I heard you two are a bit of an item," Christine said, glancing sideways.

"Oh. I wouldn't say that. We've only been out once. Has he said something?"

"No. But you know how guys are. His mates were giving him a hard time on Wednesday. He must've been a nervous wreck by the time you saw him that night."

Only after his card wouldn't work. "I'm not sure about Ricky. He seems a nice enough guy but there's something I can't quite put my finger on. He's vague about everything – where he lives, he has no phone, no car." Emily paused. "You must know something about his background."

Christine placed the empty glass on the bench. "It's not really up to me to say."

"What do you mean?"

"Let's just say he's looking for a break and I've given him one."

So there was something going on. "What do you mean, 'he's looking for a break'?"

Christine slipped her feet into her shoes. "I've probably said too much already. You really need to talk to him."

Emily frowned. "I'm not sure I want to hear any more. He's not running from the police?"

"Emily, I can't say anymore. It wouldn't be right."

Emily sighed. "Sure. I'm sorry. It's just that I don't know where I am with him."

Christine put a reassuring hand on Emily's shoulder. "As I said, you really need to ask him."

"Perhaps I will. He did mention that you might be able to help me with another matter."

"Oh?"

"I can't get hold of Stan. His phone number and the office phone have been disconnected and the website's gone. The framing on the house was supposed to begin last week, but Ricky said the crews left town and are not expected back for another month."

"Stan, that greasy guy. Never liked him."

"What have you heard?"

"All sorts of dodgy things have gone on with that company. I'm not surprised you're having trouble getting any response."

"That was not what I was wanting to hear."

"I'm going into the city next Monday if you want to come along. We could go and pay Stan a visit."

Emily rubbed her neck. "I might just do that. I'm starting to get really worried."

Christine patted her arm. "Anything I can do to help."

Having a plan in place now to find out just what exactly was happening with the house would help her get through this.

Next – could she build up enough courage to ask Ricky out?

Chapter 8

Emily woke up early on Saturday morning to walk up Red Hill again. The weather wasn't as nice as it had been on Thursday. Clouds enveloped the top of Red Hill and mist hung in the trees.

When she returned from her walk she popped into Café Steam.

Linda was wiping down the table ready to open up in half an hour.

"Hi, Linda."

"Emily, come on in," said Linda. She held the door open for her. "Good walk?"

"Yes. Although you can't see much down here and it's all cloudy up there."

"Can I get you a coffee?"

"That would be great."

"So what's the gossip?" Linda asked, as she began making the coffee.

"Work's still going well. I'm hopeless at making body butter but I had a win with some lip balm."

Linda poured the coffee into a cup and pushed the sugar across the counter.

Emily perched herself on a stool.

"Hey, I don't mean to be nosey but what was with the young fellow you were with last week."

"Ricky? Not sure. It's very early days yet. We had dinner on Wednesday night and, like here, he stuck me with the bill again, but since then I've heard nothing from him." Doubt crept over her again.

"Well, he'd be silly to let someone who picks his bill up all the time pass him by. Especially after your lot."

Emily had told Linda about what had happened with Josh and had told her on no uncertain terms what she'd thought of him. She dug around in her pocket for some change.

"No, don't worry love. On the house today."

"Thanks, Linda." She wrapped her hands around the warm mug.

Linda bustled around filling up the salt, pepper and sugar shakers while Emily helped fold up the knives and forks into the serviettes.

They both looked up when the bell over the door rang and a woman walked in.

"We're not open for another hour," Linda said, straightening up the magazines.

The woman wore a pair of distressed jeans with rips in the legs and a white hoody sweatshirt, which had a stain on the sleeve. Her mousy brown hair was pulled back loosely in a ponytail. Greasy strands escaped down the front of her face. "No bother," she said. "I'm looking for someone."

Linda laughed. "Aren't we all?"

The woman didn't think it was amusing. "You guys are obviously locals?"

Emily eyed the woman with suspicion and stirred her coffee.

"I'm the café owner," said Linda.

"I work and live here too," Emily said.

"I'm looking for a guy. He's a builder. I've heard he's worked around here. His name's Ricky Coles," the woman said.

Emily gripped the side of the stool.

Emily eyed Linda. The locals were protective of one another. Neither would say anything until this woman's intentions were clear.

"There's a bunch of builders working north of Misty Springs," said Linda, as she inclined her head in that direction. "They might be worth checking out."

Good on you, Linda. Don't give too much away.

"You visiting here?" Linda continued.

"Just up for the day from the city. I was hoping to locate Ricky."

The woman's eyes shifted to the food in the cabinet.

Emily took another sip of her coffee and studied her over the top of her cup. What did this woman want with Ricky? Could she provide a clue to his illusiveness?

"Have you got business with him?" Linda asked.

"You could say that."

The woman wasn't forthcoming with much information. Almost as vague as Ricky.

"How about you tell us your name and if he pops up somewhere we'll let him know?" Linda suggested.

"Vanessa. It's Vanessa."

"OK, Vanessa. Will he know who you are?"

Vanessa smirked. "Oh yeah, I'm his wife."

Emily's teaspoon clattered to the floor.

Chapter 9

His wife?

The blood drained from Emily's face. Right. Now it was starting to make sense.

Vanessa walked out of the café and climbed into a beat-up station wagon.

"Well," said Linda, placing her hands on her hips. "I take it by the look on your face this is a surprise."

"I… well… his wife… He's never mentioned a wife." Emily climbed down from the stool and picked up the teaspoon.

"I'm sorry, love. God, what a bastard."

Emily's mind was in a whirl. It was like someone had slapped her in the face.

"You all right, love? You look at bit pale."

"Yeah. I'm fine. Just fine." Emily sighed. She needed to get out of the café and be somewhere where she could think. "Thanks for the coffee."

"My pleasure. Hey, chin up. Maybe it's not your Ricky Coles."

Emily threw her a weak smile. Linda was trying to make her feel better and she appreciated it, but she needed some time alone.

She left the café and walked to the park. The cloud had barely lifted. In fact, it had thickened. It had a look about it that it was going to hang around all day. A tight feeling moved across her chest. It wasn't like her and Ricky were officially dating. Had she read the signals wrong? Maybe he just saw her as a friend. No. A friend didn't hold your hand or kiss you on the cheek. But it did explain a number of things. The secretiveness. Maybe his cashflow card being declined was a deliberate ploy so his wife – Vanessa – couldn't trace his spending. A pounding reached a crescendo in her ears. He'd been playing her all along and she'd fell for it like a fool. Linda was right. Ricky was a bastard.

***

Emily moped around on Sunday avoiding Marie, Andrea and Lisa. She didn't want to have to explain that she'd been used, taken for a ride. She particularly wouldn't be able to face any snide comments coming from Lisa.

Late in the afternoon the sun came out chasing away the last of the greyness and along with it, Emily's sour mood.

She checked her lavender supplies. She could do with some more. She'd prefer to use Nana Rose's lavender, but she wouldn't have time to make another visit for at least the next few weeks. But there was some old patches of lavender growing out to the south. They were part of a garden on an old block of land. An original settler's house had once been there but had been demolished years ago. The land had lay dormant and overgrown, used now only by the odd grazing horse and children acting out old western movies.

Emily hopped into her car and within twenty minutes she was rummaging around in the lavender patches cutting stalks with her secateurs. The heat brought out the aroma, which helped ease her mood even more and the comfortable feel of the blooms reminded her of summer holidays at Nana Rose's.

Every time her thoughts wondered towards Ricky she promptly pulled them back. There would be no point pursuing him now. She'd just cut her losses and move on, her trust in men dented again.

She filled the boot of the car up with all the lavender and checked the time. Seven pm. How did it get that late so fast? Her stomach rumbled. Sunday night was Andrea's turn to cook. She'd been practising whipping up rich lasagne hoping to woo Vinnie into that engagement ring. She'd be home just in time to grab a meal.

She drove down the motorway. The early evening sun threw long shadows across the road. The breeze had picked up, increasing the fragrance of freshly cut hay.

Ten minutes out of Misty Springs, Emily spotted a lone figure walking on the side of road towards her. As she got closer, the profile became clearer. The short, stocky figure, head down. It was Ricky. She entered the 80 km zone area and reduced her speed. Ricky went flashing by. Emily glanced in the rear vision mirror. *What on earth was he doing way out here? Where was he going?* She lifted her foot off the accelerator and gently applied the brakes, pulling over to the side.

The sight of Ricky was enough to make her blood boil. He hadn't been honest with her or completely forthcoming of his past life so she was going to do a little digging of her own.

She did a U-turn and drove back the way she'd come. There were no other cars on the road behind her so she could drive well below the speed limit. She squinted along the side of the road until Ricky came back into view. She pulled over the side again and hung back.

Maybe he liked to walk but walking on the side of the road seemed a strange thing to do, and it was dangerous. He was coming up to the derelict house they'd passed last Sunday. Ricky turned left and walked up the path to the front door.

What was he doing here? She inched the car closer. The front door closed behind him.

Emily turned off the engine. What should she do? Did she even care? Ricky owed her an explanation and she was going to get it now.

She opened the car door. The rusty garden gate hung on one hinge and squeaked when she pushed it open. The concrete path was littered with cracks. Weeds almost reached her waist and leaves from last autumn were piled up high against an overgrown tree. The lawns looked like they hadn't been mowed all summer. The house looked worse up close than from the road; every single wooden board had lost its paint years ago and big holes protruded. The roof was just as rusty as the gate with the guttering overflowing with weeds. One window pane had been broken and was boarded over. Cripes! If she stepped on the veranda would the whole thing collapse?

She knocked on the front door.

Inside, a dirty curtain moved.

The front door opened.

Ricky stepped out onto the porch. His face was like stone, but he held the door open.

Emily brushed past him.

The floorboards creaked as she walked into the middle of the dark and sparsely furnished room. There was a double bed in one corner and a pink Formica table with one chair pushed up against the back. A small kitchen area had a bench and an old zip water heater over the sink. Another door lead to what she presumed was the bathroom. On the opposite side of the house there was another smallish room.

Apart from that, there was no other furniture. There were no paintings on the walls, no TV, no couch. Nothing. It was clean, tidy but oh-so-bare.

"This isn't a social call?" Ricky asked.

"No." Now she was here but she wasn't sure what to say next.

"Did you follow me?"

"Yes."

No wonder he hadn't told her where he lived. And it explained his lack of comment when they'd driven past here.

God. What had she said? *The place ought to be bulldozed down.* She'd put her foot in it again.

"Why weren't you honest with me?" Emily blurted.

"Huh?"

"You have a wife."

"No I don't."

"Well, this woman claims she is."

"What woman?"

"Vanessa."

"Vanessa?"

"She came into the café the other day."

"Vanessa's here?" A shadow passed across Ricky's face.

"Oh, so you do have a wife."

"Ex-wife."

Emily stared at Ricky. Relief swept over her, but somehow it didn't make it any better. "Why didn't you tell me?"

"She's history."

"She can't be that much history. She's very much in the present."

"I didn't tell you because I wasn't sure whether we were an item." Ricky looked around. "I'm sorry there's no place else for you to sit but the bed."

Emily stared at the bed in the corner with its faded floral duvet cover. She didn't move. Ricky reached for her hand and guided her over to the edge. Her hand hung limply in his.

She sat down, her hand still in his. "Why didn't you say something to me?" Emily asked.

"About where I live? As you can tell, it's not deluxe." Ricky stroked her finger. "It's all I can do for now. No one else knows I live here apart from the mate who offered it to me."

"You haven't been honest with me. Do you want to tell me what's going on?"

Ricky rubbed his goatee. "I was married to Vanessa for three years." He ran his finger up and down Emily's thigh sending a warm wave of pleasure through her. "We had one of those relationships where we fed off each other's weaknesses.

"Vanessa was a gambler and she was pretty good at hiding the extent of it. And it got bad, real bad. I didn't keep a close eye on what was happening financially. We ended up defaulting on our mortgage payments, the credit cards were maxed out, debt collectors came calling and reclaimed my car and just about anything in the house. We-I-lost everything. And this is where I am now." Ricky waved his arm around the room.

Emily gulped. Her heart went out to him. "That's awful."

"I'm broke. I have nothing. And I live day-to-day."

"Is that why your cashflow card wouldn't work the other night?"

"I'd forgotten my wages wouldn't have gone into my bank account until the following night so there wasn't enough money for the dinner."

"And what about at the café?"

"Honestly, I did have ten dollars, but it must've fallen out of my pocket at some stage. I was gutted. Losing ten dollars is like losing a hundred."

"I'm not sure why you just didn't tell me."

"Male pride, I guess. I mean, would you've come out and said I don't have any money?"

"No. You're right."

"And I didn't know where this -you and I- were going. It's not something you tell everybody."

"Where do you think this is going?"

"I really like you, Emily."

"I like you too and I must admit I was confused about things, things that didn't make sense. You were so secretive. At one stage I thought you might've been in trouble with the police."

"Mmph. No. That I can certainly be clear about. But I don't think you want to get involved with me."

Just when Ricky was being honest with her, he was now giving her the cold shoulder?

"Is it the fact that you don't have any money, because that doesn't bother me."

"No." Ricky took in a big breath. "It's not just Vanessa who was a gambler. I am too."

Emily gasped. "Ohhh."

"I'm a compulsive gambler. God, it's like saying you have a disease or you're an alcoholic. I've shocked you."

"No. Maybe. Yes."

Ricky made a noise that was half-way between a laugh and a choke.

"Is it the pokies or horses?" she asked.

"At one stage it was a bit of everything. Pokies, poker, horses, greyhounds, casinos. It wasn't just Vanessa's problem. It was mine too. I thought cutting ties with her would 'cure' me but my addiction – because that's what it is – got worse. I didn't want to be the person that gambled. I think I did it to satisfy some sort of need. But when you're broke and have no money it's pretty hard to gamble. I joined a support group and that was helpful but as a builder there was more money to be made in Christchurch with the earthquake rebuild than in Auckland so I moved down here. The temptations of the city were just too great so here I am in Misty Springs trying to get my shit together."

"Did you try counselling?"

"No. Certainly living here is helping. I don't have an iPad or a cell phone so I can't be tempted by online gambling. The hours I'm doing building keeps me out of trouble during the day and I'm making extra money doing the odd waiting job. As you can tell I'm hopeless at it." Ricky bit down on his lip.

"Was that where you were coming back from today?"

"A fancy wedding at Hedgerows."

Emily winced. Here was a guy who'd been doing his best to make ends meet and she and her friends had made fun of his clumsiness. "We weren't very kind to you at the garden party, were we?"

Ricky laughed. "No, you were horrid. You certainly know how to kick a guy when he's down."

"I've apologised a thousand times for that. And I didn't know anything about your issues. So perhaps you should lighten up."

"Hey, I'm just having you on."

"What about us?"

"I can't offer you anything. I have nothing."

"You're talking about possessions. What about you personally? You're funny, you chop wood pretty well. You're kind hearted-"

"Keep going."

"You like flattery. I admire you for recognising you had a problem and getting on top of it."

"Have."

"Pardon?"

"Have a problem. I'm not out of the woods yet. If you take me on, this won't be an easy ride but I like you too Emily."

Ricky hadn't been avoiding her because of her hand. He'd been focused on his problems. If it was anyone's turn to gamble it was now her turn. "I'm willing to take a chance. But you have to be honest with me Ricky. No more secrets."

"No more secrets."

Emily grasped Ricky's hand firmly and gave it a wee squeeze. The response was a harder squeeze back. She turned her head to face Ricky.

He looked older than his late twenties, but also like a vulnerable teenage boy, all at the same time. What he'd been through to survive day-to-day pulled at her heartstrings.

His big, brown eyes searched her's confirming that their relationship was moving to a deeper level. Pulling her in like a magnet, he planted a delicate, soft kiss on her lips, so subtle it was like a whisper.

The early evening sun peeked through the windows bathing them in a soft, orange glow.

Emily closed her eyes and kissed him back, the bristles of his goatee caressing her. It was the strangest sensation, almost like being flicked with electrical pulses. Her hand moved up to his elbow and she clasped tighter.

He kissed harder, tingling her lips. It had been so long since her last kiss. Her mind collapsed in a warm mush as hot fire burned her stomach.

She rubbed her face against his. A musky scent mixed with a woody pine cologne drifted up. Her senses awakened with a shock. He stroked the bumps on her left hand.

He pulled away gently.

She didn't want to open her eyes fearing that she'd imagined it all. She touched her mouth. "I could've kissed you forever."

"Me too." Ricky stood up, drawing Emily to her feet.

He gave her a hug and she huddled into the shelter of his arms. "I'd better go back into town," he said, breaking away.

"Why?"

"I need to find out where Vanessa is and what she wants."

A ball and chain dragged across Emily's stomach. She walked over to the front windows. "Can you just leave it?"

"As much as I'd like to, no." Ricky's voice had a hard edge to it. "If I don't do something about it she'll be a problem that won't go away."

Emily studied the overgrown weeds peeking up around the veranda. "I don't like that she's here."

"Me neither but if I can help it she'll be off, out of Misty Springs, before she has time to get too acquainted with the locals. I'd like to keep my personal business just that."

She didn't count herself as the jealous type but if she could help Ricky to get his ex-wife out of town she was more than happy to help. "Come on. I'll drop you off."

"Thanks. I appreciate it. I know it's not the best of situations but we'll deal with it."

She liked the way he said 'we'.

Chapter 10

After their staff meeting on Monday Emily had three back-to-back massage appointments. She hummed when she could, and her face was carved in a permanent smile. She and Ricky were now together and mysteries had been solved. But having a relationship with someone who was virtually uncontactable was tough.

Had Ricky found Vanessa? What did she want? To get back with him? She'd drive out to Ricky's after work. She needed to know that Ricky and Vanessa were well and truly over.

She had her couscous salad in the staff room while checking her phone. Six missed calls. Holy heck. She scrolled through the numbers. Two from her brother, David, one each from both sisters, Bridget and Yvette, one from her mum and one from Nana Rose. Had something happened to Dad? She'd ring David first. He hardly ever rang. Something was definitely up.

"Hey Emily," Marie said, as she walked into the lunchroom and placed a newspaper on the table. "I guess you've heard."

"Heard what?"

"About Gardenway Homes."

"Ah, no. What about them?"

Marie averted her eyes.

"Marie, what?"

"You'd better read this." Marie pushed the newspaper towards Emily.

The front page headlines screamed at her.

Gardenway Homes goes into liquidation

Barry Hobbs, a director of Gardenway Homes, announced in a statement last night that liquidators have been brought in, and Peter Wilson of Wilson Smith Accountants has been appointed as the liquidators.

"It is unfortunate that this has happened. Gardenway Homes owes creditors more than $2 million."

Gardenway Homes, a South Island based project management company, has been building houses in the region for three years.

"We're doing our best to manage this delicate situation, but it appears unlikely that unsecured creditors would get paid," Barry Hobbs went on to say.

Mr Hobbs referred all questions to their liquidator.

Emily covered her mouth with her hand and sat down on the chair with a thump. "No. This can't be. I don't believe this." She shook her head. "This is awful."

That was what all the missed calls had been about. Her family worried about their investment, wanting answers.

Marie put a comforting hand on Emily's arm. "What can I do to help?"

"I don't know. That explains why I can't get hold of Stan, the office land line being disconnected, the web site gone."

"Emily, your next appointment is here," Lisa said, popping her head around the door. "What's wrong?"

"Gardenway Homes has gone into liquidation," Marie said.

"Oh, what a shock that must be," Lisa said, glancing at the newspaper. There was no genuineness in her tone.

"I... God... I don't know what to do. I suppose I should ring David." Tears trickled down Emily's face.

"How about I take your appointment and Lisa and Andrea can juggle the rest of the day. You're too upset to work now," Marie said.

"Yeah, we can do that. It'll take a bit of juggling-"

Marie threw Lisa a warning glance.

"-but we'll be fine. You go and sort this out."

"Thanks," Emily said.

Her phone rang, popping up with her lawyer, Farrah Burton's number.

"Emily. It's Farrah. I suppose you've heard."

"Yes. I've just been reading the paper. Tell me it's not true. Am I going to lose all my money?"

"I'm sorry, Emily. This has gone completely under the radar. I've just found out. How about you come to my office and we'll talk about options?"

Emily trotted down to Burton's, her stomach turning over like a boat pitching on a stormy sea, a million thoughts twirling around in her head.

Emily checked in at reception and was shown into Farrah's office.

"Emily." Farrah gave her a hug.

"I keep hoping this isn't true."

"I'm afraid it is. This is a sign of the times. These companies that haven't been operating long bite off more than they can chew and get themselves into trouble. It's greed really."

"I should've paid more attention."

"No. No. We can have all the checks and balances in place and it can still turn to custard. I'll get us some tea."

"Why do people think tea helps things?" Emily raised her voice and grasped the back of the chair to steady herself.

"It's okay, Emily. We'll do the best we can. Now, have a seat. I've set up a call on Skype so we can talk to David."

Bile rose in Emily's mouth. What was she going to say to David, to the rest of her family? They had entrusted her with their money and given her full responsibility to manage this project. And she'd failed.

Farrah's executive assistant, Gail, brought in tea while Farrah turned on the screen and clicked on the Skype icon. She dialled in and within 30 seconds David was in front of Emily. Her big brother blown up larger than life on the big screen.

"David, thanks for joining us at short notice," Farrah said.

"Hi, Farrah, Emily."

Emily gulped. Her overbearing big brother's one-word greeting said it all. She nodded.

"As you'll be aware Gardenway Homes has gone into liquidation."

"Yes. This was unexpected," David replied. "What about the house?"

"I'm going to get onto Peter Wilson after I've spoken to you and see if I can get some more information but from what I can tell so far the news isn't good."

"We're unlikely to get our money back?" David asked.

"No," said Farrah, flicking through the folder on her desk.

"How do we stand legally?"

"There's no obligation by Gardenway Homes to complete the homes."

Emily's breath caught in her throat.

"So we could end up with nothing?" David asked.

"That could be the worst case scenario."

"What about the Quality Builders Scheme?"

"There wasn't one."

"Emily, I thought you said there was one?" David asked.

"I did too. I don't know what's happened."

David fired another question at her. "Emily, did you have any idea anything was going on?"

Emily cleared her throat. "The framing crew was supposed to start several weeks ago, but they left town. I tried to contact

Stan a number of times but both his and the office land lines were disconnected-"

"Why didn't you follow it up sooner?"

"I tried but-"

"David, this is no good trying to blame anyone. Emily, the best thing now is for us to see if we can recover something," Farrah interjected.

"Okay. I'm sorry, Em. It's been a bit of a shock," David said.

Emily threw David a weak smile. Sure, he was mad. It was his money too and Bridget and Yvette's. And she'd let them down.

"How about you contact the rest of your family, explain the situation to them and I'll get back to you as soon as I have something more concrete to report on," Farrah suggested.

"All right. Bye for now," said David, already reaching for his cell phone.

"He's angry," Emily said.

"It's a natural reaction. He doesn't mean to take it out on you."

"I can't believe this is happening." Emily placed her hands over her face. Tears rolled down her cheeks. What a mess. She'd lose her money, her family's money, any credibility to manage a project as the family's baby sister and most of all she'd lost her dream – a house she could live in, call her own. She put her head on the table and sobbed.

Chapter 11

Emily struggled through the next days as the realisation of the implications of Gardenway Homes going into liquidation became apparent. The full weight of the responsibility and worry affected her work. How could she be a good massage therapist – calm, peaceful, stress-free – when every bone in her body was yelling out, why?

The days went by in slow motion. She rang Farrah at least twice a day, and the news was not good. Whenever Farrah had any extra information she would ring Emily. The latest news around the case of the disappearing timber was that it had been picked up by Culverden Building Supplies. Gardenway Homes hadn't paid any invoices for over three months.

At the end of the day, she dragged herself home, picked at dinner and crawled into bed, falling into a restless sleep. What she needed now was Ricky. But as he didn't have a phone, she couldn't ring him. She had no energy at the end of the day to drive out to his house. And what had happened to Vanessa? Had she left town? But she had to put those questions to the back of her mind and concentrate on work and how she was going to get herself out of the Gardenway liquidation mess.

***

Emily worked Saturday morning to make up for the time she'd lost on Monday afternoon.

Now that the initial shock had passed, she was more able to concentrate on providing a good treatment experience for her clients.

She grabbed some aromatherapy oils from the supply room, shut the cupboard door and jumped. "God."

Marie was leaning up against the cupboard.

"You scared me," Emily said, switching the bottles of oil from her left to her right hand.

Marie just stood there.

"What?"

Marie grinned. "Ricky's outside."

"At long last." She washed her hands and walked outside.

Ricky was sitting on the garden seat. His tanned legs showed up against his white board shorts. The sleeves of his T-shirt cut into his muscular biceps making her smile for the first time in days.

"I'm sorry about not contacting you earlier. I heard about Gardenway Homes," Ricky said.

"I'm such a failure."

"No, you're not." Ricky dug around in a plastic bag. "It's Valentine's Day. This is for you." He presented her with a single, red rose.

"Oh, Ricky. That's very sweet of you."

The rose was perfectly formed, its petals closely budded. Emily breathed in the rose scent. "And it smells too."

"No glasshouse roses for you."

She pressed her left fingers to her lips. A single rose can't have been cheap, and in his financial position. She gave a wee snort. She couldn't call the kettle black. Her own finances were now in a precarious state. "Thank you."

"And wait. There's more. I have a picnic lunch for us. I have Marmite sandwiches and two cupcakes. Apparently they're all the rage at the moment Linda said. An apple, banana and the trusty old lemonade."

"Marmite sandwiches?"

"Yes, I'm splashing out."

Emily laughed.

"Come on. We'll go down to the park," Ricky said.

It was a gorgeous summer's day. The air was scented with a wonderful combination of wild flowers and grasses from Red Hill.

They found a spot under a tree. Families were out enjoying Saturday; barbeques were being fired up, children were playing on the swings and a group was playing a game of cricket.

"I wrangled a blanket from Linda," Ricky said, spreading it out on the ground.

"Uh-huh. How did Linda get involved with this?"

"I needed her to help me, you know, woo you."

"Woo me?"

"I'm out of practise with this dating thing. I thought Linda would be able to help me. She said you like spending time outdoors so a picnic was the way to go."

Emily sat down and Ricky handed her two Marmite sandwiches.

She munched away while Ricky poured her a lemonade. When she'd finished her sandwich, Ricky presented her with a pretty pink cup cake with tiny silver balls on top.

As she ate hers, he bit down on the cake.

Emily laughed.

"What's so funny?" Ricky spluttered in between mouthfuls.

"You should see yourself. You definitely look like a man, but you eating a pink cup cake, well, it takes the cake."

"Just don't tell any of my mates. I'll never live it down." He wiped his hands on his shorts. "It's good seeing you smile. You must've had a pretty rough week."

"You won't believe it. It's been a nightmare."

"I'm sorry to hear what's happened. How bad is it?"

"Bad enough." Emily filled Ricky in.

"Man, Stan's a piece of work. No one's ever had anything nice to say about him."

"Why didn't I know? I never heard anything, and I checked them out first."

"These companies can look pretty good on paper and their staff can talk the talk. They prey on vulnerability."

"I didn't think I was vulnerable." Emily looked out over the park at two couples playing Frisbee. "I felt like an idiot. My family entrusted me to manage this project and now I've lost not only their combined sixty-thousand dollars but my own contribution – ten-thousand dollars I borrowed and ten-thousand dollars from my own savings. The eighty-thousand dollars was down payment for the framing and next part of the build. I feel like a failure." She threw a crumb out to a sparrow. "My head has been all over the place. Plus there's a small matter about your ex, which has been worrying me."

Ricky took Emily's hand in his. "And she is my ex. That's all. I'll tell you what's happened on one condition."

The sparrow hopped nearer the blanket, hoping for more crumbs.

"Yes," she said.

"You'll tell me what happened to your hand."

She stiffened. Was she ready to share the part of her that she kept hidden, locked away in her heart?

Ricky searched her eyes, willing her to take the next step. "I took a risk telling you about my gambling. I did it because I think you're worth taking a chance. Please take one too."

Ricky was right. It had taken courage for him to share his wounds – his were emotional, but her's were both emotional and physical.

"Okay," Emily said. "I'll tell you."

"Thank you."

"And Vanessa?"

Ricky rubbed his goatee. "She wanted money. She'd somehow heard via the grapevine from up in Auckland that I'd found a job and was making good money. She must've thought I was raking it in. She hitchhiked all the way down here to get a piece of the action. She wanted my money. We had a massive fight. She hasn't changed and she's still gambling, and it's pulling me down. All the bitterness I felt for her is still there. She didn't believe me when I said I had nothing to give her. She seems to have forgotten I'm still paying off her gambling debts."

"Did she want to get back with you?"

"I think she had a half-assed idea about that, but I wasn't buying it. I gave her ten bucks – all that I had, walked her to the bus depot and made sure she got on the bus. I made it clear I don't want to see her again – ever."

"So she's gone for good?"

"I sure hope so. Seeing her just reminds me of what I was, maybe still am. I want to forget that. I want to be someone else, a better me. I can't do that with her anywhere in my life."

"Well, that's good that you were firm with her."

"Emily, you don't have to worry about her. She's not coming back and I have no feelings for her."

She nodded. That would be one less complication she'd have to deal with.

Ricky rubbed his fingers over her stubs. "Now, I'd like to hear about your story. The odds that you've obviously had to overcome to be who you are today."

Chapter 12

Even though the sun was throwing out brilliantly heated golden rays, Emily shivered.

Ricky squeezed her hand tight. "Go on," he encouraged.

The day that changed her life forever was still etched firmly in her mind.

"It was a horrible day. The complete opposite to this. Torrential rain, the wind was blowing a gale. My fiancé, Josh, and I had this massive fight and I just couldn't take him yelling at me. I'd stuffed up – again! And though I loved him to bits I always seemed to be messing up. I left the apartment and went for a walk in the park, which was a stupid thing to do. The rain was driving against my face and leaves and branches were being blown all over the place." She placed a hand across her stomach and her breath came out in ragged gasps.

"A huge tree crashed down on top of me pinning my arm under one of its branches. I couldn't free my arm. I yelled for help, but nobody could hear me. The pain in my hand was incredible and I kept blacking out. I finally was able to get my cell phone out of my back pocket and call for an ambulance. I tried ringing Josh, but he wouldn't pick up. When the ambulance officers arrived they were able to stabilise me and help me with the pain, but they needed the fire brigade came and cut the tree off me."

A tennis ball that had been hit by a cricket bat struck the ground and rolled over towards them. Ricky picked up the ball and threw it back to the boy.

"The damage to my fingers was so bad they had to amputate them and so here I am with a disfigured, ugly hand."

"I don't find your hand ugly. In fact, I am intrigued by it."

"Like a person at a zoo staring at a strange animal?"

"No, not like that. It's the story behind it. You must've had some huge challenges to overcome."

"You bet." Emily sighed in relief. Ricky wasn't fascinated at her hand because of its ugliness or stared at it in a way other people did, as if she was a freak. "I had so much to overcome. First, it was the pain, the physical pain. I had to take a lot of painkillers, which I didn't want to do. It totally goes against my whole natural therapy beliefs. Then there was the emotional pain. I got depressed wondering how I'd be able to live a normal life with my missing fingers, wondering whether I'd ever be able to work again. But I had lots of physio and did exercises to build my strength and flexibility."

The doctors had encouraged her to massage the skin around where the fingers used to be to help desensitise the skin and keep it mobile. She could barely bring herself to touch her wrinkly skin. It repulsed her and freaked her out.

"It took a while for me to get comfortable with the sight of my hand."

"I have noticed you try to hide it or sit on it."

Emily smiled. "Yes, I do still sit on my hand. I'm self-conscious of it but I've had counselling and that helped. I was really worried about how I'd ever be able to be a massage therapist again, but with some re-training on how to use and manipulate my fingers and with an attitude adjustment, things have worked out okay."

"And Josh?"

"That didn't work out at all." Emily cleared her throat as the build-up of emotion threatened to overwhelm her. "He left me."

"I'm sorry." Ricky gave her hand another squeeze.

"He was great after my accident. When I was well enough to go home he looked after me. There was nothing he wouldn't do for me. Then one day I came home after a physio session. His stuff was gone and he'd left a note."

"What did it say?"

"Just that he couldn't do it anymore and he needed a break. There was a time I could've told you word for word what he said in that note. But I can't anymore. I just know he left because he couldn't stand the sight of my hand. He winced any time his hand touched mine, as though I'd just given him a disease."

"Whew!"

"I moved in with my brother, David, and I met Marie. She'd just got a job here at Misty Springs and suggested I apply for one of the other positions. Lisa took a chance on me and here I am. Slowly trying to put my life back together."

"You're doing a really good job at it. I'm no expert, but I can vouch that I wouldn't have known you had two fingers short when you gave me my massage."

"Thanks. I just wished I hadn't made such a mess of this building project."

"That could've happened to anyone. Besides I'll try and help you as best I can. That's if you still think we should make a go of this – you and I."

"I do. Now that Vanessa's out of the picture permanently it will make it easier."

"We've both got issues that we're dealing with. I think we should do something to take our minds off our troubles. Would you like to come with me to the wood chopping champs at Cooper's Creek next weekend?"

Emily stiffened and withdrew her hand.

"I've said something wrong. What did I say?"

"It's not what you said. It's just that I found it hard to watch you with that axe. It's so close to your feet. One wrong move... I'm scared you'll chop your foot off. And I don't want you to experience what it's like to lose a body part."

"Do you think that if there was such a high risk doing that all wood choppers would be walking around footless?"

"No. But you don't even wear safety shoes."

"You're right. You do have to be careful. But we wear steel cap shoes and steel socks."

"Steel socks?"

"It's a covering which goes over the top of the foot and is attached to a shin guard made of special material. When you're at my house again I'll show you."

"Have you ever hit your foot?"

"Yes. When I first started out I had a couple of miss hits."

"What happened to your foot?"

"Bruised and very sore. It makes you a lot more careful the next time."

"I don't know, Ricky. I just don't want to see you get hurt."

"I'm careful, but I'll be extra careful from now on. How about you think about it and you can let me know?"

Emily nodded. She glanced at her watch. "I need to get back."

"Sure." Ricky held out his hand and pulled Emily to her feet. "So we're good?"

"We're good."

"I'll walk you back."

They packed up and hand in hand walked back to the salon.

Emily held the rose in her other hand and couldn't resist smiling back at the sly smiles from those she passed who eyed her rose.

At the front door, Ricky kissed her gently on the cheek and promised to meet up with her on Wednesday after work.

Emily opened the door amidst frantic scurrying away from the window by Marie and Andrea.

"What's going on?" Emily asked.

"Nothing."

"Nothing."

"Were you spying on me?"

"No."

"Not at all."

Marie's head was down as she wrote something on a piece of paper, and Andrea stared at the computer screen.

"Although we couldn't help noticing Ricky-"

"-and the rose-"

"-and the kiss."

"Are you two official now?" Marie asked.

"Yeah. He's a really understanding guy. And he ran his ex out of town, which puts us on more solid ground."

"After a false start, it looks like things are working out for you," Andrea said.

"I hope so. Ricky's a nice guy." She walked down to the kitchen. Humming, she filled up a small vase with water, placed the rose in it and set it down on the counter in her room, where she'd be able to see it while she worked. Now she knew where she stood with Ricky at least she could make plans for some areas in her life.

***

"I don't know why I'm doing this," Emily said, shading her eyes against the setting of the sun. "When I used to see the house I was excited. My dream of owning a house and having my space, something I could call my own was taking shape. Now, I almost feel like throwing up." Emily pressed her lips together.

Farrah had suggested she and Emily go out to the house to check on it.

"I know that this is not the outcome you had envisaged but you can't bury your head in the sand. All is not lost. You still own the land and the foundations have been poured," Farrah replied.

"Eighty-thousand dollars has gone. How can that not be a loss?"

"We'll wait and see what the bank has to say tomorrow. Now how about you use my camera to take some photos of the site so we have records of what has and hasn't been done and I'll do a check on the rest of the property?"

Emily wandered around the section taking photos. Not that there was much to take. From every angle there was just concrete, concrete, and more concrete plus rubbish. The only thing that held any glimmer of hope was the big, lone willow tree in the corner.

"I'll get someone out here tomorrow to fence off the front, which will make it more secure," Farrah said, peering into the rubbish skip. "And I'll get the skip taken away. You're not paying any more money on something you're not using."

"Thanks for helping me," Emily said, as they jumped into Farrah's car.

"That's what I'm here for," Farrah replied, as she drove back into Misty Springs township and dropped off Emily.

"I'll meet you at the bank tomorrow at 9," Farrah said, as Emily got out of the car. "Try to get a good night's sleep."

"Okay," Emily said, getting out of the car and shutting the door.

Sleep? When she had to face the bank manager tomorrow? Emily's heart sank.

***

The bank manager, Todd Cross, showed Farrah and Emily into his office. "You've got yourself into an unfortunate situation," he said, straightening his blue tie. We're in contact with the liquidators on a daily basis, but it seems unlikely Emily or any other creditors will get their money back."

Emily gulped. It sounded worse when someone said the words out loud.

Todd riffled through Emily's file. "So you've used sixty-thousand dollars from your family, ten-thousand dollars came from yourself and we gave you a ten-thousand dollar loan at four percent interest, compounding over three years."

Emily nodded. She'd only met Todd a couple of times. He was thorough and professional but lacked any warmth which prevented her from relating to him in any way.

Pulling out the loan agreement, Todd flicked over a couple of pages, ran his finger down the page stopping halfway down. He took his glasses off. "Yes, it's our standard terms and conditions. It's not what you'll be wanting to hear. You'll still have to pay back the remainder of the loan. You've paid back five-thousand dollars so there's still five-thousand dollars plus one-thousand dollars interest."

Emily swallowed hard. "I was hoping for better news, but I guess deep down I knew there would be no way out of it."

Todd lent forward on the table. "You're not the only one of our clients who has been done out by these rogues. Normally you'd be protected by the Quality Builders Scheme, but it seems you've been taken for a ride and we certainly wouldn't have approved the loan had we known the situation."

"It appears that while the Quality Builders Scheme logo was stamped on the proposals you saw Emily, that's all it was," Farrah said.

"I was lead to believe by Stan that by signing the documents I'd automatically be covered," Emily said.

"And that's where it's gone wrong. It was an assumption. And because Gardenways Company wasn't registered with the scheme you've had no protection. This was something that should have been double-checked," Todd said, eyeing the lawyer.

"By the bank as well," Farrah replied quickly.

Tension sparked between the lawyer and the loan manager.

"I think we've all learnt some things out of this," Emily said, her voice coming out loud and strong. "I accept that I will still have to pay back what's outstanding."

He closed the file. "You did the right thing by letting us know and if you need help with extending the loan terms we can have a look at that."

"Thank you. I'll be making sure I check, double-check, and triple check all documentation before signing anything like this again," Emily said.

They all shook hands. Emily and Farrah left the bank and walked back to the lawyer's office. On arrival Gail had a tray prepared with tea and chocolate chip biscuits.

Emily sat down and stared at the painting on the wall – a landscape scene that had faded from the afternoon sun. What had once been brilliant reds and greens was now dull colours merging into the white background. What was once bright, now a dull, muted shade. *Just like my dream.*

"I honestly didn't think that they'd write the loan off, but it doesn't make me feel any better that I have to pay back money and have nothing to show for it. Part of my plan was to be able to sell cosmetics, but I would need a loan to get underway. What bank would give me one now? I'd be in the high risk category.

"Maybe I can get some more hours at the salon or maybe some waitressing. Just like when I was a student. It'll be like going backwards. I guess David, Bridget and Yvette will be wanting me to pay their money back too. I'll be in debt for the rest of my life."

"They can't expect you to do that and unfortunately they'll have to do what you've had to accept – that the money has gone."

"I can imagine what David's going to say to that."

"Let me deal with David. You don't need any more hassles."

"I'll feel obligated for the rest of my life," Emily muttered.

"One day at a time," Farrah said.

Back at work, Emily had two appointments, and she caught up with Marie and Andrea at lunch time in the staff room. In an effort to divert her misery away from herself she asked Marie about her arm.

"Look," Marie said, pulling up her sleeve. The skin was no longer angry, red, and pimply. "It's all gone since I stopped using that Nature's One moisturiser."

"Much better," Emily said, rubbing her hand lightly over Marie's arm.

"Have you had any more clients with reactions?" Marie asked Andrea.

"No, but I'm really reluctant to recommend it. I'm just worried what Lisa's going to say when she realises sales are down."

"Well, I'm not selling products to clients when their advertising is a scam. They're not natural," Emily said.

"Oh, I almost forgot. Those two lip balms you gave me which I passed on. My clients loved them and want more. You're on to something here," Andrea said.

"Really?" Emily said.

"They think the lip balm tastes divine and their lips stay silky smooth all day."

"Great. I'll have to make some more. At least one thing's going right."

"I was reading something when I was studying the other night. You know how your body butter gets mould on it? You keep them on top of the bench over here, don't you?" Marie asked. "It could be they're exposed to too much light."

Emily looked around. Sun streamed into the lunch room in the morning hitting the bench where she kept the jars.

"And the heat from the sun won't be helping either. I suggest putting them in an airtight container well away from heat and light," Marie commented.

"That makes a lot of sense. Why didn't I think of that before? I'll make a new batch and hide them away in a cupboard," Emily said, her words rushing out.

"Not before you make some more lip balm. I'll be able to charge you for commission soon," Andrea added.

They all laughed.

"The more money I make the more I'll be able to pay the loan-to-nothing off and I'll be one step closer to starting again."

Emily's heart warmed. Having Marie and Andrea as friends made the difficulties over the last week just that little bit more bearable.

Chapter 13

Ricky popped into the salon at lunch time the next day and invited Emily out for dinner on Wednesday night.

"Where would you like to go?" he asked.

"How about The Fire House?"

"I was thinking something a little bit cheaper. The meals can be expensive there."

Emily chewed on her sandwich. That was true and it wasn't just Ricky who would have to watch his spending; she would too.

"What about Red Hill Bar?" he asked.

Red Hill Bar was okay for Friday night drinks, but not her idea of a place to go on a romantic date.

"I see you're not keen on that idea," Ricky said.

"They do have cheaper light meals at The Fire House," Emily suggested.

"Sure. Let's go there. Besides, a pub meal at Red Hill on a Wednesday night might not be a good thing with my physical workload the next day."

They agreed to meet at The Fire House at six. Ricky said he'd bring a change of clothes to work and would shower at the camping grounds.

***

After work on Wednesday Emily changed into a cream blouse, black trousers and silver sandals. She spritzed her hair, sprayed on Marc Jacobs' fruity, citrusy *Daisy* and chose a pair of dangly earrings.

It was a beautiful evening with the setting sun turning the tops of the tree branches a sparkling shade of gold as she walked down the main street to The Fire House.

Ricky was waiting for her outside. He held the door open for her as they went inside. A waitress showed them over to a table by the window.

The Fire House had been converted into a restaurant five years ago. The building was where the fire brigade had been based until they moved into their new premises. The old building had been earmarked for demolition, but amidst outcry from the locals who wanted to preserve one of the only original buildings in the town, it was saved. The building was bought and turned into a restaurant while still maintaining the charm of its early days. Photos of past and recent fire crews lined the walls along with props of jackets, helmets and hoses. There was even a fire pole in the middle of the restaurant that was often used by patrons to twirl around on.

The waitress brought over a menu, which outlined fish, chicken, beef or lamb dishes served with veggies or salad, chips or potatoes. There was also a special curry section – the heat of which was graded either fire engine red, fire engine hot or fire engine volcano.

Like Strawberry Desert it was popular amongst everyone, even on weeknights. Tonight a child's birthday party was underway down one end of the restaurant and at the other end a group of females let out raucous laughter.

Ricky ordered a small serve of lamb ribs and Emily chose the fish of the day.

"Ever spun yourself around the pole?" Ricky asked.

"Ah, no. Although we've had a few late, rowdy nights here. I guess you wouldn't be surprised if I said Lisa gave a good show doing a pole dance one night," Emily said, laughing.

"No, it doesn't surprise me."

"Eventually she got told off by management who said she was being too provocative and for a family restaurant."

"Figures."

"Although she did pick up a date for the night."

Ricky chuckled.

"So have you had the chance to think about coming to the wood chopping summer carnival this weekend?"

"I suppose you're wanting a ride."

"Emily, I'm not asking for a ride. One of the guys can take me. I just thought you'd like to come along."

Emily chewed on the last piece of fish.

"You still not sure about the whole axe thing?"

"No."

"I can understand that you're nervous, but I promise you it's really safe." Ricky caught her hand. "Please come. I really need some support. A fan club."

Emily smiled. "I'll come but I want to see these metal socks."

"I'm happy to show you my socks any time."

"And I'm happy to give you a ride," Emily offered.

"Thank you. I appreciate that."

They decided against dessert and after another drink they called it a night.

The waitress popped the bill down in a black plastic holder in the middle of the table.

They both reached for it at the same time.

"I've got it," said Emily, tugging the folder towards her.

"No, it's fine. I've got it." Ricky tugged it back.

"No, really." Emily tugged it forward again.

"I'll pay."

"I'm happy to pay." Emily tugged it further forward.

"I've said I've got it." Ricky tugged it harder.

What is wrong with him? His face had gone from relaxed and happy to strained and angry. *Are we going to have a fight in public?* She didn't mind paying. She had often paid the whole bill on dates. That's what couples did. Right? Split the bill or pay it in total. She didn't expect Ricky to pay for anything.

Then the light bulb lit. She'd insulted him by implying he didn't have the money to pay. "Look, how about if you pay the next time. I'm used to splitting the bill or each person picking up the bill every other time."

She held on tightly to the holder. Ricky stopped tugging and the unexpected release caused her back to thud against the chair.

With the holder now firmly in her hands, she got up and walked over to the counter. She whipped out her card and paid the bill.

They left the restaurant and stood on the footpath.

Ricky remained silent. "Thanks for the meal," he said, his eyes downcast.

She couldn't figure out what was going on. *He doesn't sound very thankful.* "I didn't mind paying." Maybe it was best to change the subject. This was obviously a sore point for him. "How are you getting home?"

"I'll walk."

"I can drop you off."

"Thanks, but a walk on a night like this is good."

"It must take an hour each way. Don't you get tired? Working all day on building sites, walking to and from work?"

"I don't mind. It means I sleep well at night and it keeps up my fitness level so I can be match fit for wood chopping."

They made plans for Emily to pick him up early on Saturday morning so they could make a good start for Cooper's Creek, a 100 kms away.

"And I'll have my socks ready for you for inspection."

Emily grinned. "I've never been so excited to see a man's socks."

"Have a good night. See you Saturday." And he was off down the road.

Emily sighed deeply. He hadn't kissed her, not even a tiny one on the cheek like last time. *Was he sore with me for paying for the meal?* She shook her head and made a mental note for him to pay next time.

***

On Saturday Emily picked Ricky up from his house where he was already outside waiting. *Is he embarrassed that I see inside the house again?* The outside still looked a mess; it really needed a good tidy up.

Ricky popped his bag in the boot and they were off.

She desperately wanted to talk to Ricky about his house, his financial situation but he was in such a cheerful mood and obviously looking forward to the wood chopping events. *Another time then.*

Ricky explained some of the technical aspects of wood chopping, the classes and the wood used which was mostly radiata pine. "I'll be on twice today and I hope to improve on my last placing from a couple of weeks ago." He looked over the programme for the day. "I may even beat Mike. I reckon I can."

"Do you have to pay to compete?" Emily asked.

"There's a small entrance fee, but you can recoup that back if you're placed. Underhands can get one-hundred dollars for first placing."

They arrived in plenty of time for Ricky to do his preparation. He introduced her to some of the other fellow woodchoppers.

"Now you can sit here on this bench," Ricky said, "and I'll show you these socks." He rummaged around in his bag and pulled out a pair of long metal mesh socks passing them to her.

She ran her hand up and down the rough, wiry mesh.

"It helps to stop blows and deflections," Ricky explained.

It didn't seem all that much to prevent a catastrophic injury.

"You're still not sure." Ricky looked at her.

"Why can't you wear boots?"

"They're too clunky and we have to be quick on our feet."

Little butterflies flopped around in her stomach.

"You'd have to be a really bad wood chopper to hit your foot," Ricky said, trying to reassure her.

"They're tougher than what I thought they'd be." She squeezed one of the socks.

Ricky sat down on the bench beside her, whipped off his old socks, put on the metal ones and pulled on his volley steel toe cap shoes. "See. All protected." He stood up and moved his feet around settling everything down. "The first event is in a quarter of an hour. I need to find Lenny. I'm borrowing his axes, again."

Unlike the Rahu A and P Show, there were no benches for spectators, just a grass area. "I'll go and sit over here. Good luck." She found a good viewing spot, put down the blanket and took a large gulp of water.

Standing wood chopping was the first three events. By the time the third event had finished, Emily was impressed. The skill required to hit a block of wood in virtually the same place each time intrigued her. Some of the more experienced wood choppers – big, burly men – took a minimal number of swings before they switched over to the other side of the block. Muscles rippled, sweat flew and the small but awestruck crowd clapped.

Next up was the underhand, Ricky's event. She'd watched him prepare with his axe marking up the wood.

The announcer counted down the handicaps and within 15 seconds they were all chopping.

Ricky was off to a good start keeping pace with the other woodchoppers. He brought the axe down firmly and accurately between his feet, lifting the axe above his head and then powering it back down again.

Emily's stomach lurched again. One false move, one slip up. Even after feeling the steel socks and Ricky's reassurance that you had to have a good aim, she couldn't bear it if Ricky, or anyone, injured themselves knowing the long months of rehabilitation and pain that would lie ahead. But she stayed and kept watching and couldn't help but admire the strength, co-ordination, balance and accuracy the sport required. Before long, her anxiety diminished as she oohed and aahed with the rest of the crowd at the closeness of the competition. Ricky's broad, tanned shoulders ripped and his biceps bulged. The first competitor finished to loud whistling and cheering from the crowd, followed closely by the second and third placegetters. Ricky finished fourth. His beaming face reflected that he was happy with his performance.

He came over to see her at the lunch break and they shared bread rolls, fruit, raisins and nuts that Emily had packed earlier that morning.

"I should've brought more food," Emily said, as she watched Ricky devour his second roll.

"Lots of energy required. You could always starve on my behalf," Ricky suggested.

"I need food too," Emily protested. "Just remember I'm your ride back."

Ricky put an arm around her and pulled her close to him. He smelt of earth, wood and sawdust, just like the forests of Misty Springs. She leaned against his side.

"How are you holding out?" he asked.

"I'm enjoying myself," Emily admitted. "I still cringe a little when the axe gets so close to your feet, but I'm putting all my faith in those sexy metal socks."

"Atta girl." Ricky gave her shoulder a squeeze and burped. "I'd better stop eating in case I throw up."

"Eww!"

He stood up and wiped the crumbs from his mouth. "I'm first up after lunch. This time I'm going to get third." He threw a wave at her as he strode away.

He didn't get third. In fact he dropped back to fifth place. But he seemed okay with that, his smile still lit up his face.

Ricky had no more events so he joined Emily on the blanket as they watched the rest of the wood chopping, which included the double hand saw, butcher's block and the Jack and Jill swing.

It was late in the afternoon when they started back for Misty Springs. Ricky chattered non-stop all the way home, all keyed up and munching a bag of his favourite lollies, liquorice allsorts. He didn't seem to mind that he'd not placed; just that he was having to borrow equipment.

Emily dropped Ricky off back home and they made plans to catch up during the week. Even though the week had been fraught with difficulties she'd enjoyed the day out.

Chapter 14

On Tuesday after work, Emily set about making new batches of the lemon and lavender lip balm and the sugar scrub.

Making sure all the utensils were scrupulously clean, she carefully measured out all the ingredients for the body butter. The previous week she'd ordered a whole heap of airtight containers, not taking any chances this time.

She scooped the mixture into the containers. Ensuring the containers were completely airtight she carried them down the hall. The linen cupboard would be the perfect place to store them. They would be out of the light and heat from the sun.

Confident she now had the process right, she flicked through her folder looking for another recipe. Her hand stopped at one she'd wanted to try for some time – a body cream. It was similar to the body butter but was very concentrated with the promise to moisturise and leave the skin softer and silkier than store-bought moisturisers.

She whipped up the ingredients – sweet almond oil, beeswax, lavender oil and grape seed oil – in the correct quantities, spooned the mixture into jars, making sure they were 100 percent airtight. She placed the containers on a tray and popped them into the linen cupboard. One whole shelf was now taken up with her cosmetics.

Emily stepped back and ran a hand over the back of her neck. Now she had to wait.

The next day Lisa was on the war path and called an impromptu lunch time meeting.

"Let me guess," Marie muttered. "It'll be about Nature's One."

Marie was right.

"We're not selling enough of it," Lisa said. "We must get the sales up."

"I'm pushing the product as best I can," Andrea said, "but no one is interested."

"Are you using it on your client?"

"Yes."

"Then I don't understand why sales aren't growing."

"Maybe word has got around," Andrea said.

"What word?"

"I've had more clients who have used it complain that they're breaking out in a rash."

Lisa's face was stony. "I thought we'd concluded that we have no proof that it's being caused by Nature's One."

"Marie's rash completely cleared up after she stopped using the body cream," Emily said, backing up Andrea.

"That's coincidence," Lisa snapped.

"I don't think it is. Marie hadn't been using any other new products during that time."

"What about your clients, Emily? What have they been saying?"

Emily did a star doodle on her notebook stalling for time. "Nothing."

Lisa referred to her notes. "You haven't sold anything more since our last meeting."

That was true. She hadn't and that was because she refused to sell products that were being falsely sold as natural.

"I instructed you, all of you, that you'd all be required to sell more of Nature's One."

Emily put her pen down. This was verging on bullying. "What's the reason why you're pushing this stuff?"

"It's good. The overseas sales figures for a new product are exceptional. We're the first to try it in New Zealand."

A fact that Lisa hadn't told them before.

"How much commission are you getting?" Emily asked. She was sure that there was more to this than Lisa was letting on.

"You don't need to know that," Lisa said. "All you need to do is promote this product. I asked you, no instructed you, several weeks ago to use these products and sell them."

"I can't-," Emily began.

"I'm not going to say this again. I want a concentrated effort by everyone to get these sales up. In fact, I'm going to offer a weekend away in Aqua Bay to whomever sells the most product in the next month."

Bribery. Lisa must be desperate.

"Sounds good. Vinnie and I could do with a weekend away," Andrea said, missing the point entirely.

Marie gave Emily a look that said she wasn't falling for it.

But Andrea's comment had eased the tension somewhat.

"I'll give it a try," Marie said, expressionless.

Lisa's eyes bored into Emily's. "Do I have to ask you again?"

Emily wasn't going to make a promise she couldn't - wouldn't keep - but like last time she was left with little choice. Not trusting what would come out of her mouth, she just nodded, slumping into her chair.

"Great. Back to work girls. And let's get those sales up." Lisa shut her folder and bustled out of the room.

"That's an incentive," Andrea said.

"You're still going to push Nature's One?" Emily asked Andrea.

"As Lisa said, we don't have any real proof."

"You know that's not true. Your own clients have been having reactions."

Andrea's smile faded. "I can't stand up to Lisa. She scares me."

"And you just want to keep the peace."

Andrea nodded. "I hate conflict."

So did Emily. Nature's One products weren't natural, it was false advertising. Nor did the company appear to have tested the products. Clients were complaining. Her nails bit into her hand. Despite her assurances to Lisa, she wasn't going to sell any more and she would just have to bear the consequences.

***

Emily and Ricky settled into a pattern of Wednesdays being date night. Wanting to avoid another repeat of awkward 'who's-paying' restaurant scenes, when Ricky popped around to see her in her lunch hour she suggested a walk up Red Hill.

"I haven't been up there yet," Ricky said.

"All the better. I want to show you something special. How about I meet you at the bottom of Red Hill at eight pm?"

"That's late for a walk."

"It's all part of the special treat," Emily said.

"I'm intrigued."

"I'll see you then."

Ricky pecked her on the cheek and set off back to work.

***.

After a quick dinner of salad, bread and fresh fruit, Emily changed into cargo pants, a T-shirt and walking shoes. She wrapped a sweatshirt around her waist and set out down the road to meet Ricky.

He was already waiting for her, and he had changed into board shorts and a deep brown T-shirt, which matched his eyes. He took her hand and they began the gentle ascent up Red Hill.

"Is there chocolate cake at the top?" Ricky asked.

"Nooo."

"You said there was a special treat. I'm picking it involves food."

"No."

"A bar with my favourite beers?"

"No."

"A pizza place?"

"Nope. It's got nothing to do with food."

Ricky's bottom lip pouted. "I'm not sure I can make it then."

"Stop your nattering." Emily lightly battered Ricky on his arm. "You'll just have to wait until we get to the top."

"I'm sure it'll be worth it, whatever it is."

They passed a couple of people going down, but after that they had the track to themselves.

Ricky told her about the building that was going on at Morningside subdivision. "What do you think you'll do about the house and land?"

"I'm not sure. Maybe I'll sell it. That way I can at least get some of my money back and pay back my family. I won't be in debt and I'll be guilt-free." Emily sighed. "It'll mean starting all over again though."

Gradually the pine and beech trees thinned out and they entered the clearing. They wandered over to the pergola that provided shelter from the rain and sun.

Down below Emily could just make out the movement of vehicles in the streets, dark smudges moving like miniature toy cars. Long black shadows hit the roofs as the sun melted into the horizon. She leaned up against the wooden rail. Ricky stood close beside her, his body heat radiating onto her skin.

Emily lifted her head to the sky. "If you wait just a minute…"

The last chorus of the birds rang out and wind rustled gently in the trees. The golden glow of the sun stretched its rays over the land, turning the fields into deep shades of lavender, indigo and purple. Layers of soft peach, brilliant yellow and then pink beamed through the long stretch of cloud. Dusk's fingers pulled earth and sky into one. Dust motes and pollen floated, suspended in the air.

"So much beauty that lasts only a moment," Emily whispered. Every sunset she saw from Red Hill left her warm inside.

"We have to capture this moment before it disappears," Ricky whispered. He moved behind her and kissed her neck, once, twice, three times. His lips were warm as if he'd sucked up sunbeams.

Emily tilted her neck as Ricky kissed lower along her shoulder. She reached her hand up behind her and rested it on Ricky's head guiding him lower.

"Turn around," he whispered.

Emily shifted her body weight so she was facing Ricky. His arms wrapped around her drawing her in tight. She could just make out his brown eyes, the last of the sun reflecting little golden nuggets in them.

His lips played around the corners of her mouth, the whiskers of his goatee caressed her chin.

The anticipation was killing her. Her knees quivered. If he hadn't been holding her, she would've collapsed. Her heart thundered in her chest as his lips finally met hers and she succumbed. She returned his hot, moist kiss willingly and let out a tiny moan. It had been too long since her last kiss. Memories of just how good that first kiss could be, flickered like spring finally awakening after a long winter.

Emily traced her hand down Ricky's face. The light had almost disappeared, the sun nearly gone. She couldn't see his face clearly, but she didn't need to. His passion was all evident and she kissed him back with the same intensity.

He let out a sigh. "I've wanted to kiss you since I first saw you."

"Just to keep me quiet, I bet."

"It would've been the *only* way to keep you quiet."

Emily laughed. "The romantic in me always wanted to share a kiss with someone up here, with a sunset."

"Your wish has been granted. But, just someone?"

"Someone special."

She turned her head towards Ricky, his lips brushing against hers, sending tingles everywhere.

"If you were ever wondering where Red Hill got its name from, it's because of the amazing red on-fire sunsets that can be seen from here," Emily said.

"It really was something special. There were so many colours that made everything alive, but yet peaceful at the same time."

As dusk disappeared, they held hands as they made their way back down, the lights of Misty Springs shining bright. They passed Red Hill Bar, The Fire House and Strawberry Desert, all of which were crowded.

"Would you like to come in for a drink?" Emily asked, as they stopped outside her house.

"Sure."

Emily fixed herself a tea and Ricky a coffee.

They sat side by side on the couch chatting. Emily finished her tea and placed the cup and saucer on the table.

Since Ricky had kissed her, a warm glow had spread all over her. It was like all the heat of the sun had passed from Ricky's lips and melted through hers, turning her blood to honey.

Ricky kissed her cheek and in a flash their lips met again. She pressed her lips to his more urgently. His hand moved across her breasts.

"Come with me," she whispered, as she took Ricky by the hand and led him to her bedroom.

Ricky's breath hit her neck like hot embers.

She pulled him down onto the bed and straddled him.

Their lips locked again. Emily's desire met Ricky's as his wet tongue slipped over hers. She caressed the softened skin on his head. He held her arms; his hands were rough, work-hardened yet his touch was gentle somehow.

Emily quivered as she gripped his biceps feeling the strength in them.

Tugging at her T-shirt, he pulled it up over her head. He pushed her bra straps off her shoulders and kissed the mound of her breast.

Her heart pulsed in time with his. She yanked his T-shirt over his head and ran her hands down his warm body, so warm that she was sure she was about to catch fire.

There was a moan, but it hadn't come from her. And it was too feminine to have been Ricky's. Ricky's mouth moved lower on her breast. The moan came again.

Emily lifted her head up. There it was again, louder, but muffled.

Ricky stopped. "What's wrong?"

"Can you hear that?"

"Huh?"

"Listen."

This time there was another moan, louder again... coming from a male.

"What the-"

Then came the squeaking, knocking and banging, growing louder and more rhythmic.

Ricky moved off Emily and onto the bed beside her.

"Oh no!" Emily whispered, covering her face.

"Is that what I think it is?"

"Hmm mmm." Emily turned to face Ricky, his face outlined in the green glow from the alarm clock.

"Who's next door?"

"It's Andrea's bedroom. And obviously Vinnie's in there."

"Good lord."

The banging reached a crescendo, there was a squeal, a grunt and then silence.

"How embarrassing," Emily whispered. "My face is burning." She turned and buried her head in Ricky's chest. She started to giggle and Ricky sniggered.

"Talk about a mood breaker," he said then seeing the funny side of it, chuckled.

They dissolved into fits of smothered laughter.

"You know what?" Emily said, when she finally gathered her breath.

"What?"

"I really need my own space, my own house. I'm going to continue building and see it through to the end. I'll show everyone."

Ricky planted a kiss on her nose. "That's my girl."

Chapter 15

The best thing about not being able to contact Ricky was that he would sometimes turn up unexpectedly when he was on a lunch break, surprising her.

"How about we go for a swim after work?" Ricky said, biting into a mince pie. "My muscles are aching."

"Isn't it time for a massage?"

"We could do both. A private massage later would just round it off nicely."

"Not sure what Lisa would say about me giving you private massages seen as you're supposed to be a paying client as well."

"What she doesn't know won't kill her."

"Yes, but it might kill me."

A swim after work sounded great. It was well over a month since her last dip in the therapeutic pools that Misty Springs was famous for. The girls had quite often gone for a soak on Saturdays, but lately they'd all been engrossed in their own projects.

It was a gorgeous summer's evening with hardly a breath of wind. Clouds of misty steam lazily drifted up from the pools. Emily took a big breath. Sulphur and the warm, dry pine needle scent that she'd grown to love since settling in the town. She met Ricky outside the entrance to the pools after work. Now that Ricky had seen her partially naked - even though it was in the glow of her alarm clock - her damaged hand didn't seem to be an issue for him. Getting more naked didn't phase her as it may've done in the past. Still she had picked a one piece bright blue bathing costume that draped a little in front revealing her small but rounded breasts.

After she'd changed and put her clothes in the locker, she found Ricky waiting for her outside one of the four pools.

His board shorts were almost the same sea-blue, and his legs were well defined, muscular and golden brown. With all the lifting, carrying, hammering and bending day after day, he had a definite six pack of abs.

Her heart skipped a beat.

Ricky looked over at the rocks and therapy pools, each connected by a small waterfall. "Which pool first?"

"How about the sulphur pools?" Emily suggested.

They wandered over to the section where there were two large sulphur pools contained within an outer wall of volcanic rock.

"What's the temperature?"

Emily read off the sign. "Forty degrees celcius. Can you handle the heat?"

"I love it hot."

Emily climbed the natural rock steps, plunged her feet in and waded over to the seats that were immersed in the pool. "Hot is definitely what it is."

They both sat down.

Ricky let out a loud satisfied, "Ahhh."

Emily lent her head back against the rocks, letting the warmth of the water seep through her skin into the muscles, into the core of her. She plunged her hands into the smooth, velvety water. Both her doctor and physiotherapist said that the rich minerals - sodium, chloride, boron, calcium and carbonate - would help soothe her hands' damaged bones and tissues, which would otherwise stiffen up.

Emily stole a look at Ricky. His eyes were closed as he luxuriated in the heat. She closed her eyes too, the recent worries melting away as the relaxing heat drifted through her. She was half-way between the real world and an escape-to world when Ricky nudged her.

"I think we should move on before we turn into prunes," he said.

Emily reluctantly brought herself round. He was right. The heat never allowed you to stay in for long and it was important to rehydrate too.

They climbed out of the sulphur pool and washed themselves under the outdoor shower. Ricky popped into the café and bought two bottles of water.

Wrapping a towel around her, she took a sip from the bottle.

Now that the summer holidays were well and truly over, clientele had changed from families to locals and overseas tourists. Some folks had come with picnic baskets and others had a barbecue underway.

The early evening sun reached its rays through the pine trees and in the distance the sky behind the Tussock Brown Ranges prismed out into different shades of blue, finally merging into white.

"Which pool next?" Ricky asked.

"How about the therapy pool?"

This pool had a different feel to it than the sulphur pool. Rather than relaxing, this was more invigorating with large bubbling jets, which made the water roil.

Emily immersed herself in the water. "This pool should help your muscles too. The jets help decrease swelling and pain."

The water cascaded above them in a roar and bounced them up and down closer to the waterfall that linked this and the rock pool together.

Ricky bobbed over toward Emily, throwing his arms around her shoulders. Their bodies melded together Water droplets dripped off his head and down his face. She rubbed her wet cheek against his, the combination of slippery water a contrast to his rough stubbled face. He kissed her on the mouth and she returned the kiss with intensity. The more she kissed him the more it set her senses alight. *Thank goodness I'm in the water! I need something to smother the heat.*

When they'd finished in the aqua pool there was only the rock pools left, Emily's second favourite pool. These pools were a sanctuary nestled at the back of the complex. Flax, tussock grass, hebes and bright green Pittosporum lined the outside creating a striking array of patterns and colour. Behind the garden, the gorgeous yellow of the kowhai trees were in bloom. A bellbird bobbed on the branches.

By now the sun had set and fairy lights that were draped discretely in the bushes twinkled like diamonds. Coloured lights hanging over the trees danced in the gentle breeze.

The water shimmered in a colourful rainbow reflecting back in Ricky's eyes. His arm slid round her waist holding her firm and true. She didn't want him to let go. She nestled her head on his shoulder. Could they stay like this forever? Her body was relaxed beyond belief.

"I'm famished," Ricky said after a while.

"Me too."

"What do you think about getting some Italian takeaways? We could eat back at my place."

His voice was thick and heavy, the underlying meaning of his words clear.

"Sounds good," she replied.

They reluctantly dragged themselves out of the pool, and after showering, Emily met Ricky outside. As they started to walk into the village a dog up ahead let out a bark.

"Hey buddy," Ricky said, crouching down to pat the black border collie that was tied to a post. It was the same dog that had been outside Cache the day Emily had popped into the store.

The dog panted and wagged his tail vigorously.

"You been left by yourself?" Ricky ruffled the fur and the dog licked his hand. "Hey, hey." Ricky moved his hands back and forth across the fur, the pounding of the dog's tail growing more frantic. "Who's well behaved? Ay? Who's well behaved?"

The dog licked his hand again, stared up at Ricky and whined.

Ricky winced and stood up. "Gotta go buddy."

The dog barked twice.

"You obviously like dogs," Emily said, as they crossed the street.

"I love dogs. I miss my dog. I had her since she was a puppy."

"What happened to your dog?"

"Another consequence of Vanessa's gambling. I brought my dog with me when I came to Christchurch but the flat I was staying in wouldn't allow animals so I gave her away to the SPCA," Ricky said. "I wonder what Toto is doing now."

"I'm sorry to hear about Toto." She stopped outside Dolce, the Italian takeaway shop. "Dogs adapt easily."

"Life's still a bitch," Ricky said, bitterly. He pulled his wallet out of his pocket and rummaged inside. "Here, this is what she looks like."

The cutest golden ball of fluff with mischief written all over her face peered up at Emily.

"She's really cute. Why did you call her Toto?"

"From my all-time favourite movie. There was never a question when I got her what her name would be." Ricky took a deep breath and put the photo back in his wallet. "Maybe one day I'll get another dog."

"That sounds like a good idea. You're obviously good with dogs."

Ricky held the door open for her as they went inside the shop.

Emily ordered Gnocchi di Patate. She played it safe by paying for her meal leaving Ricky to pay for his. She exhaled quietly when his cashflow card worked without a hitch.

They grabbed their meals, popped into the supermarket to get a bottle of wine then walked back to Emily's house.

Before long they were out on the road zipping along in Emily's wee hatchback and then parking outside Ricky's house.

Ricky carried their packages inside. Emily held the rusty gate open for him, wincing as it screeched. It hung lopsidedly in her hand as she put it back on its latch carefully. If she pushed too hard the whole thing might fall right off.

Ricky juggled the house keys in his hand and opened the front door.

Warm, cloying heat hit her face as a result of the windows being closed all day.

"Phew!" Ricky said. "I think I'll leave the front door open." He flicked on the light, placed the meals on the pink, Formica table and shoved a few windows open.

"Are you okay with eating out of the packets?" Ricky asked. "I don't have many plates. And they need washing."

Emily glanced at the bench where a few dirty plates and cutlery stood. "That's no problem."

"And I don't have any wine glasses so it's going to be a bit tacky, sorry." Ricky reached up into the overhead cupboard and pulled out two coffee mugs.

"This'll be a first," said Emily. "Maybe it'll take off."

Ricky poured the wine and they wandered out on to the veranda.

She would've preferred to stay inside; it was much cleaner. The porch needed a good sweep, but she found a reasonably clean spot clear of twigs, leaves, weeds and stones.

"Aw. This is so good." Emily said. "I hadn't realised how hungry I was."

"It's all the swimming we did."

"Swimming? It was more like lazing around."

"Well, it was all that lazing around. Tiring." Ricky feinted a heavy sigh.

Emily took a sip of wine and screwed up her nose. Although the cup was clean it was tainted slightly with the taste of coffee. *Maybe if I swallow it in one go it won't taste quite so off.*

They chatted about the day as they finished their meals and wine.

Emily slapped at her arm. "I think I'm being bitten."

"It's that time of night for the mosquitoes. Here, let's head back inside. I think the light inside is attracting them too."

Ricky switched off the light.

"Hey, I can't see." Emily stood still waiting for her eyes to adjust to the darkness.

"Let me take these off you." Ricky took her empty package and coffee cup over to the bench.

Fuzzy images became more distinctive. Ahh! There was the outline of the Formica table, the bench and the door to the bathroom. Moonlight shone through the threadbare curtain beside the bed. Now that her sight was limited her other senses were heightened. The zit-zat of a few katydids travelled on the air and the strong scent of the flowers from the overgrown jasmine lingered.

Ricky moved towards her, the moonlight shining off the top of his head like silver. "Finally, alone," he whispered. He kissed her, sending shockwaves through her.

Every part of her was like a tightly wound coil about to release at any minute.

He nibbled at the sides of her mouth gently pushing her back.

Moving with him, her feet shuffling backwards, her legs hit the bed.

Ricky slid the straps off her shoulders and slowly undid the zip until her dress hit the floor in a swirl of fabric.

She pulled his T-shirt over his head while he yanked off his shorts and underwear throwing them out to the side. She was mesmerised. Even in the half-dark, half-moonlight, Ricky's chest made her heart skip – again. She ran her fingers over the firm muscles.

He nuzzled her neck, reaching around behind her to unhook her bra. He pushed her back gently on the bed and laid a kiss at the base of her throat. The light feathery touch made her skin shimmer. His mouth was hot and moist, moving lower, his hand cupped one breast and his mouth teased a nipple while he grew harder against her.

Emily clenched her thighs revelling in the exquisiteness of the sensation. She clasped Ricky's shoulders and let out a low moan.

"Open up for me, baby," Ricky said, in that husky tone that drove her mad. His hands had moved down, gently easing her thighs apart. His fingers explored gently and she widened her legs. She kissed his arm, breathing in the light mixture of sulphur and water from their swim.

"Ricky," she murmured. Every nerve in her body pulsed. Her whole world was vibrating.

He moved his hand away and lifted his head, tensing his muscles.

The broken contact was like a lifeline disconnecting.

Ricky stiffened and turned his head towards the window.

"What's wrong?" Emily asked.

The vibrations became stronger.

"Ahhh!" He moved off her and leant back on his elbows in frustration.

The light in the room was changing. No longer were they bathed in soft moonbeams, but another harsher light hit the side of the wall. The vibrations, which had started on the ground, grew in intensity and now travelled up the bed.

"Is that a…?" Her voice was drowned out by a long blow on a horn breaking the spell of the night.

The light in the room changed again to flashing red followed by a clang of bells.

"Here's the midnight train," Ricky said.

Emily looked around, flung her head back and giggled. She hugged Ricky to her closer and acted terrified. "Is that the Misty Springs Monster?"

"God, what a mood killer." Ricky flopped onto his back.

The ground shuddered violently. The cups and plate shivered, shook and clinked together. The continuous wail of the train horn blared.

The house shook as the first of the carriages thundered past in a symphony of squealing, metal and clinking couplings.

She buried her head in Ricky's arm, her giggles turning into full-on laughter. The house shook and the front door rattled. She was sure it was going to fall apart any minute, any minute. Surely the old past-its-use-by-date house couldn't possibly withstand such a shaking.

Was this the longest train in history? It went on into infinity, the carriages rocked and rolled as they hurtled north.

Finally the red lights stopped, the bells ceased clanging and the room settled back down.

The train passed through into the night taking with it not only its cargo but a passionate moment lost and trailing far behind.

***

"So what happened next?" Marie asked, her eyes almost popping out of her head.

"Well, nothing," Emily replied, sipping her tea as she perched on the bar stool in the kitchen.

"No!"

"The moment was there and then," Emily waved her hand, "it was gone. After my initial fright and relief that the house wasn't going to collapse on top of us, I got the giggles. I just couldn't stop laughing."

She'd buried her head in Ricky's arms. Her laughter became infectious and soon Ricky was quivering as too he saw the funny side.

"We called it a night then. Ricky said that the train comes back again with new carriages going south. You know, I'd never given much thought to those night trains. Occasionally if I was awake at night I'd hear them but, gosh, they sound so much closer and nosier than here," Emily said.

"What an awkward moment."

"Not as awkward as the first night here when Andrea and Vinnie were in an amorous mood. God, I just wanted to melt into the bed."

"You were lucky you've only experienced that once. When they'd first met, they were going at it every night. Until Lisa told them to get a room – a different room."

"Hmm, too much information." Emily tipped her mug up and swallowed the rest of her tea. "How are your studies going?"

"Good. I'm just delving into the first assignment which is the history of aromatherapy. I was wondering whether you'd be able to help me with a few of the practical components," Marie said.

"Sure. How about after work tonight?"

"Perfect."

The phone rang and Emily picked it up.

"Midge, is that you?" A creaky voice asked.

"Nana Rose, hi. If I wasn't here and you asked to speak to Midge nobody would know who you would be talking about."

Nana Rose had always called her Midge, short for midget, from the moment she was born as she'd been a prem baby. And she was still calling her Midge after all these years. Emily didn't mind. It was part of their own special bond, Emily being Nana Rose's favourite grandchild.

"I've been calling you Midge for so long now I almost forget your real name," Nana Rose huffed out.

Emily frowned. "You okay, Nana Rose? You sound a bit wheezy."

"Oh, I've just been out in the back paddock cleaning out some of the bushes."

"Nana!" Emily scolded. "You shouldn't be doing that."

"Oh, it's good exercise. Keeps the muscles and bones moving. Do you want some more lavender, my dear? There's heaps of it here. Some of its past its best but I'm sure you could use some for those gorgeous handmade creations."

"That sounds lovely, Nana. Maybe I could come up tomorrow and stay the night."

"It would be lovely to see you again."

Emily had a sudden idea. "Nana, could I bring a friend?"

"Yes, of course. I'd like to see Marie again."

Emily half-smiled. "Actually Nana it's not Marie. It's a guy – Ricky."

"You've met someone? Of course, bring him too. It would be nice to have a man round here again."

"Thanks, Nana, I'll see you sometime Saturday."

"Okay dear," said Nana, as she rang off.

"I couldn't help overhearing," Marie said. "Time to meet the family already?"

"I feel really good with Ricky. My hand doesn't bother him. He takes me for who I am and I'm starting to feel like I can trust him."

"You do look so much happier since you've been seeing each other. I'm pleased for you." Marie touched her friend on her shoulder. "We'd better run for it or Lisa'll be on our backs."

***

Ricky called into see Emily at lunchtime.

"How would you like to come away with me tomorrow to my Nana Rose's?" Emily asked. "I know its short notice."

Ricky bit into a donut and chewed.

Why is he taking so long to answer? Emily turned away. *It was too soon. It was a silly idea.*

"I... going... to." Ricky munched away.

What is he saying? Emily leaned forward to hear better.

"... hoping... prize money."

"Ricky," Emily exclaimed. "Finish your mouthful. I can't understand a word you're saying."

"Sorry." Ricky swallowed hard. "What I was trying to say is there's a wood chopping competition this weekend. I thought I'd go."

Emily's shoulders slumped. *He'd rather spend time wood chopping than spend a weekend away with me. And how precisely was he going to get to his competition?*

"But I'd rather spend a weekend away with you." Ricky grasped Emily's hand.

"Really? I was so sure you'd say no."

"I could do with the comp practise, but a missed weekend isn't going to hurt me."

"Thank you. Nana Rose lives in this gorgeous homestead surrounded by fields of rambling grass and flowers and there's heaps of lavender I can pick. It's like an oasis. You'll love it."

"A weekend in the country sounds very relaxing." Ricky caught Emily around the waist and kissed her on the mouth. "We both need to get back to work."

"I'll pick you up at nine on Saturday morning," Emily said, as she waved Ricky off. Spending a whole weekend with Ricky and her beloved Nana Rose was just what she needed.

Chapter 16

Emily and Ricky arrived at Nana Rose's property, Paix, just before lunch.

She hopped out of the car and took a deep breath. The breeze was ladened with fragrance. There was definitely honeysuckle. That would be coming from the branches draped lazily over the veranda. The cloying headiness of jasmine, growing wild towards the back of the house and then the creamy, vanilla scent of wisteria that trawled up towards the bedrooms on the top storey. And, of course, the lavender that lined the drive. Somewhere, mixed in, was the aroma of homemade baking. It was then that Nana Rose poked her head out of one of the three upstairs windows.

"Midge. You've arrived. Come on inside, I'll be down in a bit. I've just made a fresh batch of scones."

"Midge?" Ricky looked at Emily.

"It's Nana's nickname for me. Because I was small. Am still small."

"Midge. huh. I like it." Ricky patted her on the butt.

"Don't you go getting any ideas," Emily said. "And behave." She unclasped Ricky's hand.

Emily opened the front door and stepped into the kitchen.

Nana Rose had just reached the bottom of the stairs. "Oof." She placed a wrinkled sun-spotted hand on the small of her back. "That's getting harder."

Emily frowned. Nana was in good health, but the house and the land was a handful for just one person. The family had tried to persuade her to sell up, move into something that required far less maintenance, but she refused. Emily was kind of glad in a way. She loved this place. It had a special rustic yester-year charm and memories that she wanted to hang onto forever. She greeted her grandmother with a kiss and a hug.

"You're too thin, my girl. You need to put some meat on your bones."

"There's enough meat on my bones."

"You can have some of mine then." Nana Rose tapped her ample hips. "And who's this then? Where's your hair?"

"Nana. Don't be rude!"

"That won't warm you in winter. You're Ricky?"

"Yes. Pleased to meet you." Ricky stuck out his hand.

"I don't need any of that. If you're a friend of Emily's, you get a hug. Come here. And call me Nana Rose. Everyone does." Nana Rose held her arms out wide and Ricky moved into them. "Well, you've got a bit more padding."

"That's muscle," Ricky said.

"I can tell you don't sit behind a desk all day. Let's feel those biceps."

"Oh, Nana. You're embarrassing him."

"No worries. I get a lot worse from the guys I work with," Ricky replied.

"And what's that bit of fluff on your chin. Not like in my day when a man grew a beard it was full, big and bushy."

Ricky turned red.

"Enough Nana," Emily scolded.

"He can take as good as he gets." Nana grinned and Ricky grinned back, an immediate understanding sealed.

Nana Rose lumbered over to the coal range. "I've made chicken pie and salad for lunch and there's homemade bread. There are scones too. Have a seat."

Emily and Ricky sat down at the large, wooden table.

Ricky ran his hands over the kauri wood. "Nice table you have here, Nana Rose." He ducked his head under the table to take a closer look.

"Oh, that's been in the family for years. You know something about wood then?"

"I'm a builder."

"Ahh! So that's where the muscles come from. If I was younger..."

"Nana," Emily warned.

Nana Rose cackled as she cut up the pie and served the salad onto old Royal Dolton plates.

Emily smiled. Everything from years past spoke subtly of nostalgia. Nothing much changed here. It was like stepping into a museum. And she loved every bit of it. The kitchen was full of the comforting smell of baked bread and chicken pie.

"Here's some lemonade." Nana Rose placed a large pitcher on the table, lemons slices bobbing up and down.

Emily and Ricky devoured the pie and salad in no time. Nana Rose didn't have to work too hard to convince Ricky to have another slice.

"Nana Rose, that was lovely," Emily said, placing her knife and fork down on her plate. She patted her stomach. "Whew!"

"Good on you. What do you think you'll do this afternoon?"

"I'd like to collect the lavender," Emily said. "Maybe show Ricky around the property."

"That'll give you a chance to build up your appetite for dinner." Nana Rose said, standing up and removing the plates from the table. "How does roast lamb, vegies and apple and blueberry crumble sound?"

Ricky rolled his eyes in ecstasy. "I'm ready to move in permanently."

Nana Rose laughed. "Men need a good feed. Keeps them happy."

"Is there something we can do to help beforehand?" Emily asked.

"How about making some Herbes de Provence? I'll put it on the lamb tonight."

"Sure." Emily stood on tiptoes to reach the mortar and pestle on the top shelf.

"Need some help there, Midge," Ricky said, a cheeky grin creeping across his face.

"No, I don't," Emily replied, and then poked her tongue out. "And don't call me Midge."

"It's kinda catching."

Emily groped around inside the top shelf of the pantry for the small bottles she was looking for and placed them on the table. "You must have a nickname. Baldy?"

"That'd be too obvious."

"Well?"

"Hmm… I'll tell you later."

"You're just avoiding telling me."

"What's Herbs de Provence?" Ricky asked, struggling to get his tongue round the words.

"It's a mixture of dried herbs that can be used to flavour meat, chicken, and fish. You can put it in stews and sprinkle it into omelettes." Emily measured out dried thyme, rosemary, lavender, flowers, summer savoury, oregano, mint, basil, sage and fennel seeds. She picked out an orange, grated the rind and added it to the mixture. She ground away with the pestle so that the herbs and orange rind became tiny balls.

Ricky moved closer and breathed in. "Smells good."

"You wait until it starts roasting. That's when the aroma is unbelievably scrumptious."

Nana Rose hung up a tea towel. "Thanks, my dear girl. Now you two go and get some good country air."

"We have good air in Misty Springs too."

"Ahh… but it smells different here."

And she was right. There was nothing wrong with the light, slightly sulphurous, odour that hung round Misty Springs, but the country air did make for a nice change.

Emily and Ricky wandered off down the front path and past a rusty old skeleton of a Ford truck. Knee high grass grew round the abandoned hulk. The windows had long gone and the headlights dangled off the barely-there wires.

"Geez. This is a surprise. Nana Rose keeps an immaculate kitchen, yet here is this rust bucket," Ricky said, standing with his hands on his hips.

"Don't let her hear you say that. This was Grandad's. She's refused to do anything about it so it's just been left here year after year to disintegrate. I think it provides a link to the past," Emily said, pointing back towards the house. "She can see this from the kitchen window. See Grandad."

"How does she cope? Paix is really big to look after."

"The neighbours help out. Kyle Bannister, who has the land next door, keeps an eye out on her." Emily looked over in the distance where she could just make out the two-storey house on Kyle's land. "Kyle spends a lot of time in Christchurch. He comes out here on the weekends to escape the rat race."

She and her brother and sisters had spent long summer holidays with Kyle and his two sisters playing in the streams dividing the property, chasing rabbits in the fields, running wild, and toasting marshmallows over the fire on balmy nights. She'd practically grown up with Kyle.

"Let's take a look at the boundary fences. They night need some maintenance," Emily said.

They took the dirt track that meandered down towards the rear of the property.

"Okay. This is more my area," Ricky said, bending down to inspect a couple of posts. "I might not know much about Herbs de Provence, but I do know this post and these wires need replacing." Ricky pinged the fence, which made a dull thump.

"Do you mind fixing it?" she asked.

"No, not at all. Where does she keep the tools and equipment?"

"In the barn. Come on, I'll show you."

They continued down the track and past a bank of trees. A big red barn rose up to meet them. It was in a sad state of repair. In the heat of the sun and the lashings of rain, most of the paint had cracked and there were a couple of boards missing off the top section.

"It should be open." Emily lifted the latch and shoved on the door. "It can be a bit stiff. There," she said, giving it a final heave.

Something scuttled away. Probably a rat or mouse; they frequented the barn regularly. "I'll need to send Kyle's cat over here to do some pest control."

They located a couple of fence posts. All the tools were placed neatly on a shadow board. Ricky grabbed what he needed and they returned back to the fence.

Before long they were working together to make the repairs. The heat in their little part of the valley increased and Ricky pulled his shirt off.

Emily sat down on the grass tilting her sunhat back off her forehead. Ricky's rippling muscles gleaned with sweat as he pulled out the rotted wooden post.

"Hey, you're supposed to be helping," Ricky said.

"I'm enjoying the view," Emily teased.

"Well, don't stare too long. I might charge you."

Emily laughed. If only the girls could see her now. Her own piece of heaven.

Nana Rose turned up with a flask of coffee, lemonade and more scones wrapped up in a towel. "You're doing a great job there, Ricky"

Ricky put up his hand in acknowledgement.

"That's a good lad you've got there. He's a keeper. Better than that other guy you were set to marry," Nana Rose said.

"Josh?"

"Do you ever hear from him?"

Emily sighed. "No, and I'd like to keep it that way. He walked out on me, remember?"

"Hmm… mmm."

"These are nice scones."

"Oh, that wasn't for the scones."

"Pardon?"

"That was for your shirtless fellow."

"Nana Rose!"

"I'd better get back to the kitchen before I pull up a comfy chair and join you."

An hour later they'd finished. Posts were replaced, the fence was fixed. As they returned the tools to the barn, Emily picked up the old basket she used for collecting lavender and two pairs of secateurs. Long gently swaying lines of lavender bordered the track back to the house.

"Here," Emily said, handing Ricky a pair secateurs. "You can help me cut some lavender." She bent down and cut a small handful. Picking off the stalks and rubbing them between her hands and over her arms, she then scattered them back over the dry earth. "Do you know there's not much lavender can't fix?" She bent down to cut another bunch. "Roman soldiers used it to dress their wounds, and it was used as a disinfectant in World War I. And it can also be used to prevent disease, and stave off insects, treat headaches and hysteria."

"I'll remember that the next time I feel the urge to go mad." Ricky stood up and placed his bunch of lavender in the basket.

"Oh… and embalm corpses."

"Thanks for sharing."

A solitary bee buzzed by and landed on a lavender flower. He busily got to work crawling all over the haze of purple.

"The oil which I use for my massages relieves stress and anxiety."

"What type of lavender is this?" Ricky asked. He crumbled a flower head and breathed in its scent.

"This is Augustifolia. It's originally from France. It has the highest quality of oil." Emily tucked a strand of hair behind an ear. "It's said lavender is also an aphrodisiac."

"Is that so?" Ricky grabbed Emily round the waist. "I'd be keen to test that theory."

Emily placed her hands over Ricky's arms. His lips brushed against hers and she responded eagerly. He bent her backwards until her knees gave way and she landed on the ground. The combination of sweat, his woody aftershave and the dirt brought out her animal instincts. She pulled at his top while his hand travelled up under her T-shirt and fondled a breast. His tongue shot into her mouth and she played with it. She wanted to go much further – now. The sexual tension had built up to almost a crescendo after two failed attempts to make love. *Could I lose myself now? Out in the open. Exposed.* It would be so reckless and so unlike her. But it was the perfect place. She moaned, opened her eyes and watched the purple haze of lavender sway over Ricky's head, enveloping them, closing in on them. He moved his hand down over her stomach, his fingers light, barely touching her but then he hit a delicate spot and she giggled.

"Oh, so we're ticklish, are we?" Ricky teased.

"Nooo."

Ricky plunged his fingers into her side and fumbled.

She giggled again. "Stop." She slapped his hand away.

"Now I know I can have you completely under my control." Ricky tickled harder.

Emily doubled over begging for him to stop, but really wanting him to continue. She pushed down on his hands, but he was too strong and he increased the tickling.

Her giggles became full-on laughter. "Stop!" she pleaded again, "or I'll wet my pants."

"Hey, Emily is that you?" A male voice boomed out.

Who on earth? She struggled to sit up, pushing Ricky off her. She bounced to her feet, smoothed down her T-shirt and flapped her hands across her shorts.

"Kyle." Emily coughed. "Oh... um... hi."

"I was just checking the fences. I thought I could hear laughing."

Emily's ears burned. She looked down. *Had he seen anything? Exactly what had he heard?*

Kyle wrapped his arms around Emily, encircling her in a big hug that lasted for a beat too long.

Ricky popped up onto his feet.

"Oh," Kyle exclaimed, quickly releasing Emily. "You're not alone."

"Ah… no. Kyle, this is Ricky. Ricky, Kyle."

The two men shook hands eyeing the other up like lions about to circle each other. "Just down for the weekend?" Kyle asked, shaking his blonde hair.

His hair was longer than she had seen it before. She ran her eyes over his T-shirt and jeans. His white cap was turned around backwards, his blonde curls turning up at the edges. *Who would've thought he was a big-time investor during the week?* Faithful, his huntaway dog, ran up to her.

"Yes. I needed some more lavender and I wanted to check on Nana." She stroked Faithful's head.

"She doing okay? I haven't seen her for a while."

"She's doing well, but this place…" Emily looked out over the fields. She curled her fingers up on her left hand.

"I know, it's a lot for one person."

Ricky bent down to pat Faithful. They sparred, the dog's tail wagging non-stop.

"She's not considering selling?"

"Never. This place is in her heart. And she wants to feel close to Grandpa."

"Thanks for replacing the fence post." Kyle nodded towards Ricky.

"No problems, mate." Ricky rubbed Faithful's tummy as she rolled onto her back and stuck her four legs in the air.

"There's a few further down that are looking a bit dodgy. I'm just going down that way," Kyle said.

"Let us know if you need a hand," Emily said.

"She'll be right. I'll let you two get back to whatever you were doing."

Emily drew an arm across her chest and watched the smirk intensify on Kyle's face.

"Um, you've got…" Kyle indicated to the side of his face.

Emily reached up and pulled out a few stalks of lavender that had got caught up in her hair.

"See you later. Faithful, come," Kyle yelled.

Emily waved as Kyle and Faithful trotted back down the hill.

"Come on, lavender lass," Ricky said in a Cockney accent. "We should head on back or Nana Rose will be wondering what's happened to us."

"Lavender lass?"

"It suits you. I love how when you're close to the lavender, it contrasts with your black hair. Almost mysterious. So, you're my lavender lass." Ricky reached for her hand and they strolled back towards the house.

"Lavender lass," she whispered to herself. She liked the sound of it. And she liked it even more because Ricky had said it.

Chapter 17

Emily spread the paste over Nana Rose's face.

"I really think it's too late for any concoctions to make me look any younger."

"Hush, Nana. Just enjoy."

It was early evening. Dinner had been devoured and Ricky declared it was the best meal he'd eaten in a hundred years. He was now laid out on the couch snoring softly.

"I think we've worn out Ricky," Nana Rose said.

Emily looked over towards him and smiled. He had a look of contentment that seemed to suggest that, like her, this was the place he needed to be.

He'd been intrigued with an old gramophone player that had been in the family for years. He'd picked out a record and now the refined voice of a woman singing "La Vie En Rose" lilted with the slight breeze blowing through the open doors.

"Do you think he's bored? Maybe he wished I had a TV," Nana Rose mumbled.

Emily smeared the homemade paste of oats, rose petals, ground almond, honey and chickpea flour over Nana Rose's face. "He doesn't have a TV." She hadn't told Nana the whole extent of Ricky's situation.

"I see he doesn't even own one of those phones you young ones seem to be playing with all the time. Won't he be missing Facetube?"

"YouTube."

"Pardon?"

"It's YouTube or Facebook."

"Facebook? People's faces have been on books for years. What's new about that?"

Emily giggled and wiped her hands on a towel. "It's okay, Nana. Now I'm going to leave this on your face for twenty minutes. It'll remove the build-up of dry skin and exfoliate your beautiful face." She loved sharing this time with Nana. Even as a kid Nana had helped her choose plants and flowers from her garden and with kitchen ingredients they whipped up all sorts of mixtures and smothered themselves. Sometimes they even ate what they'd made just to see what it tasted like.

Soon the country air blowing through the windows was filled with Ricky's snores. The last weekend of summer and the trees were throwing larger shadows across the driveway. Dusk was creeping in earlier.

Emily helped herself to some lemonade and set it down on the kitchen table. Pulling out her new house folder and placing all the notes on the table, she fired up her iPad. *Can I still build my house?* Over the next half-hour she punched figures into her calculator, rejigged numbers on the spreadsheet and jotted down notes.

"What are you doing?"

Emily jumped. "You gave me a fright."

"Sorry," Ricky said, rubbing the sleep out of his eyes.

"I'm trying to work out how I can still build my house."

"It looks complicated." Ricky peered at the handwritten notes Emily had made.

"I can budget really carefully and maybe even ask David, my brother, to help financially although that might take a bit of work. He's still sore with me. I could approach another building company and maybe the bank could give me another loan," she chatted on, doodling frantically on her notes.

"Whoa," Ricky said. "Slow down. Be careful about rushing into this. You don't want to make any more mistakes."

Emily winced. Mistakes? She'd done what she thought was right. It wasn't her fault Gardenway Homes had gone into liquidation.

"You'll need to have a solid plan to present to the bank."

Emily sighed. Ricky was right. What had got her into some of this mess was that she'd taken things at face value and not checked things out properly. This time it would be different. She would check, double check and triple check everything.

"I'm happy to help," Ricky said. "Maybe I can look at the building plans and see if we can cut some costs somewhere."

"That would be fantastic." This time she would do it right. Ricky had offered his help and she'd take him up on it.

"I'd better get that paste off Nana's face," Emily said. It had been almost an hour since she'd applied it. She roused Nana Rose who was quietly snoozing away.

"Oh sorry, Midge," Nana said. "I must've dozed off."

Emily sponged the paste off Nana's face. "There you go. Beautiful."

"Hah!"

"Let me help you up." Emily pulled Nana up to the tune of creaky bones as she struggled to her feet and wheezed. "Nana, that's not sounding so good. Does that happen often after you've been lying down?"

Nana waved a hand dismissively. "It's just me getting old." She clutched her chest.

Emily bit her lip. "I'll help you up to bed. Lean on me."

Nana held onto Emily's elbow as she escorted her up the stairs and along the landing.

"I'm sorry that you and Ricky will have to sleep in separate bedrooms. I know what you kids are like these days – sex before marriage."

There she was, as blunt as ever. Emily glanced into the bedroom she stayed in and at the single bed. "It'll be fine."

Many years ago when Emily and Josh had stayed a few weekends, Emily had crept into Josh's bed late at night to steal a kiss. The bed was old and the springs squeaked. Making love quietly was almost impossible. They had been happy – her and Josh. That was before the accident, before he'd left her.

Nana sat on the bed while Emily pulled the blinds closed and turned on the antique bedside lamp.

"Where's your nightie?" Emily asked.

"Just under my pillow." Nana fumbled around until she laid her hands on her nightie. "I might read for a while before I turn out the light. It helps me to settle. Could you get my night jacket for me? It's in the third drawer of the dresser."

Emily walked over toward the dresser. On top were photos of Grandpa Thomas, family photos of Mum, Dad, her brothers and sisters and one of her when she was five. Her hair was long and straight then. She'd only cut it off to below her collar after she'd left school. Little Emily, and then a laughing Emily crunching on an apple stared back at an older Emily, eyes shining bright. She squinted further at the photo, at a blonde head peering out at the corner. Kyle. Even in those days before the term photo-bomb was even heard of Kyle found a way to get into everyone's photos. Apart from the photos, old trinkets lay on top of lacy doilies. A bouquet of red roses from Nana's garden was drying.

Emily opened the drawer and gasped. Beside Nana's bed jackets were piles of twenty dollar, fifty dollar and one-hundred dollar notes. What on earth was all this money doing here? "Nana."

"Hmm."

"I don't mean to pry, but why do you have all this money in your drawer."

"Oh. You can't trust the banks these days. All these financial institutions that're going bust."

Emily ran her hands over the money. "How much is here?"

"I think about two-thousand dollars."

"Oh, Nana." Emily pulled out one of the bed jackets and helped her into it." It's not a good place to keep it here. What if there was a fire? Or the place was burgled? You could lose all the money."

"That's a very small risk."

"I don't know." Emily frowned. "It's a lot of money to lose if something happened. Your money *is* safe in the bank."

Nana put on her glasses and peered over the top. "I do worry about having the money in the bank, but it's a worry having it in the drawer too. Look what happened to you with those building people."

"That was different. Your money will be perfectly safe in the bank. It should be there so it can earn you interest as well."

Nana sighed. "I don't know what I should do."

Emily walked over to the bed and sat on the side. "How about I put the money in my bank account for you and when you need some I can transfer it back into your account? I'll look after it for you."

"I wouldn't want to bother you."

"Nana, you're not bothering me. It makes sense."

Nana studied a point somewhere above the dresser. She reached over and patted Emily's hand. "Okay, dear. You're right. You can look after it for me. I trust you."

Placing a hand on Nana Rose's shoulder she said, "It's for the best, Nana. If I'd known that money was there I wouldn't have been able to sleep at night. How about I put it in my bag for safe keeping?"

Nana nodded.

Emily went back to her room, emptied out one of her backpacks and returned to Nana's room. She carefully put the stacks of money in the backpack. *Why do I feel like a bank robber?* She pulled the drawstring tight, flipped the flap over and then bent over to kiss Nana good night. "Have a good sleep."

"You too."

Emily was almost at the door when Nana Rose said, "Midge?"

"Yes."

"You're a good granddaughter."

Emily smiled. "And you're the best nana."

She was almost out the door when Nana added. "No bed hopping. Those beds aren't built for too much activity."

Emily shut the door and covered her mouth to quieten a giggle.

Downstairs Ricky was closing the windows and doors and drawing the blinds.

"I was just about to send out a search party," he said, as he put the record back in its sleeve.

"I got the shock of my life when I opened Nana's drawer. She doesn't trust the banks so she's been hiding a lot of cash."

"That's not particularly safe. How much is there?"

"Two grand."

"Whoa!"

"Hmm. I've convinced her to give the money to me and I'll put it in my bank account."

Ricky's face had turned grave.

"Ricky?'

"Yes, sorry."

"Have you locked up?" Emily turned out the hall light.

"Yep. One of the locks on the door is a bit loose. I'll tighten that up for Nana tomorrow."

"You've been great today. Nana will have appreciated what you've done, me too."

"It's the least I could do. I feel spoilt. And I'm glad I didn't go wood chopping this weekend."

Emily tapped Ricky gently on the tip of his nose. "See, I told you. Now I'll show you to your room."

They walked up the creaky stairs together. Ricky's room, which would've been her dad's boyhood bedroom, was decorated in soft browns and still had some of her dad's softball trophies on the dresser. He had been a keen sportsman but something she hadn't inherited. Ricky put down his bag. "So where do you sleep?"

"In the room next door."

Ricky pouted.

Emily drew him in close. "I know. But would you be up for a midnight visit?"

"Up?"

"Sorry." Emily giggled. "Wrong choice of words."

"You can visit my bed any time," Ricky whispered in her ear, sending a wave of delicious shivers over her. "I'm not sure I can stand this waiting much longer."

"Me neither." Emily traced her hand over the back of his neck.

Ricky pressed his lips to hers. Every time he touched her now he sent shockwaves through her body.

She gently pushed him away. "Soon," she whispered. "Sleep tight."

Ricky kissed her on the forehead. "Sweet dreams, lavender lass. And I'll be waiting."

***

What woke me up? What time is it? The summer sun streamed in through the crack in the curtains. What sounded like a million birds were chattering. She sniffed. Bacon and eggs. Nana must be cooking breakfast.

Emily reached for her phone – 9.00. *Did I sleep right through the night?* Ricky… Oops! She'd promised a midnight visit.

Springing out of bed and grabbing a towel, she headed for the bathroom. By the time, she'd had a quick shower, made her bed and had wandered down the stairs to the kitchen a half hour had passed. Ricky was already sitting at the kitchen table shovelling bacon and eggs into his mouth.

"Morning." Emily kissed both Nana Rose and Ricky.

"Morning, sleepyhead," Ricky said, as he munched away.

"I'm sorry I'm late."

"Well, you've never been an early riser."

"It's the weekend, Nana."

Nana Rose handed Emily a glass of freshly squeezed orange juice and a plate of French toast adorned with blueberries, raspberries and strawberries.

"You've had a good year for the berries?" Emily asked.

"A bumper crop. It must be that new organic fertiliser I've been using."

"What time did you get up to do all this cooking?"

"Normal time. Remember I'm used to feeding a big family and lots of men."

"So what have you two been talking about?" Emily asked.

Ricky put down his coffee cup. "Oh, we've been trying to solve the problems of the world."

"And?"

"We narrowed the problems down and decided that the lock on the door is all we need to worry about today," Ricky said.

Nana Rose busied herself at the kitchen sink with the dirty dishes.

"What happened to you last night?" Ricky whispered.

Emily poured maple syrup over the French toast. "What happened to you?" she whispered back.

"I was waiting for you!"

"I was waiting for you! I slept right through. I poked my head into your room at six, but you were out of it."

"Oh." Emily bowed her head. Another chance gone.

Nana clinked the dishes in the sink.

"I'll dry," Emily said, as she finished off her breakfast.

"And I'll go and fix the lock." Ricky took off outside and Emily grabbed a tea towel.

"That's a nice lad you've got there, Emily. I like him."

"I like him too Nana – a lot. I really hope this will work out."

"And the future?"

"It's much too early to tell, but I feel positive."

Ricky banged, cracked and tinkered around with the lock. "There, Nana Rose. Much more secure."

"Thank you. When do you think you will head back home?" Nana asked, directing her question at Emily.

"Probably mid-morning, but first I want to check out my favourite thing."

"Yes, I haven't seen you on it yet. I knew you'd be itching to have a go.'

"What on earth are you talking about?" Ricky asked, frowning.

"Follow me," Emily said. She took Ricky's hand in hers and led him outside down the stairs and over towards the massive gum tree. And under the gum tree a homemade swing rocked gently in the wind. She skipped over to the swing and climbed on the old, wooden seat. The original swing, along with the rope, had been built by Grandpa and had been replaced many times over the years. Leaning back and putting her feet down, she pushed slowly then building momentum, pushed harder and then she was flying, higher and higher. The wind whooshed past her, elevating her into the sky where she almost reached the sun. Back now, the sun retreated. The long grass rushed beside her again and the top of the red barn came closer then receded. She closed her eyes, put her head back and squealed in delight. Ricky laughed. A strong hand on the small of her back pushed her.

"Higher," she yelled. And she flew higher. Darkness and dizziness. A sense of falling, floating and freedom. The strong hand pushed again. She was now five-year-old Emily with her long black hair coursing out behind her, Kyle pushing her and giggling. "You're flying like a bird," he'd yell out. "Push me higher," she always insisted.

"This rope is looking frayed," Ricky said, breaking into her thoughts.

"It's fine," Emily said dreamily. "It'll last for years." Her dress went flying up over her knees, exposing her legs. She no longer pushed. Gradually the momentum slowed and she leant back, coasted on the ride down till her feet touched the ground. She opened her eyes. Everything was still but somehow she was still flying. And there was Ricky standing in front of her.

As she hopped off the swing, Ricky pulled her towards him. "You don't know how gorgeous you looked with your dress flying out all over the place. You looked like you were lost in some moment. I think I'm falling in love with you, Emily."

Emily held her breath and rubbed her face against his cheek. Those words. How much they could change everything. She melted into him. "I'm falling in love with you too." There, the magic words were out. How long she'd waited to say those words. How long had it been since someone had said them back? The someone she could now finally trust.

Chapter 18

Emily and Ricky prepared to leave Paix after Nana Rose had fed them with leftover lamb, lettuce salad and peach muffins.

"Thank you for a lovely weekend," Emily said, giving Nana Rose a hug.

"It was wonderful seeing you again, Midge. Don't leave it so long next time."

"I won't."

"And you, young man, look after my precious granddaughter."

"Will do, Nana Rose. I'm sure I'm leaving a couple of kilos heavier."

"You'll work it off and keep those muscles bulging."

Emily smiled as Ricky and Nana Rose hugged each other.

"Safe travels."

"Bye, Nana Rose."

But the good weekend feeling vanished quickly on Monday morning when Lisa called Emily into her office.

Emily's stomach dropped. There was only one thing that this was going to be about.

Lisa didn't even say good morning. She got right to the point. "We had a staff meeting a month ago about the sales of Nature's One. I've been looking through your sales figures and you haven't sold anything." Lisa flipped over pieces of paper.

"No. No, I haven't," Emily said, stalling for time.

"Do you remember what I asked at that meeting?"

"You wanted to see an increase in my sales."

"And there's nothing." Lisa glared at Emily.

"What about the other girls? What about their sales?"

"I'm not concerned about their sales. It's yours. Not only has there been no increase, you haven't sold anything." Lisa yanked a piece of paper off its staple and shoved it in front of her. "See. Zero."

Emily remained silent. *How far should I go in telling Lisa exactly what I think of Nature's One?*

"Well?" Lisa asked.

"I don't think the products are as natural as what they claim to be. The labels clearly state synthetic ingredients plus we've had clients who've had skin problems."

"We've been over this a number of times. There's no proof these skin problems are related to Nature's One."

Emily sighed. She was fighting a losing battle.

"You've left me with no choice. I'm giving you a verbal warning. If I don't see any products sold by the end of the week I'll start disciplinary action.

Emily gasped. Was Lisa that desperate? "I don't know why..."

"I've given you plenty of opportunity and this is bordering on downright insubordination," Lisa snapped.

Emily stared at the ceiling and squeezed her eyes shut. *God, I can't afford to lose my job now. Not when I owe money. Not now when I have a plan in place to get building my house back on track.* She had to play this safe. "I'm sorry. You're right." Every bone in her body was screaming out, *this is wrong, this is wrong.* "I'll do my best to make up sales."

"Good," Lisa said. "I'll look forward to seeing an improvement."

Emily left Lisa's office mentally trying to work out how she could sell Nature's One to her clients. It would mean each one would have to buy at least one product to meet Lisa's sales target.

The day went from bad to worse. When she checked on the body butter in the cupboard all of the samples had mould on them. Emily hung her head in despair. Her third batch and she still hadn't got it right. Once again she scooped the mixture out. What had gone wrong? She'd kept everything away from the sun and heat and had made sure everything was completely sterilised. She had only two products – the lip balm and the body scrub – that worked. She had so wanted the body butter to be a success. Three good products would provide a base for her to start selling her range commercially, but with the body butter she'd have to go back to the drawing board again. She stared out the window. The leaves on the trees were starting to turn a pale shade of yellow, signalling the end of summer.

Leaves floated down and with them, the distant memories of the weekend past.

Her mood hadn't changed when Ricky popped in after work.

"Why the glum face?" he asked.

"The third batch of body butter turned out like the rest – mouldy. I just don't think I'm much good at making cosmetics."

"What about that lip thingy you were telling me about?"

"The lip balm and the body scrub are fine. I just wanted the body butter to work. I just know it would be a great product."

Ricky gave Emily a hug, drawing her near. "It will. I know it. Now, we've got some work to do."

"What do you mean?"

"Have you already forgotten that you wanted to get that house of yours back on track? You've got a business case to prepare."

Emily nodded. Maybe if she focused on the house first and then thought about how this whole cosmetics thing was going to work. She suggested Ricky come back home with her. They could have an early dinner and then she could start pulling together her plan.

Together they threw some salad leaves of rocket, boiled eggs, tomatoes, cheese, and avocado into a bowl, sliced up some cold chicken and cut up some bread.

After the meal Emily fired up her laptop and together they went to work on a revised plan for her house.

Ricky helped look at the original plans and suggested where she could reduce costs. "Unfortunately the foundations have already been laid so you can't reduce the size of the house. He looked at some calculations he had written down. "But we've still managed to reduce costs down to two-thousand dollars per square metre."

"I need to be thorough about this. Let's go over the figures again."

They redid the figures with Emily double-checking they'd not made any errors.

"You know," she said, leaning back. "I'd always had this wild dream that I could make my own lavender oil. It would be a great add-on to the cosmetics, to be able to say the oil came from locally grown lavender. But I don't know..." Emily wavered. She sat on her left hand.

"You're doing it again," Ricky said.

"What am I doing?"

"You're hiding your hand."

"No, I'm not."

"You are. It's something I've noticed about you. Every time you have any smidgen of doubt you sit on your left hand."

Emily stared at Ricky. "I can't help it. It's what I do sometimes. It's just that I think people will judge me as a person and my capabilities."

"The only person who is judging you is you. Stop letting your hand come between you and what you want."

Here was the encouragement she'd been waiting for. She could do this. She'd worked hard to not let her disfigured hand get in the way of her life. And here was someone who believed in her. Ricky was so sweet, he was willing to help her, encourage her, stand beside her.

"What are your plans for the cosmetics?" Ricky asked.

"You're going to be sorry you asked." Emily laughed. "I have so many ideas."

Over the next two hours they threw ideas back and forth testing validity. Ricky brought Emily back to earth when she started to get too out of control.

They were studying a web page that sold distillers. "Look!" Emily said, pointing at the screen. "How cool." She was referring to a 40-litre column distiller with a brass thermometer. "It would cost one-thousand-nine-hundred-and-fifty dollars, which I can finance. I might not need a loan."

"Yeah, but have you read this? These smaller units won't achieve and keep the temperatures required to extract good quality oils. It looks like," Ricky clicked to the next page, "if you want to do it properly you'll need something more than a table top unit and that will set you back between ten and twenty thousand dollars."

Emily's stomach sank. "I don't know whether the bank will lend that much money plus what I need to borrow for the ingredients to make the bigger quantities."

"I think we need to look at other ways you can make income from the lavender. That would show the bank that you're not relying on just one source."

"Great idea!"

Before long they had a list of other ways to make the lavender products that would be more profitable, everything from selling the products at the farmer's market, making pot pourri sachets, using lavender in food recipes, selling plants and making a moth repellent. They estimated the value of the potential income streams and produced a spreadsheet that laid it all out.

"I'm so excited. I'd never even thought of all these ideas," Emily said, a rush of adrenaline passing over her.

"Well, if it all comes off you're going to be one very busy lady."

"Let's take one final look at the figures."

They'd produced a number of scenarios with the most expensive options being the bigger distiller right down to the tabletop distiller option which would need less money for Emily to borrow.

At 11 pm the final page was printed out. Emily stapled together the papers for both her new plans for the house and the cosmetics business and placed them into two folders. "I know I've done a thorough job researching this time. I'm confident I've checked everything over at least twice. The bank is going to find it hard to say no. Thanks for your help. It was great to have a second opinion. Would you like me to run you home?"

"No, No. It's okay," Ricky said, standing up. "I'll pop over to Red Hill Bar. Jake lives out that way and he'll be finishing up."

Emily walked Ricky to the door.

"You sure we couldn't…" He cocked his head towards the bedroom, his voice thick as he put his arms around her.

"It's late," she whispered. "I don't want to wake the girls."

"How loud do you think we'd be?"

"Hey, I want to as much as you do. I promise. But the timing never seems to be right."

"Come back with me. Stay the night." He nibbled on her ear. The tingling in her breasts almost drove her over the edge.

Emily pulled away from him. "It's getting late. Maybe we could work something out this weekend."

He kissed her again. "Definitely. See you tomorrow."

Emily watched Ricky as he walked down the path and out onto the street, his heavy footsteps echoing into the night. She had no doubt that she wouldn't have been able to get as far as she had tonight without Ricky's help.

Chapter 19

There was an upsurge in clients wanting massages during the week which saw both Emily and Marie run off their feet. Lisa extended the salon's hours to three late nights to keep up with demand.

Emily fell into bed at the end of each night exhausted.

"Let's promise we'll give each other a massage when this crazy upsurge has died down," Emily said, as she and Marie shared a bleary-eyed breakfast on Friday morning.

"How's Ricky?" Marie asked, buttering her toast.

"I haven't seen or heard from him since, must be, Monday. I hadn't realised it had been that long," she said, frowning.

"He normally pops round for lunch."

Emily stared at the wall. "He does. He must be really busy too. It's frustrating with him not having a cell phone. He's not easily contactable."

But it was out of character and they'd missed their usual Wednesday date night. Emily brushed it aside. No doubt they'd catch up with each other on the weekend. *Was it really a whole week since they'd been at Nana Rose's?* It was the best weekend she'd had in a long time and she was sure Ricky had enjoyed it too.

After a long sleep-in on Saturday morning, Emily had a look at the business case she was going to submit to the bank.

Marie, with her marketing expertise, offered to give it a once-over too.

"Emily, this is really good. You've done your homework and you've researched it thoroughly. I'd find it hard to believe that the bank wouldn't support you," Marie said, handing the folder back to Emily.

She took a deep breath. "I hope so. This is the only way I can see to get my life back on track."

Getting more worried, when Emily still hadn't seen Ricky by the end of the day, she drove out to his house. She pulled up outside and stared at the dilapidated structure. What would it be like to lose everything and have to start all over again? It had nearly happened to her. At least she had somewhere decent to live. As autumn began to make a subtle appearance the days would begin to get colder. The house would be freezing in winter. Maybe Ricky would find something better beforehand.

Biting her lip, she got out of the car and entered through the squeaky rusty gate. There was no sign of life around. The front door was shut and the windows were closed. She rapped on the door. When there was no answer she peered through the dirty front window but everything was hazy. She turned around and put her hands on her hips. *Where was he? Why hasn't he been to see me? Things had been going so well. Have I done or said something wrong? Was he having second thoughts?*

Emily drove back into town and out to Morningside subdivision on the off-chance that Ricky was working today. The building site was empty, drawing another blank.

She grew more worried resulting in a sleepless night.

Her first appointment on Monday morning was with Christine, Ricky's boss. This would be the perfect opportunity to find out whether Christine knew anything.

"Morning," Emily welcomed Christine.

"I so need your hands to work magic on my tired, old muscles. We put in some big hours last week. I've been driving those boys hard. Twelve to fourteen-hour days."

Ahhh! So that's why I hadn't seen Ricky. He'd been just as busy at work as she had.

Emily led Christine into the treatment room and offered her a seat.

"How's Ricky feeling?" Christine asked.

Emily frowned. "Good, I think."

"There's been some nasty flu bugs going round. And it's only just the end of summer. The flu seems to have knocked him around. He's been off work since Tuesday. I do hope he's back at work soon. I can't really afford to have one man down."

A week? He sounded okay on Monday night. He hadn't been complaining about feeling ill then, but maybe it was one of those fact-acting bugs – the one that hits you within a couple of hours of the first symptoms.

Emily handed Christine a robe and selected her favourite oils from her box. "How did he let you know he was ill?" A knot twisted in her stomach.

"A woman rang on Tuesday morning and said he was sick and would be taking a few days off."

Emily clunked the oil bottles together. "A woman?"

"At first I thought it was you but I still don't know who it was. There was a lot of noise in the background. It was almost like she was ringing from a party."

A hazy red mist swept over Emily's eyes and she grabbed the bed for support.

"Are you all right?" Christine asked.

"Yes, yes, I'm fine," Emily stammered. Her mind raced at a million miles an hour. What woman? Who'd be calling on Ricky's behalf?

"Maybe it was his sister. He did mention she was coming to stay with him." Christine's voice appeared to be coming at her through a fog. Ricky had never mentioned a sister who was coming to stay. What was going on? Something wasn't right. Something had changed.

"I'm sure that's right. Yes, his sister," Emily said.

"Anyway, he'll need to provide me with a doctor's certificate if he's going to be off work for any longer. Not that I don't trust him." Christine placed a reassuring hand on Emily's arm.

Trust. Emily gave Christine a half-smile. *Why is that word sending not-so-good- shivers up her spine?*

Emily left the room so Christine could undress and when she returned she set about giving Christine her usual massage. Her hands stroked up and down. The more her hands moved, the more her thoughts tumbled over in her mind keeping pace with her busy hands. Concentration was difficult, but she focused hard on working on Christine's sore spots.

At the end of the hour, Christine was all glowing "thank yous" and "that feels sooo much better."

After Christine dressed, Emily gave her a glass of water. She took a deep breath and braced herself for what she reluctantly had to do. "We've got a brand new range we're using at the moment. Would you like to try some?" Emily squeezed a glob of hand moisturiser into her hands.

"Always up for trying something," Christine said, holding out her hands.

"This is Nature's One. It's quite a rich moisturiser and really good for your hands."

"Well, as you can see mine need all the moisturising they can get. I don't have what you'd call lady's hands."

Emily massaged the moisturiser into Christine's brown, work-worn hands. Days helping out her staff building houses had resulted in callused, blistered and dried out hands.

"Smells all right." Christine wrinkled her nose. "Smells very natural."

Emily swallowed hard. *What can I say?* None of what was in the moisturiser was natural. "Oh, it's a combination of gardenia and freesia." She grabbed at some names. Christine would have no idea that they weren't in the product.

Christine rubbed her hands together to absorb the moisturiser. "These are the softest my hands have been for ages."

"Would you like to buy a tube?" Emily turned away. *How can I look Christine in the eye and sell her a product I don't believe in?*

"I'm not sure I'll need it. I can't see a man wanting to hold my hands in the near future."

Emily's shoulders slumped. She was no closer to selling just one Nature's One product. *What dressing down would Lisa give her now?*

"But why not? I can only pray that one day my knight in shining armour will come riding into Misty Springs."

Emily breathed a sigh of relief. At least Lisa would be able to see that she was trying. She took Christine out to the front and cashed up the sale. "I've made another appointment for you for two weeks' time." Emily wrote the details down on the card. "Enjoy your new hand cream."

"Thanks, Emily. And you tell that man of yours we need him back at work," Christine said.

The mystery around Ricky was complexing, but she couldn't focus on that now. She had to prepare herself for this afternoon's appointment with the bank.

* * *

"And you can see where I've worked out the profit based on projected sales for the first two years," Emily said. She ran her fingers across the back of her neck. The sun was streaming into Todd Cross's office and the heat in the confined space was suffocating.

"You've been very thorough, Emily," Todd said. "Both with your business case and with your plans to press on and finish your house."

Emily smiled. All the hard work and determination and meticulous research had been worth it. "So when do you think you'll be able to let me know?"

"In a couple of weeks. Both cases will be reviewed together at our next Loan Approvals meeting." Todd stood up. "You have a very good case."

"Thanks for your time." She walked out of the bank. The sun streamed down, but a bracing wind greeted her and she pulled her cardie round her. She'd done all she could and now her future was in someone else's hands.

Chapter 20

By Saturday, and with still no word from Ricky, Emily was growing increasingly worried. Ricky must really be sick. But if he was that sick then why wasn't he at home? Maybe he'd been at the doctor's when she'd dropped around. When everything seemed to be going okay between them something happened to cause her doubt and confusion. *What do I really know about Ricky?* She picked up her phone and Googled 'Ricky Coles'. She logged onto Facebook and typed in his name. His page came up. His profile details told her no more than what she already knew and his last post was over a year ago.

At a loss of what to do next, she headed down to Café Steam for a tea fix.

Emily perched on a stool as she watched Linda fill up the cabinets with the food for the day. It was still half an hour before opening time.

Linda put the heels of her hand on her back. "God, the day hasn't even started and my back's aching already."

"You really ought to go see someone about it," Emily said. The words would fall on deaf ears. Linda had been complaining about her back for months. "How about you come and see me? A deep tissue massage might help or it might be a nice, relaxing aromatherapy massage to help you."

"Sounds lovely, love, but I can't afford those kind of luxuries. It's all I can do at the moment to keep this place going."

"How about a months' worth of tea for one massage?" Emily suggested, raising her teacup.

Linda let out a belly laugh. "You're on. We can start now. Let me fill up your cup."

Emily held out her cup to be refilled.

"You know that woman who dropped in here a month ago when you were here?" Linda said.

A chill ran up Emily's spine.

"She was looking for Ricky. Wasn't she the wife?"

"Vanessa. It was his ex-wife." Why did the words sound like someone else was saying them?

"Ex-wife. Thank goodness for that." Linda poured sugar into the little containers on each table. "I was going to ask you about that. You want to make sure the last relationship is well and truly over before you go entering into the next one. Believe me. Been there, done that. This Vanessa obviously still thinks she has some claim on Ricky."

"Why?" Emily cocked her head.

"I'm sure I saw her wondering around town the other day. If not, it could have been her twin. But I don't think it was a coincidence. She got into that same old beat-up car she was driving last time."

The chill had turned into a cold sweat. Vanessa? Back in town? No. Ricky was adamant that he'd seen the last of her. But if she was back what did she want? Linda was right. She needed to be sure Ricky's relationship with Vanessa was finished for good. She'd needed to find Ricky and this time she'd wait outside his house until he came home. "Thanks for the tea, Linda. I'd better go. I've got a few things to sort out."

"No worries. Cross fingers for you it wasn't Vanessa."

Emily trotted back to the house. Was Vanessa the woman who had called Christine earlier in the week? Enough of the mystery. She grabbed her car keys off the bench and was almost out the door when Andrea called out to her.

"Hey, Emily. I almost forgot. Your Nana called a couple of hours ago. Can you give her a call back. She said it was urgent."

"Oh?" Emily turned around. "Did she say what it was about?"

"No. But she sounded quite stressed."

Emily picked up the phone and dialled Nana Rose's number. The phone was answered on the first ring.

"Nana Rose. I'd a message to call you. Are you OK?"

"Yes, I'm fine Midge but I'm just a little worried about the money.'

"Money. What money?"

Nana Rose's voice sounded tired and strained. "The money I gave you to put in the bank for me. I had a bank statement yesterday, but there's no deposit for the $2,000."

Emily's hand flew to her face. She'd completely forgotten about the money. The backpack. Where was the backpack? She must've absent-mindedly thrown the backpack in the wardrobe forgetting that she needed to bank the money.

"I've been really busy, Nana Rose. I'd completely forgotten about it. I'll pop to the bank first thing on Monday morning and deposit the money for you."

"Thanks, dear. I know you have a busy life, but I'd just wanted to check to make sure you hadn't forgotten."

"No. I hadn't forgotten. I'll sort it all out for you and give you a call on Monday. Thanks for reminding me."

"OK, Midge. You have a good weekend."

Emily rang off and sprinted to the bedroom. Her overnight bag was right at the front of the wardrobe. There was no backpack. Maybe it had fallen behind the suitcase. She moved it out the way. No, it wasn't there. It was dark at the back of the wardrobe. She tossed shoes, a tennis racket and a sleeping bag aside. She really needed to have a clean out. But no amount of moving stuff around revealed what she was looking for.

She threw everything back in the wardrobe trying not to give into a rising sense of panic. She must have left the backpack in the boot of the car. She ran outside and shoved the key in the lock, unlocking it and throwing up the lid. Empty. There was no backpack. A sickening flood pooled in the pit of her stomach. Where else could it be? Maybe she'd left it behind at Nana Rose's. No. Ricky had taken the bags out to the car. Then the backpack must've ended up with Ricky by mistake. And, of course, she hadn't seen him all week so he hadn't had a chance to give her the backpack.

She hopped in the car and drove on out to Ricky's. She pulled up outside the house, ran up the path and banged on the door. The place looked exactly the same as it had when she'd been here earlier on in the week. Her hand clenched her car keys. She'd drive back into town and keep driving until she found Ricky. If Vanessa was in town maybe Ricky was with her.

For the next hour, Emily drove up Main Street scouring for beat-up station wagons, for Ricky and Vanessa. Women with brown ponytails were everywhere. She stopped a couple of times ready to jump out of the car and confront Vanessa, but all turned out to be false alarms.

Turning off the main street, she went back down to the Morningside subdivision. She drove around every street in Misty Springs and even past the desolate, concrete foundations of her barely started house, but Ricky was nowhere to be found. There was only one thing left to do. Go back out to his house again and wait. He had to come home sooner or later. And she'd sleep in her car overnight if she had to.

She drove back out to Ricky's and as she got closer to the house she spied the station wagon parked outside his house. Ricky got out of the car, slammed the door shut and Vanessa drove away in the opposite direction to Misty Springs. So he had been with Vanessa.

She parked the car on the grass verge. A flame of heat flushed through her hands. What had been going on behind her back?

Ricky's shoulders were slumped forward and his chin dipped down on his chest.

Guilty. Caught in the act. Ricky owed her an explanation. Big time.

He looked up when she got out of the car and slammed the door shut.

"I've been wondering all week why you haven't been to see me or contacted me and now I know why," Emily said, as she walked up to him.

"It's not what you think."

"Oh, spare me. That's what they all say."

"Come inside. Let me explain."

Emily glared at him but followed him up the path and through the front door. "Christine told me you haven't been at work all week. That you've been sick. Was that true? Had you been sick?"

"No."' Ricky's eyes studied the floor.

"Was it Vanessa who'd called Christine and told her you were sick?"

"Yes."

A one-word answer man. She glared at him then she spied the backpack lying on the floor under the kitchen table. She strode over to it, picked it up and unzipped the bag. It was empty. The money was gone.

She swallowed hard and fought a lightheadedness that threatened to overwhelm her. "Ricky," she stammered. "Where's the money?"

There was no answer. Ricky's head hung low.

"Ricky, answer me," she demanded.

Rick's head slowly tilted and his eyes were filled with tears.

"Where's the money?" She was almost yelling. Her stomach rolled and a wave of nausea swept over her.

"I'm sorry Emily."

"Sorry? What do you mean sorry?" Her heart filled with dread. Was Ricky about to say what she had suspected and then confirmed in the last few moments?

"It's gone," Ricky said. Tears trickled down his cheeks.

"What do you mean it's gone?"

Ricky stared out the window and she watched a tear drop onto his T-shirt staining the material.

Emily looked in the bag again. Maybe if she stared hard enough the money would reappear. Then she had a moment of clear vision.

"It's Vanessa, isn't it? You gave the money to Vanessa."

Ricky spluttered and Emily caught the slightest nod of his head.

"I can't believe this," she whispered. "I thought you said she was out of the picture."

"She was. But she had debts to pay off and she was being threatened."

"So you thought you could take my money, Nana Rose's money." A loose window pane rattled in the wind.

"I was going to pay it back, I promise."

"How? You hardly have enough money now to look after yourself."

"I was going to go into the city..."

"To gamble?" The fuzziness returned. Red spots swum in front of her eyes.

Ricky barely nodded. "I thought I'd be able to get it back within the week and return the money to you. You wouldn't have even noticed."

"Except I found out. You've been seeing Vanessa again after you told me you and her were finished, and now you've stolen from me."

Ricky blanched. "I'm so sorry, Emily." He moved towards her, reaching out his hand to take her's.

"Get away from me," Emily said.

Ricky's hand stopped in mid-air.

The tears she had been fighting spilled out of her eyes and she sobbed loudly. "I trusted you." The words coming out between racking sobs. "I trusted you with the money and with my heart. I'll never forgive you." She threw the backpack down on the floor and ran out of the house.

Somehow, through blinding tears she managed to get into her car, do a U-turn and drive back to Misty Springs. She clutched at her stomach as pains shot through her.

How could she have been so foolish? The one man, the one chance she'd had to find love again had forever undermined her trust in him and betrayed her.

***

The sun had well and truly set behind Red Hill when Emily pulled into the drive. Fortunately Lisa, Andrea and Marie were not home. She couldn't face anyone seeing her like this. To see what a fool she'd been. How she'd been betrayed.

Her stomach growled. It had been over eight hours since she'd eaten. If she ate now she'd throw up with all the churning that was going on. She undressed, threw a Winnie-the-Pooh nightie over her head and crawled into bed, pulling the covers up, almost smothering herself.

The full extent of Ricky's betrayal hit her. It would be unlikely that she'd see the $2,000 again. She sniffled and wiped away a tear that, like a dripping tap, refused to stop. *What would I tell Nana Rose?* Nana Rose had taken her advice, had trusted *her* and now her money was gone before it had even been banked. Her head thumped. She couldn't tell Nana Rose It would be too embarrassing. She'd have to use her own money to replace Nana Rose's. She'd deposit the money into Nana's bank account tomorrow and ring and tell her everything was all right. That she didn't need to worry anymore. Her money was safe and sound and would appear on her next bank account statement.

But now she would be $2,000 out of pocket. She'd be dipping into her last remaining savings. Emergency money she'd put aside. *How will Todd react if they know I'd had to use $2,000 of my own money?* Her plans to get on with her life had ended in disaster and she'd slide further into debt. She almost laughed at the irony of the situation. Ricky had stolen from her to help Vanessa pay off her debts sending Emily backwards. A bile taste rose in her mouth. She'd learnt her lesson. And anything she'd do in the future she'd now do on her own. In a misty haze she fell into a troubled sleep.

***

How she got out of bed, readied herself for work and massaged her clients she couldn't say.

Each day she went through the motions and each day she fell further and further into despair.

She rose early each morning and was at the salon before anyone else, making an excuse to Marie that she wanted to do a thorough clean of her treatment room and get an early start on the stocktake. She booked clients after her normal finishing time just to keep both hands and mind busy.

On Monday she'd transferred $2,000 into Nana Rose's bank account and rang her to let her know.

She pressed her lips tightly together as Nana Rose prattled on about her week, all Emily wanted to do was cry and spill the whole story but she hung on and "hmmed" and "aahed" at the appropriate times as silent tears trickled down her face. Emily made a promise to ring again next week. Nana Rose wanted to hear all about her plans and how she'd got on with the bank. She hung up and burst into tears.

***

Marie had asked Emily to help her with a marketing assignment so on Saturday afternoon the two of them were buried at the kitchen table amongst laptops and paper.

After an hour they took a break. Emily wandered out to the kitchen to prepare some snacks. She opened a packet of nuts, some raisins, cut up some cheese and some fruit. Now she needed a large plate to put it all on. Lisa had one she used frequently when she was entertaining. It would be the perfect size. But where did she keep it? She opened a few cupboards and up on the top shelf was the yellow and red flowered platter. It was just beyond her reach, but if she stood on tiptoes she could just reach it.

"You OK there?" Marie called out.

"Yes, fine." Her words rasped out as she strained to grip onto the edge of the plate. She reached higher. Her left fingers finally wrapping firmly around the plate. She pulled the plate to the edge of the shelf. But it was heavier than she had anticipated. She'd underestimated the weight and as she pulled

241

the plate towards her, her weakened fingers were unable to bear the weight.

"Oh no!" She scrabbled with her right hand, but it was too late. The plate overbalanced and crashed to the floor. Emily squealed as bits of ceramics hit her in the face.

Marie jumped up out of her chair. "Are you all right?"

"Yeah." She surveyed the damage. Bits of broken plate lay everywhere. "The plate just slipped out of my hand." She covered her face. "I'm so clumsy."

Marie placed a reassuring hand on Emily's arm. "No, you're not. Silly place to put something we always use."

"Lisa's going to kill me," Emily said.

"Let's get this cleared up and worry about Lisa later."

Emily found a pan and brush and together they swept up the broken pieces. *Broken pieces, like my heart.* She rubbed her left fingers.

"How's the hand?"

"Sore. The plate bent them back as I lost my grip. I was too ambitious."

"Anything to do with what's been going on with Ricky?"

She hadn't told Marie the whole story. She'd been too embarrassed.

"Ricky and I are over. He stole Nana Rose's money and gave it his ex-wife to help her pay off some debts. The money's gone. No doubt gambled away."

"That's pretty serious. I thought you'd just had a disagreement."

"I wish, but it goes a lot deeper than that. Ricky's a gambler and I guess for gamblers there's always that attraction of wanting to make more with what little they still have left."

"I'm sorry that things didn't work out. He seemed like a nice guy."

"I thought so," Emily said. The tears were blinding her vision again. It was no use crying over spilt milk. She'd just have to work harder to replenish her bank account. And as for her love life, well, she'd just flag that. She emptied the broken plate pieces into a paper bag.

The doorbell rang.

"I'll get it," she yelled out to Marie.

Emily pulled open the front door. And there standing in front of her was a tall, dark, handsome man. Josh, her ex-fiancé, was back in her life.

Emily squeezed her eyes tight. This couldn't be. She opened her eyes, but Josh was there in front of her. He hadn't changed. Well, maybe a few extra frown lines, the brown hair at the edge of his temples had a sprinkle of grey in them. He was still slim. One side of his collar was tucked under his jersey. The way it used to drive her crazy in a good way. She'd always be tugging the corner out joking that he still needed her help to get dressed in the morning. She took a step back. "What, what are you doing here?"

"I came to see you," Josh said, giving her that winning smile.

Her heart skipped out of time. *Don't do that.* She willed her heart to behave. "How did you know where to find me?"

"Can we go somewhere we can talk in private?" Josh asked. He leaned up against the doorframe as if he lived here. As if it hadn't been four years since she'd last seen him when he walked out on her.

"Yes, we could go to Red Hill Bar. It'll be pretty quiet this early on Saturday." The words were out of her mouth before she could stop them. *Why on earth would I want to talk to Josh?* She had nothing to say to him. But maybe she was just a little bit curious as to why he'd suddenly reappeared. "I'll grab my bag." She left him standing on the doorstep. She wasn't going to invite him in that was for sure.

They walked down to Red Hill Bar. Thank goodness it was only a five-minute walk. Josh chatted about the weekend traffic driving up to Misty Springs. He'd always been a talker, which for now was good. She was finding it difficult to make small talk.

She was right. There were few people inside but that would change later tonight. As it got darker earlier and the weather grew cooler, people would start to fill the bar.

"Can I get you a drink? Lemon and ginger tea?" He remembered. After all this time he still remembered what kind of tea she drank.

"Yes, please."

Josh ordered at the bar and they sat in a booth. "So how you've been?"

The waitress brought over their drinks.

"After all this time you suddenly turn up. No word for the last two years and now, here you are."

"I needed to see you in person. Would you've seen me if you knew I was coming? Would you've talked to me if I'd rung you?"

"No." She stared into Josh's blue eyes. The kind of eyes that were such a dark blue they were almost black.

"Okay. I deserved that." The smile that had radiated from his face had disappeared.

"How did you find me?" Emily took a sip of tea but flinched as the scalding liquid burnt her tongue.

"I called David. He told me you were here now."

Damn David! Typical that he'd just give out her private details without asking her first. Not thinking of the consequences. "Are you still living in Christchurch?" she asked.

"Yes, I'm a realtor with Redwood Homes. I've only been doing it for eighteen months but I've achieved top sales agent four months in a row."

"That's very good," Emily replied. Josh had always wanted to sell houses. He saw the good returns for the hard work and how he could put his commerce degree to use.

"And what are you doing here?"

"I got a job as a massage therapist at Serenity Spa." Emily held her head high. She wanted Josh to know that she'd picked herself up after he'd left and had the guts to carry on.

"And your hand?" His voice was almost a whisper.

"My hand is fine." She put her cup down with a clink and pushed her hand under her thigh. "What do you want, Josh? I need to get back."

"I wanted to say I'm sorry for walking out on you the way I did. Leaving a note was cowardly and I've always regretted it."

"Regretted leaving me or telling me in a note?"

"Both."

It was going to be one of those days when only just a little thing someone would say or losing her grip on a plate would set her off. "You're right. Leaving the way you did was not only cowardly but cruel. The fact that you'd dump me because of my deformed hand was really shallow."

Josh winced. "No. No. I didn't leave you because of your hand." Josh scrambled to cover her right hand with his large, tanned hand. She snatched it away.

"I blamed myself for what happened that day. The argument we'd had over something so trivial. I shouldn't have yelled at you. If we hadn't argued you wouldn't have gone out in the stupid storm and been knocked over by that tree. It was all my fault."

The frown lines that Emily had noticed earlier had deepened. He looked older now, weary. Josh drew in a big breath. "I came here to say I'm sorry."

After all this time he was now saying sorry. And what she'd believed all along hadn't been true? Josh hadn't left her because of her ugly hand; he just couldn't handle the guilt of the consequences of their argument

Josh's shoulders slumped forward, and her heart went out to him. "Emily come back to Christchurch with me." He reached for her hand again and this time she didn't pull it away. "I'm making good money. I can buy you a house, everything you've always wanted. We can travel together, maybe one day get married. And I can help pay off your debts."

"What?" Emily straightened up.

"David said you were having financial problems." Damn David again! Man, was she going to give him a piece of her mind later. "David had no right to tell you that." Emily's voice was low.

"It doesn't matter. I can help you."

Emily wrestled her hand away. "I don't need your help. I've managed this far without you and I'll keep managing. You were right on that day. I didn't plan the trip to Wellington properly and I'd forgotten to book the accommodation so we had to cancel our trip and that's what we argued about. But I've learnt from my mistakes. I'm a good planner now and I research thoroughly. I don't take chances and I check everything. I won't be taken for a ride anymore. I don't need your money to help finance your guilt trip."

Josh was unfazed. "Please tell me you'll think about it."

"No, Josh. I need to go." Emily stood up.

"Emily, please. I still love you."

She sat back down with a thud, and the air went whooshing out of her lungs. "I would've thought you'd be married by now."

"I've had a few relationships but nothing serious. I keep coming back to you and me. What we had was good."

"Until you left me."

"Emily, I said I'm sorry. Can't we move on together?"

She'd never forgiven Josh for leaving her, but this was the man that one day she was supposed to have married. But she'd closed her heart off, too scared she'd get hurt again. She'd just been betrayed by one man and here was another wanting her back. She shook her head.

"Please, Emily. Give us another chance. Let me make it up to you."

She was falling under his spell again. The nights he'd sat beside her in hospital, the care he'd given her while she recovered at home. He'd been there for her. He'd cared about her, still cared about her.

"I don't think so," Emily said, avoiding his eyes.

"Emily, look at me."

She raised her head and stared at him. A mixture of pain and love was written on his face.

"Just say you'll think about it," he said.

It had been an emotional day. She bit her lip. If she said anything now, she'd start crying. She nodded.

"Thank you."

And because she couldn't resist it any longer she leant over the table and tugged his collar out of his jersey.

Josh laughed. "I still forget about that."

"Are you staying in Misty Springs long?"

"No. I'm going back now."

"You came all this way just to see me?"

"Yes."

"And what if I wasn't here?"

"I'd have hung around until you showed up."

Just like what she'd done with Ricky.

Josh stood up. "Will you give me your cell phone number? So we can stay in touch?'

Emily rubbed the back of her neck. Was that going to be a good idea? Josh now able to contact her?

"I promise I won't text you early in the morning on weekends. You still like to sleep in?"

"Yes."

Their body clocks had often clashed. She, the late riser, Josh up as daylight overtook night.

They walked outside. Emily hung back. The hello had been awkward; the good-bye more so.

"My car is parked up the hill. I'll ring you later. I hope you'll reconsider and think about us, Emily."

All she could do was nod at the man she'd once loved.

***

There'd be nobody back at the house. Lisa would be out, no doubt with Hunter or whoever else was flavour of the month. Andrea and Vinnie were going to be catching up with friends and Marie had mentioned she'd be doing research at the library. An empty house wasn't what she needed now. A crawling mist swirled around the middle of Red Hill. It wouldn't be long before it reached the township, the dampness creeping its way down the streets, encroaching on your sight, blinding your way, making it difficult to see too far ahead.

She wandered across the road to Café Steam.

Linda was stacking up the chairs outside.

"Let me give you a hand," Emily offered.

"Hey, thanks," Linda said. "I feel like an old woman struggling away here."

"You really should get your back looked at." Emily folded up a couple of chairs and stacked them inside the café.

"Did you find out any more about Vanessa?" Linda asked.

"Oh, yes."

"Hmmm. Sounds suspicious to me."

How much should I tell Linda?

"Well, that's the last of them." Linda put the chairs on the pile. "Now I can lock up, go home and have a bath."

"If you want to drop by the salon, I can make up some oils for you to help you enjoy your soak."

"Well, speak of the devil." Linda was staring out the window.

"What?"

"Over there by the reserve."

Emily squinted. The mist was thickening, descending. Under the tall, gum tree in profile were three, no four, men and a woman. They were in deep discussion. One of the men, wearing a black T-shirt and trousers, was gesturing. The woman turned, her ponytail bouncing in agitation. One of the men stepped forward. The mist pulled back and a shard of light hit the top of one of the men's head. The profile was unmistakable – it was Ricky. An emptiness filled her heart. He had come into her life quickly and had left just as quickly. He obviously had moved on, back with Vanessa.

"That's not who I think it is." Linda moved closer to the window.

"Yes, it's Ricky and Vanessa."

"No. Not them. The other two undesirables."

"I don't know who they are. I've not seen them around here before."

One of the men flicked the butt of a cigarette onto the ground, the burning end pulsing out sparks in the mist.

"I should hope not. Those two are good-for-nothings from the city who come up to supply."

Emily frowned. "Supply?"

"Well, I'm not talking about ice cream."

"Please don't tell me you mean drugs."

"Yes, I do. And I'm sure the police will want to know they're back in town. Do you know they were trying to sell drugs from my café? Were trying to use it as a base. When I found out what they were doing I called the cops. That was a couple of years ago."

One of the men handed a packet to Vanessa. She gave him something in return, then she and Ricky hurried away. The two men walked off in the opposite direction.

Emily squeezed her eyes tight. Was Ricky involved in drugs? Why? Or was this something that his ex-wife was dragging him into? *How much do I really know about Ricky?*

Apparently not everything. God, she hadn't learnt anything. She had been so busy making sure the business case and her house loan application would pass all tests that she hadn't done a thorough check on Ricky. He hadn't told her everything.

Linda tied up the strings on a rubbish bag. "It's a good thing you're not involved with Ricky anymore. You don't want to get mixed up in his shoddy business. He doesn't look like a drug user, but the police told me people buy off those two thugs and then on-sell it to make a profit."

And the money they earned would be gambled away. The picture being painted was perfectly clear. Maybe she had got out just in time. This was more than she could stand. Her head pounded and her stomach churned.

"Well, that's one thing you won't have to worry about anymore," Linda said. She grabbed the keys.

Emily followed Linda out of the shop. Everything was happening in a daze. Too much happened today for her to process. She said good-bye to Linda and walked back home, clutching her hands.

The mist was thicker and tiny beads swirled and eddied. The sulphur seemed more pungent and suffocating, invading her nostrils, almost choking her.

She misjudged the kerb and her foot landed heavily on the road throwing her off-balance. Her ankle turned over. Putting her hand out to break her fall, her fingers on her left hand twisted and crumpled under her. She yelped out in pain. The tears that had been hiding under the surface exploded, releasing both her physical and emotional pain. She'd truly hit the ground, the bottom, and had nowhere left to fall.

Chapter 22

Every part of her body ached. She stretched herself out cautiously and swung her legs over the side of the bed. She tested her ankle, putting as much pressure on it as she could and hobbled a few steps. It was still sore but once she got moving it would loosen up a bit.

After she'd picked herself up off the ground yesterday, she'd limped the few metres to the house, applied ice to her ankle and bandaged it. Her two fingers had bent right back when she fell. She couldn't tape them together – they were too far apart. She'd just have to do the best she could, but it made everything that much harder. She grabbed a T-shirt from the drawer. Nothing with buttons on it; that would be too challenging today.

She wandered out to the kitchen and made a cup of calming chamomile tea. Picking up a notepad, she idly doodled, her hand drawing lines and sketches that eventually became lavender stalks. One lavender became a bunch and soon the whole page was filled with little bunches of lavender. She closed her eyes, seeing the lavender bushes at Nana Rose's gently swaying in the wind. That was where she needed to be now. Nana Rose would make it all right.

It was 7.30 on Sunday morning. Nana Rose would be up, pottering around in the kitchen. Emily pulled the phone toward her. If she left now, she'd be at Paix by 10.30. She'd have the whole day and, if she left no later than six, she'd be back in Misty Springs before dark.

A quick phone call to Nana Rose, who sounded tired, to let her know she was coming up for the day, a shower and a bite to eat and she was on the road within half an hour. She stared straight ahead as she passed Ricky's house. She wouldn't look. She didn't care. That relationship was over, over before it had hardly begun.

Her heart soared when she drove down the long drive, past the trees that sheltered the garden on either side and pulled up outside Nana Rose's house. She was on the veranda repotting her herb plants.

Emily got out of the car and breathed in the country air, free of sulphur and full of fresh grass and flowers.

"It's such a lovely surprise to see you. And so soon after your last trip." Nana Rose kissed Emily on the cheek. She looked over Emily's shoulder. "Where's that young man, Ricky? He didn't come with you?"

"He had some things to take care of so it's just me." Emily reached down and picked up the old, dead plants that Nana Rose had discarded. She wasn't ready to tell her that Ricky and she were over.

"That's a good thing. That gives us some time all to ourselves. You're pale and look like you need feeding up. I quickly whipped up a batch of those scones you like so much, and we can have a salad for lunch."

"You spoil me."

"You deserve it. Now, I know you're not telling me all that's going on. Did I see you limping?"

"Let me get rid of this rubbish in the compost for you and then I'll tell you about my slight accident."

Over lunch Emily played down her accident. Her ankle had held up in the drive and if she didn't move her fingers too much they were okay.

"You need to be more careful, Midge. We can't have you falling over like that."

Emily was eager to change the subject and asked Nana Rose about the fences.

"Kyle came over to see me yesterday. He's fixed the last two posts. I may need to borrow Dusty."

"Are the mice getting out of control?"

"There's been a few more in the barn lately. That cat will have a ball in there."

"How about I go and visit Kyle this afternoon and bring Dusty back?"

"That'd be lovely. Here, have another scone."

Emily buttered her second scone and afterwards helped Nana Rose with the dishes.

"Okay, Nana. I won't be long," Emily said. She grabbed her straw hat, limped down the stairs and set off down the path past the swing that hung limply in stillness. She looked away. The swing had always meant happy memories but today represented sadness. Some of the petals on the sunflowers had sunburn marks on them. Other petals had fallen off, along with the seeds. The flower heads had grown so full and round that they were almost bent over under their weight, like a stooped old lady. White yarrow dotted the grass like clusters of snowballs.

She poked her head into the barn. The light disturbed the mice and they scampered out of sight. She ventured down to the bottom paddock and inspected the new posts. She pulled on the wires that Ricky had fixed, the low deep twang ringing out. Ricky and Kyle had both done a good job.

Clambering down to the bottom paddock she was soon out along the road and turning into Kyle's drive. Why was it that old farmsteads always felt like you were taking a step back in time? The rusty old cylindrical letter box must've been the original one. The lid hung open and Emily peered inside. There were a few letters so she pulled them out. She and Kyle used to leave each other notes in the letter box when they were kids, playing postman and Indians. The letter box had survived years of baking sun and driving rain. An old cartwheel below the letterbox added to the rustic charm. She continued up the drive and was greeted by a woof.

"Hey, Faithful. Where's Kyle? What've you done with Kyle?" She ruffled the dog's head and his tail wagged in response. "Let's go see. Come on." She walked up the steps of the old house. "Hello? Anyone home?"

"In here. Is that you Emily?"

"Yes, I'm back again." She wandered into the lounge.

Kyle was sprawled on the couch. He clutched some papers in one hand and a can of beer in the other.

"Working hard, I see," Emily said, sitting down.

"Trying to catch up on some work. The only time I can do that these days is here without any distractions."

"Oh, well seen as I'm a distraction," Emily teased.

"Hey, you know that's not what I meant. You're welcome here any time. Let me get you a drink. How about a wine?"

"Perfect."

Kyle headed out to the kitchen and within a few moments was back with a glass of wine, another can of beer, chips, nuts and dip. "Cheers." They clinked their glass and can together. "So what brings you back out here so soon?"

"Just needed a day away. We need to borrow Dusty."

"That mean old cat. You got a mouse problem?"

"A wee one, but I don't want it to get out of control."

"Sure. We can go look for Dusty. He'll be around somewhere. I'll just need to find the cage to put him in."

Faithful let out a whine and thumped down on the floor.

"Where's your other half?" Kyle ran his fingers over his blonde unruly curls.

"I'd rather not talk about it."

Kyle frowned. "You have a squabble? You looked like the ultimate love birds."

Emily bit her lip. "Well, you know…"

"Yip. I do. Here I was thinking I'd be married by now with a barefoot and pregnant wife."

Emily rolled her eyes. "Typical."

"Made you smile though, didn't I?"

Emily nodded.

"Seriously. I'd always imagined a car load of ankle-biters running around enjoying these long, hot summers. Doing all the things I – we - loved to do as kids. Remember that summer we caught those little frogs and let them out in Bridget and Yvette's room?"

"I can still hear them screaming," Emily said, laughing.

"Yeah. We weren't too popular after that."

"And we weren't allowed dinner until all ten were found."

Kyle laughed. "Bridget and Yvette refused to sleep in their room."

"Yeah, we had to instead. I must admit, I was a bit scared. Frogs in the daytime are fine, but jumping around at night, that's a different story." Emily got up and stretched. She swallowed the last of her wine and wandered over to the dining table. There were papers strewn everywhere and a lap top hummed away. "What's all this?"

Kyle jumped up. "Highly confidential investment stuff. I really should've put it away."

"I know you're involved in business investments but what exactly?"

"You don't really want to know. It's boring to most people."

"No, I do."

"Okay. But be prepared to be bored silly." He swept the papers off the table and into a briefcase. "Here have a seat and I'll show you."

Kyle brought up Kyle Lester Investments' website. "So this is us. And we look at businesses who are wanting to grow and need some extra capital to get them underway for the next step. We also help those who want to start a business and need some start up dough."

"Really?" *Could Kyle's company be an option for the lavender business?"*

"Sure. They have to have a solid business plan." He stared at her. "What's going on in that head of yours?"

Should she tell Kyle about her plans? There was probably no point. Todd said she had a very good chance of getting approval. But maybe it was worth getting Kyle's point of view too. Over the next hour and a couple more glasses of wine and beer, Emily outlined her plans to make cosmetics, buy a distiller to make her own oil and the other ways she could use lavender to supplement her income. She was able to log into the computer back at home and show Kyle her business case.

"This is good, Emily," Kyle said, after poring over the documents and punching a few figures into a calculator. "You've obviously done a lot of research."

Emily beamed. Another compliment that proved the thoroughness of her work.

"This is a business I'd definitely invest in."

"Well, hopefully the bank will think so too," Emily said, as she munched on the last of the nuts. "Anyway I'd better get back. Nana Rose will be wondering where I've gone. Do you think I could take Dusty back with me?"

"No worries. I think the cage is down in the basement. Give me a tick and I'll be back."

Emily waited on the veranda. She looked out over the fields in front of the house and the huge plum trees that lined the drive. It was so peaceful here. She didn't want to go back to Misty Springs, back to her troubles.

"You look just like you did the last year of the summer holidays."

Emily turned around.

Kyle was staring at her, a far-off longing in his eyes. He moved closer. "The last summer. Remember? When we were seventeen, you moved to the city and I went to uni and we went on to live our adult lives. We hardly saw each other after that. Maybe a weekend every now and again."

"Yeah, I do remember. It was a sad weekend. You said goodbye to me on this veranda. And I kissed you."

Kyle was that close now, his breath tapping her cheek. "And we promised to stay in touch, but we didn't really." He wrapped a curl behind her ear. "You know, I always imagined you'd be my wife and those kids I talked about, they would be ours. Maybe that's why I haven't found anyone yet. It's the vision of you I can't get out of my mind."

She stared into his blue eyes, mesmerised by Kyle, the blonde dare-devil boy and Kyle, the older man. Like steel to a magnet, she was pulled closer to him until their lips were almost touching. But this wasn't what she wanted. She didn't want Kyle. They were just good friends, sometimes neighbours. She wanted Ricky but Ricky didn't want her. Josh wanted her but she didn't want Josh. God, what a mess!

"No. Stop. I can't." Emily pushed Kyle away. "I'm sorry." Her hands flew to her face.

"Damn! I said too much." Kyle placed his hands on the railing and looked out over the fields.

Emily gulped. She'd hurt his feelings, but it all happened so quickly. She put out her hand and covered his. "I had no idea you felt like this."

"I've always felt something for you, Emily. Ever since we were kids. But the feelings have grown stronger since I saw you last. It's you I've been waiting for."

She had to stop this. "I don't feel the same way. I love you Kyle but like a brother. Not anything more."

Kyle blanched, pain travelling across his face. "Maybe I've had too many beers." He pushed back off the veranda, trying to hide his embarrassment. "Don't worry about it. It was the beer talking."

That was a lie, but he was trying to save face.

She needed to change the subject quickly. "Did you find the cage?"

"Ah, no. I think it's in the shed. Let's have a look." Kyle took off at a quick pace and Emily followed behind. Before, their conversation flowed freely and was light, now there was silence. She hung back outside the shed giving Kyle some space to gather his composure.

Bangs and thumps and muttered words came from inside and finally Kyle emerged with the cage. "Right. Found it. We're off then."

"Um, haven't you forgotten something?" Emily asked.

Kyle stared at the cage.

"The cat? Dusty."

"Oh, yeah." He laughed, and at that moment the tension was broken. "Okay, let's get that grumpy cat."

After some calling and checking out his favourite places, Dusty was found sunning himself in a pot under the clothesline.

Kyle swiftly picked Dusty up and plonked him in the cage before he could bite and spit. "Mission accomplished," he said, snapping the latch shut. "Let's take the shortcut through the stiles. Save us having to go out along the road."

They wandered down through the fields, climbed over the stile that separated the two properties and came out behind the barn.

Kyle was overcompensating for his revelation and was chatting away non-stop. He'd break out in song every now and again, his verses punctuated by growls from Dusty.

"Okay, Dusty. Go and do your stuff." Kyle unlatched and opened the door and a relieved Dusty jumped out. "We'll leave Dusty to hunt in peace. I'll leave the door open a fraction so he can come and go."

"Hey, look who's found us."

"Faithful."

Faithful wandered up to Kyle and sniffed him.

"Come and say hello to Nana Rose," Emily said. "She'll want to thank you for your pest control."

"And maybe she'll send me home with those well-known scones."

"How do you know I haven't eaten them all?"

"If you have you'll have to bake me some."

Inside the house, Emily poked her head into the lounge. No Nana Rose. She wasn't in the kitchen, and the house was eerily quiet.

"Nana Rose," Emily yelled out. "We're home."

No reply.

"Maybe she's out the back. I'll go have a look." Kyle poked his head took out the back door. "No. She's not out there."

"Nana Rose!" Emily yelled out again.

There was a thundering crash from upstairs as something hit the floor accompanied by a loud cry of pain.

"Nana Rose?!" Emily yelled out.

Kyle and Emily bounded up the stairs along with Faithful.

"Nana Rose!" Emily yelled out again. She ran from room to room calling out, but there was no sign of her. She'd almost reached the end of the hall. Where was Nana? In front of her, the ladder, which was normally tucked away, was standing tall and reaching up towards the attic.

"She's up in the attic," Emily said. She hurriedly climbed up the ladder, Kyle close behind. It was dark with only the shards of the late afternoon sun shining through the gaps in the curtains. She squinted. Dark bits of furniture and boxes were starting to take shape in the shadows.

Emily fumbled in the dark. Where was the light switch? Her fingers finally found what she was looking for and she flicked on the light. She squinted again against the bright light.

"Nana," Emily said, as she raced over to the crumpled form lying on the attic floor. "Are you alright?"

Nana Rose moaned. "My hip." She moved an unsteady hand over to her left side.

"Let's see if we can turn her over onto her back," Kyle said.

Emily took Nana Rose's hand and gave it a comforting squeeze.

Nana moaned as they gently turned her over.

"What happened?" Emily asked.

"I was standing on a couple of boxes trying to get something. The boxes must've collapsed and I fell." Nana Rose's eyes filled with tears. "I'm a silly duffer."

"Don't you worry. We'll get help."

"I'll call for Dr Jones. I don't want to move her too much." Kyle fished around in his pocket for his cell phone, punched in a few keys and was immediately connected to Dr Jones.

"Nana, I'm just going to get you a blanket and a pillow so you don't get cold," Emily said.

"Okay, dear," Nana Rose replied, wincing in pain.

Emily went down the ladder, gathered what she needed and was back just as Kyle was finished with Dr Jones.

"We're in luck. Dr Jones is just down the road. He's going to swing by. Should be here in about half an hour."

"That's good timing." Emily covered Nana Rose with a couple of blankets and lifted her head so it could rest it on the pillow. She comforted Nana Rose, who every now and again let out a little moan.

Kyle went outside to wait for the doctor.

"What were you doing up here in the attic?" Emily asked.

"Books." Nana Rose wheezed. "I was getting some books for you."

Emily frowned. *Books?* She wasn't a reader.

"Can I have a cup of tea?" Nana Rose asked.

"How about we wait until Dr Jones sees you and then we'll get you a drink?"

Faithful, who had settled himself down at the foot of the ladder, barked indicating that the doctor had arrived.

Loud clanks on the ladder and Kyle and Dr Jones emerged.

"Emily. I haven't seen you for a while. You're looking well," Dr Jones said.

"Thank you," Emily said. The doctor's once black hair had now turned completely grey and he'd put on weight around his middle. His black-rimmed glasses reflected the golden glow from the uncovered light bulb.

"Now, what have you been doing, Nana Rose?"

"She's had a nasty fall," Emily explained.

"That's no good. Let's see what damage you've done."

Emily and Kyle stood back and watched Dr Jones examine Nana Rose and ask her questions. "Well, I'm pretty sure she hasn't broken anything. I think she's fallen quite heavily on her hip so it's bound to be badly bruised. But I'd like her to go to Culverden for X-rays, just to make sure."

"We can take her," Kyle said.

"But how safe is it going to be to move her? We have to get her down the ladder," Emily said.

"Let's see how Nana does sitting up and then we'll see if we can get her on her feet," Dr Jones suggested.

It took a while to get Nana up, and in a carefully planned manoeuvre all three of them managed to support Nana and get her back down the ladder.

"Dr Jones said he'd call in on Nana again tomorrow and discuss the X-ray results," Kyle said.

Emily guided Nana Rose into a straight-backed chair in the kitchen and made her a cup of tea.

"Oh, that's better," Nana Rose said, her voice a little stronger than an hour ago.

Once Nana Rose was feeling better, they settled her into Emily's car. Kyle drove while Emily sat in the back seat holding Nana Rose's hand. When Kyle hit bumps Nana Rose let out little groans. Emily frowned at Nana Rose's pale face. Within half an hour, Kyle pulled into the car park of the region's small hospital.

Emily grabbed a wheelchair, helped Nana Rose into it and wheeled her into the waiting area.

Fortunately it was a quiet day so Nana Rose didn't have to wait long. She was given another painkiller, then Emily and Kyle accompanied her to the X-ray department. After the x-rays were taken, they had to wait half an hour to see the doctor, but eventually Nana Rose's name was called.

"Mrs Seymour, I'm Dr Cook and I've just been looking at your X-rays? How are you feeling?"

"Sore."

"Hopefully the painkiller will help with that. You'll be pleased to know you haven't broken anything; we don't want that happening at your age."

Emily breathed out. That was a relief. A broken hip would not have been good news.

"You've just badly bruised your hip. So I'll write you out a prescription. And you'll need to rest up for a while."

"I'll try. I don't like sitting around and doing nothing," Nana Rose grumbled.

"I think it's a good opportunity to have a rest." Dr Cook winked at Emily. "I think you'll probably find you won't feel like doing much anyway. You're going to be tender for a while."

They both thanked the doctor and met Kyle out in the waiting area. Emily got Nana Rose's prescription from the pharmacy and before long they were on their way back to Paix.

Nana Rose, knocked out with painkillers and tiredness from the stress, slept most of the way home.

It was just after six pm when Kyle turned the car into the drive.

Emily, with Kyle's help, manoeuvred Nana Rose out of the car. After a quick discussion, it was agreed that Nana should sleep on the big couch in the lounge, rather than try and navigate the stairs.

"I'll stay the night. I don't want to leave Nana on her own. Not until she's feeling better," Emily said.

"I'm not going back to the city until Wednesday so I can check in on her too," Kyle replied.

"That would be great and thank you for your help today."

"No worries. I'd better get going. I've got some sheep to feed." Kyle whistled for Faithful who'd parked himself by the front door. "I'll catch up with you tomorrow."

Emily watched Kyle head down the drive to the back part of the property. He had been a good man to have round in an emergency. A good man... she shook her head. She couldn't dwell on Kyle now. She had things to do.

Chapter 23

Emily rang Lisa, explained what had happened and requested the next day off work. Would Lisa say no given that things between them were a bit frosty? She hadn't even had time to tell her about the broken plate, but she didn't care. Nana Rose needed her now and if she lost her job then she'd figure that out later. Lisa grumbled about being a therapist down but reluctantly gave her the day off and mumbled something about hoping Nana Rose got better soon.

Emily helped Nana get changed and got her onto the couch.

"Now you're not to worry about a thing," Emily said, as she ruffled up the pillows. "I've got tomorrow off work. I'm here to look after you."

"Thank you, Midge. I don't know where I'd be without you."

Nana fell asleep almost immediately. Emily, also exhausted from the day's events, locked up the house and went up to her room.

The attic door was still open. She'd better shut it and put the ladder away. Nana wouldn't be going up there for a while. She climbed up into the attic. The light had been left on, accentuating the squashed boxes that Nana had toppled off.

Books. That's right. Nana had mentioned she had been looking for books for her. There were a number of books lying higgle de piggledy on the floor. She bent down and picked up some of them: Growing Lavender; Lavender Gifts; Lavender in Provence. One remaining book had fallen open when it'd landed on the floor. Emily crouched down. The page that was staring up at her was a recipe for Lavender Body Butter. She turned the book to look at the front cover. *Lavender Cosmetics for the Cottage Market*. It was an old book – maybe 30 years old with a musty, dusty smell. She flipped to the inside cover page and in beautiful cursive writing was the following: *To my darling Rose. May you long live in a garden of lavender. From your loving husband, Thomas.*

Tears formed in Emily's eyes. Nana Rose was going to hand these books down to her so she could use them to make cosmetics. She flicked through the old pages. Nana must've used these recipes. Splotches of ingredients stained some of the pages. Bits of lavender flowers were scattered between the pages emitting a slight fragrance. There were recipes for soaps and moisturisers with Nana's pencil notes in the margins.

Emily stopped at a page for a moisturiser. She scanned the ingredient list. It and its measurements almost matched Emily's recipes. But there was one extra ingredient – coconut oil. She wasn't using coconut oil in her recipes. Down at the bottom of the page, Nana Rose had made a note. Use coconut oil or grapefruit seed oil as an anti-microbial; it will destroy bacteria and make the moisturiser last longer. Was that the missing ingredient from her products that were causing them to fail? She flicked over several more pages and there were more notes. Vitamin E and Rosemary Oil extract; antioxidant; will help prevent products from spoiling. Nana Rose had been onto it. Even after all her training, it hadn't clicked that she had been omitting crucial ingredients.

Emily hugged the book to her chest and grinned. This could well be the answer to her failed products. As soon as she got back home, she'd start some new batches. But first she needed to make sure Nana Rose was over the worst of her fall.

***

Next morning Emily was up early. She prepared a big breakfast for both her and Nana and it seemed Kyle must've smelt the bacon and eggs. He appeared in the kitchen just as she was plating everything up.

"How's the patient?" Kyle asked, as he took off his cap.

"She's sitting in her chair in the lounge." Emily prepared a third plate and they carried the full plates into the lounge so they could eat with Nana Rose.

Despite her sore hip, Nana had slept well.

"I'll try and get up and move around after breakfast. If I stay in one place for too much longer my bones will completely freeze up," Nana Rose said.

"Just a little bit of movement. Remember the doctor said you need to rest up. I'll run some laundry through for you, I'll cook some meals, which I can freeze, so all you'll have to do is to take a container out and heat it up each day and your dinner will be ready for you."

"I'll go check on Dusty," Kyle said, standing up.

"What's wrong with Dusty?" Nana Rose asked.

"We put him in the barn yesterday to have a go at the mice."

"That was very thoughtful."

"I'll be back soon." Kyle popped his cap back on his head, called to Faithful and wandered down to the barn.

"Nana, I wanted to ask you about these books." Emily picked up the lavender books that she'd brought down from the attic.

"Oh yes." Nana Rose adjusted herself in her chair and grimaced.

"Were these the books you were talking about?"

"I forgot I had them – Alzheimer's," Nana Rose joked. "But all your talk about making your own cosmetics, I remembered I'd a go at doing my own years ago. The recipes worked well and I'd had a dream, just like you, to maybe supplement the farm income by selling cosmetics at places like the farmer's markets. But life got too busy and I only ever ended up making enough for myself and some I could give away as gifts. I thought these would be helpful to you."

"They will be, Nana." Emily planted a big kiss on her cheek. "And thank you so much. I've already worked out that I may've been leaving out a vital ingredient and I can't wait to get back home to use your recipes."

"I'm glad to see you smiling again, Midge. I know something's been bugging you. You sure you don't want to tell me what's going on?"

Emily stood up and picked up Nana's plate. "Not yet, Nana. Don't you worry about me. You just need to concentrate on getting better."

She spent the rest of the day washing and drying dishes, doing the laundry and sprucing up the lounge. Gathering the remainder of the summer vegetables from Nana's garden, she made a big casserole, a couple of pasta dishes, a potato salad, and cut up some cold chicken with a salsa for Nana's dinner.

Dr Jones turned up early afternoon. After examining Nana Rose and making sure she had enough painkillers, he declared he was happy that no major damage had been done. Emily packed him off with some scones and he promised to make another visit on Wednesday.

By four pm, and Nana settled back in her cosy chair, Emily finished up the last of the tasks. "I need to head back home now. Will you be okay?"

"Yes, of course. I've had too much fuss made of me." Nana patted Emily's hand.

"Now, you phone me if you need anything, but I'll ring you tomorrow morning. And remember Kyle is next door. He's here until Wednesday."

"Was that my name I heard?" Kyle popped his head inside the lounge door.

"I'm leaving and just letting Nana know you'll be around."

"Yip. I'll come over and check on you tomorrow." He turned to Emily. "I'll walk you out."

She gave Nana Rose a kiss goodbye, carefully bundled her books into a bag, and walked out to the car with Kyle.

With all that had been going on she'd pushed the incident that had occurred between them aside. She jingled the car keys in her hand. "I really appreciate what you've done over the past few days." She stared into Kyle's blue eyes.

"Like I said no probs, but hey…" Kyle shuffled his feet and pushed his cap further up on his head, "…are we, you know, good?"

"Yeah, yeah. Sure. Forget about it," Emily stammered. She opened the car door and climbed inside. She couldn't look Kyle in the eye anymore. It was too embarrassing.

"Drive safely."

Emily started the car, put it in reverse and swung around and down the drive. Kyle grew smaller and smaller in the rearview mirror till he was just a blur. If she only saw Kyle as a brother, then why was her heart crying?

Chapter 24

There was little traffic on the road heading back to Misty Springs. It was just as well. Her mind was in such a whirl. She flew through the little towns without watching out for the quaint artists' houses she liked to stop at occasionally.

Coincidence was a funny thing. Three months ago there was no one in her life. Now, why did Josh think he could just waltz back into her life like he'd never left? She had to admit seeing him last week brought back memories of their life together; before it had all fallen apart, before he'd walked out on her. They had been in love, ready to start a life together. But in an instant everything had changed forever. She'd been left alone, left to cope with both the physical and emotional scars and to pick up the pieces again by herself. She couldn't deny that seeing Josh had made her tingle just a little bit. Maybe him being sorry now was better than him never saying he was sorry.

She zoomed past the signpost that indicated that she'd be entering Misty Springs within 10 kms.

And what about Kyle? That had hit her like a bolt out of the blue. She'd never known he'd felt that way. She'd been completely honest when she'd told him she saw him as a friend, a brother. She'd had a closer relationship with Kyle than with David, her own brother. But after he'd made his feelings clear, did that change how she felt about Kyle? Had she dismissed him too quickly, without really examining her own feelings first? Maybe she was too scared to think about it. Her disfigured hand didn't bother Kyle either. And wasn't that what she'd been looking for?

She slapped the steering wheel in frustration. Why now? Why Josh? Why Kyle? When all she really wanted was the man who'd taken her trust and then taken her for a ride.

How did things get to be so complicated?

Tomorrow she'd make two important phone calls – one to Nana Rose and the other to Josh.

***

During her lunch hour on Tuesday, she rang to check on Nana Rose who was feeling better. Kyle had popped over as well, had prepared her meals for the day and made sure she was comfortable and taking her medication.

The next phone call was more difficult. She drew in a deep breath and phoned Josh's number.

"Emily, I didn't expect to hear from you so soon," the delight in his voice obvious.

"When can you come up and see me?" She kept her voice low and steady.

"I could make the trip on Saturday. We could spend the day together."

"That would be OK for me. What time could you get here?"

"If I left at 7 am I could be in Misty Springs by 8.30," Josh said, the words tumbling out.

"That's early for Saturday."

"Oh yeah, you sleep in."

"It's Okay though." She needed to get out what she wanted to say to Josh and she wouldn't be able to stand too long a wait.

"Let's make it 9.30. I'm really looking forward to seeing you again."

Emily said, "Bye," and then rang off.

***

When Saturday arrived, Emily could hardly sit still. Her nerves were tightly bound like a spring itching to be released.

She'd made sure that the girls were going to be out of the house. She didn't want an audience. Oh, for when, if ever, she'd have her own house.

There was a knock on the door just before 9.30. Emily let Josh in. His was wearing blue jeans and yet again he had one corner of this collar tucked into his jersey. She ignored it.

She offered him a drink and made herself a cup of tea while he merrily chattered away telling her about his week.

"So, how's your week been?" Josh finally asked.

Emily sat down at the kitchen table opposite him.

"I went to Paix. While I was there Nana Rose had a fall."

"Is she Okay?"

"She's slowly recovering. I do worry about her though. She has such a large property to look after. But Kyle is keeping an eye on her."

"Kyle. I haven't seen him in ages."

Josh had met Kyle a number of times when they'd stayed over at Nana Rose's. "How's he doing?"

"He's running his own investment business now. He's doing really well." Emily jiggled her leg. *OK. Enough of the small talk.* "Josh…"

"Emily, before you say anything. I just wanted to say again how sorry I am for my poor behaviour, the way I treated you. I can make it up to you. We can be good together."

"Stop."

Josh jumped.

"I don't really know why you've suddenly reappeared in my life wanting to make amends. Maybe it's guilt."

"I-"

"I suspect that there's something more going on that you're not telling me. But you can't just expect me to pick up where we left off. I've moved on and so should you."

Josh wrung his hands.

She had deliberately sat far enough away from him so he wouldn't be able to reach her.

"I want to help you," he said.

Emily frowned. "What do you mean 'help me'?"

"With money."

Emily gasped. "Is that what you're trying to do? Buy me?"

"Don't say it like that."

"But that's what you mean. It's guilt. The way you think you can fix this – 'make you feel better' – is by throwing money at me."

"You make it sound like it's a bad thing."

"I've learnt a lot since my accident. I've learnt I can stand on my own two feet. Sure I've made mistakes. But I'm fixing them."

"You're right. You have changed. And I admire the strong woman you've become. No other woman measures up to you."

No other woman lost her fingers and then had her fiancé walk out on her. Her determination was fading. The longer Josh sat here and kept trying to convince her they should be together she couldn't be sure she wouldn't cave in. She didn't love him and she certainly didn't want his guilt money but at least he wanted to make a go of it. But enough of this. This had to stop now.

Emily got up from the table, walked over to a drawer, pulled out a small box that she'd hid earlier. She sat down again. She slid the box in front of Josh.

"What's this?" Josh whispered. The confident composure of five minutes ago was crumbling.

"You don't recognise it?"

Josh frowned. "Is that...?

"Open it."

Josh tentatively opened the box. "It's your engagement ring." The sun reflected off the diamonds, but as a cloud passed over, the twinkling faded like a candle snuffed out by the wind.

Tears trickled down Emily's face. The pain that she'd buried so many years ago resurfaced again. "This was supposed to signify love, a life we would have together. But I couldn't wear it anymore after you walked out. It was too painful. And what made it worse was I would never be able to physically wear it. I had no ring finger anymore."

Josh's face was as pale as the lining in the ring box. "I don't know how many times I can say I'm sorry."

"You don't have to say sorry anymore. I wish you'd never come here. And the only way I can truly move on is to give you your ring back. I should've done it years ago but I was too scared to see you again. It would've been too painful. Please take the ring and go."

Josh closed the lid on the box, the moment of hope now trapped again. "I'd completely forgotten about the ring. You should keep it."

"Josh, you're not listening to me. I don't want it. It's of no use to me. We're not engaged anymore. Please, I want you to go." Emily ran a hand across her forehead.

"Okay." Josh stood. "If that's what you want."

"Yes, it is what I want."

Emily walked towards the front door. She needed to get Josh out of the house and out of her life as quickly as possible.

He stood on the steps outside. "Could we still be friends?" He looked down at the box he was still holding in his hands.

"I don't think so. And please don't call me anymore."

She closed the door before Josh had the chance to respond. And as suddenly as Josh had reappeared in her life, he was out of it again, this time for good.

Emily's daily calls to Nana Rose assured her that she was getting better. She was up and moving around and the previous night she'd managed to get up the stairs and had slept in her bed.

At work she'd sold only one more Nature's One products, falling well below Lisa's sales target for her. Her stomach churned over at the thought of what might happen.

She'd not seen Ricky – or Vanessa – around. Whatever mess Ricky had got himself into he needed to sort it out himself.

On Friday afternoon she had a call from Todd, the bank manager, asking her if she was available to pop in at 4.30. *Why can't he tell me over the phone?* His voice didn't give anything away. Fortunately her last client was at 3 pm, which gave her enough time to prepare the treatment room for Monday's first appointment, then get to the bank.

Emily hurried to the bank. The end of March sun had dipped down below Red Hill. The giant pine trees that lined Main St lurched back and forth in the strengthening wind, their branches trembling as they clawed at the air. She pulled her cardy closer around her.

Todd was waiting and ushered her into his office. "Thanks for seeing me so quickly. I wanted to give you the news I'd just received from the Loans Committee."

Why is he not smiling?

"I'm sorry, Emily, but your applications have been declined."

Both of them? She shook her head. If she hadn't been sitting she would've fallen down. "I don't understand. I did a business case. I worked hard on the figures." Her bottom lip trembled.

"You did a great job, but the bank thinks there's an element of risk they're not prepared to carry."

"But the income I could get from the lavender…"

"It's not just the cosmetics business, it's the house as well. The bank noticed a drop in your funds of $2,000."

The money she had to use to pay Nana Rose back after Ricky had gambled it away.

"I can explain…" The words trailed off. It was no use going into all that. In fact, it was probably better that she didn't say anything. The bank wouldn't want to hear money and gambling mentioned in the same sentence.

Todd was saying something, but the ringing in her ears blocked his words. She nodded and bit her lip hard. She wouldn't cry. Strong, professional business women didn't cry.

"We'll keep your application on file and maybe in a year's time when you've got some more equity we can look at it again."

Emily stood up and shook Todd's hand. "Thank you for your time and I understand what you've said." She didn't understand at all. She'd done it right this time, but it hadn't mattered. She walked back home in a daze. All that work. She wouldn't be able to do what she wanted with the cosmetics business, and she had concrete foundations to a home she'd never be able to build.

Marie was inside and asked, "Why the glum face?"

Emily put her bag down on the table and let out a big sigh. "I've just been with the bank."

"I gather the news isn't good."

"No. They turned me down." Her cell phone rang. She looked at the screen. It was David. Not good timing. He would want to know what she was doing with the house, but she had a bone to pick with him. Giving out contact details to Josh was not on. "Hi David."

"Emily, hi." His voice was weaker than his usual booming voice. "I have some news."

It would be about the house. "I've just been to the bank-"

"I have some sad news."

"Oh."

"I wish I didn't have to tell you this over the phone. Nana Rose passed away this afternoon."

"What? I don't understand." Her knees weakened, and bright lights flashed before her eyes.

"Dr Jones went to check on her just after lunch. She had been lying on the couch, probably resting. She died in her sleep."

"Oh no. I just spoke to her this morning. She sounded fine." Somehow she'd wandered over to the couch. She sat with her head between her knees, rocking back and forward, a keening sound coming from between her pressed lips. Marie sat beside her rubbing her back.

"I know it's a shock. Mum and dad are flying out from Sydney today. I'll bring them up to Paix tomorrow. We can talk more then. I'm so sorry, Em. I know how close the two of you were," David said, then rang off.

"Nana Rose died," Emily said, as she dissolved into tears.

"Oh, Emily, I'm so sorry." Marie hugged her tightly while she sobbed her heart out.

***

Marie offered to come with her to Paix, but she said she'd be fine. She needed some time alone to think.

She set off early the next morning. She'd hardly slept the night before, lost in the blackness of her grief and replaying over and over in her mind the memories of Nana Rose and the wonderful times on the farm. And Grandpa Thomas. All of them – Mum, Dad, David, Bridget, Yvette, Kyle and his folks – sharing a meal in the summer at the big, long table under the eucalyptus-scented gum trees. The laughter, the telling of stories, the scrapes and bumps that were miraculously fixed by Nana's 'magic' first aid. She smiled at the memories and cried again. By the time she got to Paix she was sure her heart had splintered into tiny pieces.

David, Bridget, Yvette, Mum and Dad had already arrived and were having a conversation in the lounge. Just seeing all her family together brought on a new flood of tears.

"Oh, darling," said Mum. "It's okay. Come and sit down."

"It's not okay," Emily spluttered.

Her mother took her by the hand and lead her to the couch. She couldn't see. Her eyes were so wet from crying, maybe she'd drown.

Somehow over the next hour, in a combination of family stories through tears and laughter, funeral arrangements were discussed. Nana Rose would be buried in the cemetery down the road next to Grandpa and Grandpa's family.

Emily had cried herself out. Exhausted from the emotion, the emptiness of a hollow heart, she needed to busy herself with something.

There was a knock on the front door.

"I'll get it," Emily said, jumping up.

Kyle was standing in the doorway. Seeing him brought on another flood of tears. Kyle wrapped his arms around her shoulders and led her outside, down the path to the barn, and out of sight of everyone.

They sat down, leaning up against the warm wood. Emily dropped her head onto Kyle's shoulder as he patted her head soothingly. It was like when they were younger and they'd both been there for each other when they'd taken a tumble while exploring the fields, tramping through streams or climbing trees.

Eventually there were no more tears left to cry and all Emily could do was let out a desperate sigh every now and again. The tissue she was using to wipe her eyes was wet, shredded and wrecked.

"Hey, Nana Rose would be looking down on us now and telling us to wipe those tears and get on with it all," Kyle said.

"I know. I guess it's just been such a shock. I never wanted to think about that one day she wouldn't be here. I know it's silly, but I just thought she'd be here forever."

"At least now she'll be with Grandpa Thomas. Just think about all they'll have to catch up on."

"Yeah. He'll want to know whether she got rid of his rusty, old broken-down truck."

They chuckled softly.

Emily turned at the gentle rustle of the grass. Faithful plodded over towards them.

"You found us, you old mutt," Kyle said, ruffling the dog's fur.

Faithful plopped his head down on Emily's lap and looked up at her with mournful eyes.

"He knows," Emily whispered. "You might be an old mutt, but you're a wise mutt as well."

Emily, Kyle and Faithful sat in silence for a while. Emily lifted her head to the breeze, to Nana Rose's spirit.

"We should get back," Kyle said, gently lifting Emily's head off his shoulder. "I'm sure your family are discussing things and making decisions that you should be involved in too."

Back at the house, neighbours had joined the Seymour family in remembrance. Baking and cooked meals jostled for space on the huge kitchen table.

Late in the afternoon the funeral director arrived and the arrangements were slowly spun together for a funeral that would honour Nana Rose. At some point someone would be overwhelmed by the tears, then comforted by a hand. At other times, the house was filled with laughter as Nana Rose's idiosyncrasies were remembered.

The funeral took place on Wednesday at the small cemetery down the road. The day dawned sunny and bright but the autumn wind ran keenly through Emily's thin black dress. She pressed her teeth together to prevent them from chattering as she stood with the rest of the family and the small community at the edge of Nana's grave. The dullness inside her grew heavier and heavier. The celebrant's words washed over her as her own memories came to light. People took turns at laying flowers on top of the coffin. Somehow Emily was last. She had a bunch of lavender in each hand. She placed one bunch, tied together with a matching ribbon, on top of the roses, Nana Rose's namesake. "Goodbye, Nana," she whispered. She kissed her own left hand and stroked it across the lavender.

Strong reassuring hands pressed on her shoulder. Kyle. His ever-present steadying force.

Bit by bit people left in their cars to drive back to Nana Rose's for refreshments.

"There's room in David's car for all of us," her mum said, her eyes misty with tears.

"Thanks, Mum, but I'll walk back"

"Okay. We'll see you back at the house." Her mum gave her a quick peck on the cheek.

"Can I walk back with you if you feel like some company?" Kyle asked.

He looked so different in his suit. Older, mature. Even his curly surfer-blonde hair was behaving today.

"Of course."

Together they walked along the grass verge off the road cutting back through Kyle's property.

"What are you going to do with the lavender still in your hand?" Kyle asked.

"Watch me," Emily said, as they were about to pass the tree with the swing.

The swing moved gently in the breeze. The last time she was on it she had been happy. Happy with Ricky, happy being at Nana Rose's, happy despite some rocky patches. Now those rocky patches had become more like mountains, with jagged peaks and sharp shales.

She placed the lavender on top of the swing and gave it a gentle push. "Be free, Nana," she whispered. The frayed rope creaked as if in answer. She stood and watched the swing until it slowly lost momentum. She gave it a final small push, the rope creaking out again.

She turned back around. Kyle had been keeping his distance, giving her some space. "Your suit will need dry-cleaning."

Kyle looked down at his dirt covered shoes, and muddied trouser bottoms that were also covered in wet grass and what looked like sheep poo. "This old thing. The only time I wear a suit these days is at funerals." He brushed off the wet grass, walked over towards Emily and slung his arm across her shoulder. A good friend. Like a brother and that was okay.

By now people had made their way back from the cemetery and were helping themselves to cups of tea and food. Marie had come up too from Misty Springs and Emily thanked her for her support.

Gradually people left until it was just the immediate family again.

"So what's everyone doing now?" Kyle asked, after Emily thanked the last of the mourners.

"Mum, Dad and David are staying here. Bridget and Yvette are going back to the city."

"And what about you?"

"You know, this is the one time I don't want to be here. There's just too many memories. Nana is everywhere I look." Emily swept her eyes around the kitchen. The old preserving jars, the mincer, glass bowls, Nana Rose's apron, all waiting for her touch.

"Besides I need some space to have a think about things. The bank declined my application for a loan so I'm back to square one or maybe it's square zero." She let out a half-laugh, half-cry. She wasn't usually sarcastic, but today everything looked bleaker than usual.

"Really? Well, that's a surprise. I would've staked my life on you getting approval."

She shrugged her shoulders. *Should I tell Kyle about the $2,000 that had probably clinched the decision?* No, it was no point now and her only hope at getting herself back on her feet had disappeared.

Kyle appeared to be studying something out in the garden, lost in thought.

"Anyway, I should get on back," she said. She kissed everyone goodbye turning down her parents appeals to stay the night.

Kyle walked her out to her car.

"Here we go again. Me thanking you for your help. You've been a rock," she said.

"Nah. Just doing what anyone else would do." Kyle ducked his head.

They swapped cell phone numbers chuckling as to why they'd taken so long to do so. Emily gave Kyle a quick hug and then she was off down the drive and out to the main road. Back to Misty Springs, back to... what?

Chapter 26

The weeks passed. March turned to April and with it the gradual nudge further into autumn. The trees were well and truly in their full colourful magnificence that Misty Springs was famous for. The mixture of fiery red leaves mixed with tawny browns and gold painted a landscape of vibrant colour. It was Emily's favourite season, but she drew little joy from the splendour. She walked home from work each day kicking the crinkly old dead leaves into the gutter that was already overladen. Any significant rain now would run into the gutters and be trapped by the leaves, which no longer had a purpose.

The days somehow seemed to grow longer in contradiction to the decreasing daylight. When Christine had come in for one of her weekly massages, Emily had received an update on what was going on with her builders. She'd rather not know, but deep down inside she was curious as to what was happening with Ricky. As far as she could tell, Ricky had miraculously recovered from the flu and he was still being seen around town with Vanessa. She had been keeping a low profile, not wanting to bump into either of them.

"You know that boy used to have a good work ethic, but the rumours I'm hearing about him are worrying. He seems to have got himself mixed up with the wrong crowd. He barely makes it to work on time and I have to inspect everything he does. He's just not been the same since you two broke up."

If Christine had told her that a month ago maybe there would have been some hope in a rekindled relationship, but now she had her own issues to work out. Her heart was a lead balloon, dull and dead like Nana Rose. Loneliness cut through her. There'd been numerous times when all she'd wanted to do was jump in the car, drive to Kyle and tell him, why not? They'd spent summers growing up, side by side. They always looked out for one another. They could make it work. Maybe in time she'd develop more than just brotherly love for Kyle. But every time she almost called him, a different image played around the edges of her mind. The image of a man who had somehow lost his way. Who was still attached to his ex-wife.

Marie had been great support. Trying to lighten her day by telling a joke, cooking a meal for her or giving her a foot rub. She'd even shouldered the blame for breaking Lisa's plate.

"Oh, Marie. You didn't have to do that," Emily said.

Marie had convinced her she'd needed a night out with the girls. It was Easter Saturday night and they were putting the final touches to their make-up before joining Lisa and Andrea at Red Hill Bar.

"That's what friends are for. We went shopping at Cache so she could choose herself a new plate. She's happy. That's all we need."

Emily blotted her lipstick and threw her phone and lip balm into her handbag. "I don't know if I want to go out."

"Don't be silly. You've had a tough time over the last few months, but it's time to be happy again.

Emily sighed. "I suppose."

They arrived at Red Hill Bar and spotted Lisa and Andrea in a corner booth. The bar was humming with rock music from the stereo. As Emily looked around there were many familiar faces. Not unexpected on a holiday weekend when the townies escaped the city to recharge with all Misty Springs had to offer – long soaks in the hot pools, relaxing forest walks, mountain biking, drinking coffee in one of the cafes or letting your hair down at the hottest bars.

Emily and Marie grabbed a drink and sat down.

"Well, stranger," Lisa said. "Welcome back to your social life."

The girls lifted their glasses to toast Emily. Her glass was slipping, but she held onto it tightly.

Lisa seemed content to people watch. Every minute that passed was another she didn't have to worry about Lisa playing her 'get the phone number game.'

After her second drink, Emily relaxed a bit more.

"It's good to see you ease up," Marie said. "You've smiled more in the last half an hour than you have all month."

Emily smiled and took a sip of her wine. She had to admit the tension that had been dragging across her shoulders over the last few weeks was slowly disappearing.

After a couple of hours the tiredness hit her and, as usual, she was the first one to excuse herself and head on home.

"Shall I come back with you?" Marie asked.

"No. I'll be fine. There are heaps of people around."

She said goodbye to the girls and ventured into the chilly night.

As she passed the reserve, a couple of loud shouts rang out; a shout of surprise, then a squeal of pain.

She squinted into the darkness. She could just make out four shadowy figures. There was another thump, then another followed by a shout of pain. Three men were laying into a fourth man, who was lying on the ground. They were kicking and punching the living daylights out of him.

She rushed forward. "Hey," she yelled out.

The three men turned around in surprise. One of them had his fist held in mid-air.

"We don't want to be seen, man," one of the men said to the others.

"Yeah, this would be all we need." A big burly man dropped his fist. He grabbed the T-shirt of the man who was on the ground. "You're lucky this time, dude. But we know. And we'll be back. That's a warning." The man shoved his hand in the helpless guy's face, then scampered away, his two mates following him.

As she moved closer, the guy on the ground shifted onto his knees, crouching and retching. The trees shifted in the wind. The light of the moon shone a path in front of Emily towards the injured guy. The light gleamed off the top of his head.

"Ricky!" Emily stooped down.

Heavy, laboured breathing indicated Ricky had been hit hard and he was gasping for breath.

"Just breathe deeply," she said, placing her hand on his back.

Ricky sputtered, let out a groan and clasped his stomach.

"Can you turn over?"

He twisted over onto his butt. Blood from his nose coursed down his face and through his goatee. "Ouch!" he said, touching his nose gingerly. A cut above his forehead was also oozing blood.

"Does it feel broken?"

"No," came Ricky's garbled response.

"Here, stand up." She reached out her hand, helping Ricky up off the ground. She stared at him. *What mess has he got himself into now and do I really want to know?* But she couldn't leave him here. Besides, those thugs might come back. She didn't want to take him back to her house, the girls would be home soon and they'd be curious, asking question which probably, for Ricky's sake, were best left unanswered.

"I'll run you home," she offered. "Do you think you can walk to the car?"

Ricky nodded.

They left the reserve and within five minutes were in Emily's car. She took the first aid kit out of the glove box and pulled out a large gauze dressing. "Here, hold this on your nose to stop the bleeding."

They arrived at Ricky's house. She followed him up the path, the rusty gate singing out a mournful song in the night. The wind whistled around the corners of the house and a draught blew in under the front door.

Ricky turned on the light.

She squinted. The wind whistled around the corners of the house and a cold draught blew in through the open front door. Somehow the room seemed more desolate than ever, the bareness mirroring the lone occupant who lived there. "Why don't you sit over here?" she suggested, avoiding the bed and the memory of what'd almost happened there.

"I'm in trouble, Emily."

Silence.

"I've got to the end. I don't know what to do." The pleading tone in Ricky's voice forced her to look at him. His face was illuminated starkly in the one lonesome street light shining through the window. He looked like he'd aged a million years. His forehead was furrowed heavily, like a field that had just been ploughed, and his goatee was matted with dried blood. But it was his eyes that held so much pain.

Emily almost choked. "I don't think I should get involved." Her words said what her heart didn't believe.

"I've no one to turn to, who'd understand." A sob punctured his words.

"What about Vanessa?" Emily said softly.

"She's what's got me into this mess. I'm through with her. And this time I mean it."

"Ricky, I've heard all this before. Why should I believe you now? Vanessa got you into this, she should be the one to get you out. Thanks to you I've enough troubles of my own."

Ricky removed the bandage from his nose.

She sighed. "Do you think it's stopped bleeding?"

"Yeah," Ricky sniffled.

Emily rummaged around in the kit and pulled out another bandage. This one was wrapped in plastic. She grasped the packet with both hands but couldn't get a proper grip with the fingers on her left hand. She pulled hard, but the packet was sealed tight.

"Here, let me." Ricky took the packet, tugged harder and the bag popped open.

Emily dipped her head. She'd wanted to show she was in control, but her left hand still let her down at times when she really needed it to perform – to show she could function like any able-bodied adult.

"There. I think that part's done." She cleaned up his nose and applied some disinfectant cream to the cut on his forehead. "From what I saw it looked like your stomach took a beating too."

"It'll be fine. Nothing less than what I deserved," Ricky said softly.

Emily rose from the chair.

Ricky's hand snaked up and encircled her waist. "I stuffed things up, didn't I?"

She tried to pull away but couldn't. For the first time, Ricky was apologising and sounding sincere.

"Yeah, you did Ricky."

"I never meant to hurt you. I've been working hard to try and pay back the money I took from you. But I've got myself into a hole I can't get out of."

"Did you know Nana Rose died?"

A look of pain and regret travelled across Ricky's face. "Yes, I did. And I can't help thinking that she died because I took her money." Ricky dissolved into a flood of tears. He was crying so hard he shook.

The mind could be cruel in times of distress, playing tricks, twisting things. She couldn't bear to see Ricky do this to himself. Blame himself, but he needed to realise the pain he'd inflicted on her. "I never told Nana Rose that you took the money. In fact, I haven't told anyone." She took his hand in hers.

Ricky's head gradually lifted. "I don't understand. I thought…"

"Yes. I was angry and hurt at what you did, and I could've told people what you'd done, but it would've made things worse."

"Worse for me." Ricky gulped.

And still she would not tell him that by protecting him she'd also lost her only chance to build a future for herself. Somehow her hand found his and it hung loosely, wrapped in Ricky's.

"God, I've been such a fool." Ricky tugged on his goatee. "I don't know where to go from here. I don't know what to do." He seemed smaller, vulnerable, lost.

"Don't blame yourself for Nana Rose's death. She had a fall. She died less than two weeks later in her sleep. It was just one of those things. It had nothing to do with you."

"Nana Rose was a good person. Just like you. You take after her in so many ways.

Emily's lip trembled.

"I know that I shouldn't be asking this of you. And you have every right to tell me to buzz off, but I could really do with a friend right now." Ricky's tears reflected back her own. They were both grieving, they'd both lost something, but it was time to move forward.

Ricky was reaching out to her, asking for her help. *Can I help him? Do I want to help him?* She didn't want to get hurt again and if their relationship was to continue she would go in it with her eyes wide open.

The smile that was returned was filled with anticipation and hopefully, a silent promise.

Chapter 27

Emily put the groceries, which included a pack of liquorice allsorts, and some plates and cutlery in the back of her car. The least she could do at this point would be to feed him.

When she arrived at Ricky's and knocked on the door, he opened it looking no better than the night before – unshaven, bleary eyed, and with fresh blood around the bandage on his nose. He was still in the clothes he'd worn yesterday and had obviously slept in. He was crumpled, wrinkled, dirty – the image screamed out, "down on your luck."

"I brought breakfast," Emily said, holding up the groceries.

The corners of Ricky's mouth turned up ever so slightly. "Good. Someone who can make a decision because I'm lost."

"How about you take a shower and I'll cook up some breakfast?"

"Do you think food will fix what's wrong with me?"

"It's a start, but I can't cook while I'm still on the porch."

"Sorry." Ricky opened the door letting Emily in.

Ricky pulled a T-shirt and jeans out of his drawer, mumbled something and walked toward the bathroom, his movements were slow and shoulders slumped.

Emily turned her focus back to getting breakfast prepared. Before long the bacon and tomatoes were cooking while she made scrambled eggs. She squeezed fresh orange juice and made a pot of coffee.

Before long Ricky emerged and sat down at the table.

"How are you feeling?" Emily asked.

"I forgot what a shower, shave and a fresh change of clothes can do to make you feel better."

"Here. Dig in." Emily placed a full plate in front of him along with the coffee and orange juice. She smiled as he devoured his meal as though it was the last supper.

"Whew! That's better," he said, patting his stomach. "Thank you."

Emily was only half-way through her breakfast. "Your sense of humour appears to be back too."

When Emily had finished they took their coffee and sat on the back porch. "How's the nose?" She brushed the ever-present dirt away before sitting down.

"Still sore. I think a good shiner's going to come up."

She watched a bunch of dried up grass roll past; it almost resembled tumbleweed, making Ricky's garden look like a ghost town.

They sat in silence for a couple of minutes, both of them quietly sipping their drinks.

"I didn't sleep much last night," Ricky began. "I've wondered how I've got myself into such a mess and why you're the one who's saving me."

"Only you can save you," Emily said. *But here goes.* She drew in a deep breath. "I'm willing to give it a go again. I want to help you. I didn't know much about this addiction you have, but it seems you started off on the right track by going to a gamblers' support group.'

"When I moved here obviously there was no group in Misty Springs, so my support disappeared."

"You need to get you some kind of professional help. I'm not willing to just hear you say, 'It'll be okay', or 'I'm away from the distractions of the city' because that clearly didn't work before."

"Actually, I think the best place for me *is* here. Knowing that there is someone I can rely on is enough."

"I care but don't think you can rely on me Ricky. I'll help but I still don't trust you. How can I? You need to earn back my trust. I do have an idea but I'm not sure how you'd feel about it."

Ricky clasped his hands under his chin. "I'm willing to try anything."

"After the accident with my hand and after Josh left me, I got depressed and as part of my recovery I received counselling." Emily watched Ricky's reaction. Would he be man enough to see counselling as an option or would he dismiss it?

Ricky studied his hands. "Did counselling help you?"

"Yes, it did. I was dealing with a lot of issues. I felt worthless and at times I wished that tree had killed me. But I was able to break through that thinking and see that life wasn't over. I opened myself to the physiotherapy so I could work again." Emily set her cup down on the ground. "It's worth a shot. Like most things, there's usually something deeper that's going on."

Ricky opened his mouth but shut it again.

Was he about to tell her something that he'd kept hidden from her?

"There are a few counsellors in Misty Springs. Their rooms are in the health hub on Main Street. You should check it out," Emily suggested.

"I'll swing by there tomorrow after work."

Emily threw Ricky a weak smile. This would be a test of his commitment. If he made an appointment and followed through it would be a good step forward. A way for him to prove that she could trust him again.

"But if there's any chance for you and I to start seeing each other again, you have to promise me that Vanessa is out of the picture for good. I won't even consider us if she still has some kind of hold over you."

Ricky shook his head. "I thought she was gone when I put her on the bus. I was sure I'd seen the last of her. Every time she comes back into my life it's like I take two steps back."

"I had a visit from Josh a couple of weeks ago. He wanted to get back together."

"Oh?" Ricky's eyebrows shot up. "And what did you say?"

"I told him he needed to move on because I had."

"I don't have a cell phone so maybe that's a blessing in disguise but I can show you what I can do." Ricky reached inside his jeans pockets and drew out a piece of paper and tore it in half. He kept going until the pieces were almost the size of confetti.

"What was that?" Emily asked.

"Vanessa's phone number."

Emily's hand shook slightly. A link to the past gone. Maybe now they could move on – together.

***

They had managed to get the chimney cleaned in the old house and one afternoon went hunting for pine cones and wood that could be used for a fire.

"I don't know how you can live here," Emily said.

"I have to make the best of my lot. And if you think it's cold now it's going to get a lot colder, my lavender lass." Ricky tweaked her nose.

Lavender lass. His special name for me. It sent tingles down her spine.

He walked past her to put wood in the basket by the fireplace, the scent of forest following him.

Two weeks had gone by since Emily had rescued him from the fight. He seemed happier as he attempted the first steps in turning his life around.

He had kept his word and had attended counselling sessions that were helping him get to the root of his gambling addiction.

Emily sat on the edge of the bed and watched Ricky light a late-afternoon fire. Within minutes an ember flared, caught and an orange light glowed.

He joined her on the bed putting his arms around her and kissing her deeply. She was sinking, the flames warming her as desire pulsed inside her.

Emily held onto the bottom of Ricky's T-shirt and began pulling it over his head.

Ricky pulled it back down.

What was he doing? Emily lent back on her elbows and studied Ricky in the dancing firelight. She swung herself up off the bed. This was rejection. She would leave now. Ricky obviously wanted a relationship that wasn't physical.

"Emily, wait." Ricky pulled her back down on the bed.

"I thought we were… together."

"We are-"

"It's my hand, isn't it? It'll always get in the way."

"Stop that!" Ricky scolded. He picked up her left hand and kissed her fingers and the stubs. "You're blaming your hand again. I love you because you're you. Your hand makes you, you. You make a bigger deal out of it than what it is."

"Then why? Why won't…" She couldn't even say the words. *Why doesn't he want to make love to me?* Emily watched a tiny spark fall onto the wood where it smouldered.

"Emily, look at me."

She met his brown eyes filled with compassion.

"I want to make a promise to you. When I feel better about myself and I know I can get through this, then we'll take our relationship to the next step, okay?"

Emily nodded. "I want to be a bigger part of how you're healing, but I feel like you're not sharing things with me. I want to be able to understand." She bit her lip.

"What can I do then?"

"Will you tell me about your counselling sessions?"

Ricky hesitated for only a moment. "If that will help you feel more a part of what's going on then, sure, I can do that. I'm not comfortable with spilling. Some of it's really private, painful even, but I think it's something that could bring us closer together."

"Thank you. I know it's not easy bringing up the wounds of the past, but we can help each other, till then you'll just have to take cold showers."

"As long as you take a cold shower with me." Ricky beamed.

Emily leant over and kissed the top of Ricky's head. It would just have to do in the meantime.

Chapter 28

Emily checked herself in the mirror. Her short black hair had lost its angular structure and would need a trim soon. She'd chosen a darker eye shadow and lipstick than usual now that winter was chasing autumn away. Her heavy plum jersey would protect her from the cold mountain chill, and she'd pulled on a pair of new jeans.

Tonight was her and Ricky's first official proper date since getting back together. She'd suggested a meal at Red Hill Bar. They'd both been working hard over the last month and there had been little time to get together. Ricky had taken on waiting jobs on Saturdays, if a catering event was booked in town, to help him earn some extra money to pay her back the money he had gambled.

Ricky was catching up with a mate, Jake, after work at Red Hill Bar so Emily met him there. She pulled the collar of her jacket around her neck to block out the cool night air.

Jake was just leaving as Emily arrived.

She pulled off her jacket and sat down in the booth opposite Ricky.

"Hey, my lavender lass." He leant over and kissed her on the mouth. "I've ordered you a lemonade."

"Thank you."

"I really need to come up with an appropriate nickname for you."

"Try and do something more original than 'baldy' or 'goatee'."

"Who calls you that?"

"My work mates."

"I was thinking something a little more romantic," Emily said, pulling a menu out of the holder.

"Please not honey-bum or sweetie-pie."

"Hmm, no. That's not really my style." She handed the menu to Ricky.

The waitress came over and they ordered their meals and drinks.

"It's quiet now on weeknights. I guess people don't want to go out as much when it's cold," Emily said.

"Well, I'm looking forward to my first winter in Misty Springs."

"You might change your mind once you're wearing skimpy shorts on the building site in sub-zero temperatures."

"You want me to stop wearing my skimpy shorts?"

Emily laughed. Ricky's sense of humour had helped them both stay positive through the last few challenging weeks.

"We haven't had much time to talk," Emily said. The promise from Ricky that he would share with her what had been discussed at his counselling sessions had been ignored. Work had been the main focus for both of them, but Ricky seemed happy and focused and was putting an effort into their relationship.

"Would you like another drink?" Ricky asked, eyeing her empty glass.

"A lemonade would be good."

Emily watched Ricky as he walked over to the bar. She still couldn't figure out what it was that she found so physically attractive about him. He was different from Josh, Kyle and other men she'd dated. His strong biceps always enveloped her when he gave her a big hug. The bald head and goatee was what made Ricky different.

She looked around at the bar. She'd never really studied the décor but the red bricks, and old western-type photos on the walls grabbed her attention and she realised the way the room was furnished and decorated contributed to the feel of the place. She fumbled around in her bag for a pen. She pulled a serviette out from under her glass and sketched a room with a bed.

"What are you doing?" Ricky asked, as he placed her lemonade down beside her.

"I just had an idea. I've always been sketching and doodling ideas for what my massage rooms would look like in my own business. Lisa insists we have this red colour, similar to the tones in this bar. But when you're massaging, you want to create a relaxing atmosphere – soft greens, blues, lavender colours." Emily sketched some more. "See, I need windows to let in lots of natural light, but I can pull net curtains over to make it darker. And here..." Emily sketched some more. "I could have fairy lights or candles."

"You're really passionate about this," Ricky said, studying the rough sketch.

"It's been my dream to do this, but it hasn't worked out. But maybe one day..."

Ricky placed his hand over her's and gave it a slight squeeze. "With your determination I'm sure it will."

Their meals arrived and Emily put her scribbling aside. They caught up with each other's news; Emily really wanting to ask Ricky how the counselling sessions were going but it would be inappropriate in a public place.

The waitress cleared the plates away.

Emily yawned.

"So it's an early night then?" Ricky asked.

"Yes, sorry." Emily searched around on the table.

"No worries. I'm feeling a bit the same," Ricky said. "What are you looking for?"

"The serviette that I did the drawings on."

Ricky looked under the table. "Can't see it. Maybe the waitress took it away."

"Maybe." Emily peered under the table too. "Not to worry. I'll draw it again."

The waitress brought the bill over to the table and Emily picked it up.

"How much?" Ricky asked.

"Don't worry. My shout."

"No, no. I'm paying."

"No, really. I want to pay for both of us."

They'd reached the front counter. Ricky began pulling out his wallet.

"Ricky, I can pay." Why was he making such a big deal out of this?

The waitress stared at them.

Ricky seemed to be studying something on the wall. His face was going from a pale pink to beetroot red, then he turned and walked out of the bar.

Emily stared after him. This was reminiscent of when they were first dating. The whole money thing was obviously a really sensitive issue for him. "Gosh, sorry," Emily said to the waitress.

"Don't worry. It's not the worse example of fighting over who's paying I've witnessed."

Emily paid, took the recept and left the bar. What had been a nice relaxing meal had turned pear-shaped. She strode past Ricky who was kicking stones into the gutter.

They walked back to the house in silence, got in the car in silence and headed out to Ricky's place in silence.

Emily kept her eye on the road carefully planning what she'd say.

When they arrived at his house, she followed him through the front door. "What was that about?"

"I said I'd pay."

"And I said I was happy to pay. This is not the first time this has happened." Emily crossed her arms.

"I'm quite capable of paying. I don't want your pity."

Emily stepped back as though she'd been hit. "Pity? I wasn't offering to pay out of pity. It was because I wanted to. I don't see why you have such a problem with it." Tears were welling in her eyes.

Ricky collapsed onto the bed and put his head in his hands. "I'm sorry, I'm sorry, I'm sorry," he said over and over.

Emily's shoulders dropped. What was going on? She sat down on the bed beside him. "This is about something more than money, isn't it?

Ricky nodded. "Shit!" He rubbed his eyes. "I guess it's a male thing."

Emily frowned. What was he trying to say? "You mean about letting a woman pay?"

He nodded.

She let her arms fall to her side. What kind of century was he living in? Hadn't everyone gotten over that? Men could pay, women could pay, or you go Dutch. "Why is it such a big deal?"

"I guess it's the way I was brought up. Men had their jobs, women had theirs. Ours was a typical, traditional family. I never saw my old man in the kitchen cooking. He wouldn't have been seen dead doing any kind of housework. But Mum was happy with that. She didn't mow the lawns, repair anything. Dad even filled the car up with petrol. Mum never had a job. Her job was the house and raising us kids. They were both clear on their roles and they lived a happy life."

"But surely you know that the world has changed. It doesn't work like that anymore."

"Of course I know that. But when you've had those values instilled into you, they're very hard to break."

"So you've felt it wasn't a done thing for me to pay for your meal?"

Ricky shook his head. "No, I just felt really uncomfortable and I was embarrassed."

"Well, you embarrassed me at the bar. I couldn't understand why you just wouldn't let me pay. You were making a scene."

Ricky swallowed hard. "How does one change what they've been led to believe all their life is right?"

"You can't change that thinking over night, but it's an equal world now."

"It's not that simple, Emily. I've been brought up to believe that a man provides for his family. And if he can't do that then he's not a man."

"Do you really believe that?" She held his gaze.

"Yes. I love you, Emily but I've nothing to offer you."

"But you don't have to offer me anything. I have my own money, I'm independent. Relationships are partnerships." Emily was rushing to get the words out. Were they about to fall apart because of some old tradition?

"My worth is tied up in wanting to feel as though I'm contributing. That's why I have a problem with this money thing, with you wanting to pay."

"Are you saying there's no future for us?"

"What I'm saying is that money and being able to provide is part of who I am."

This was a big hurdle. How could they get past this? She'd always believed that a man and woman would contribute where they could and once married, they'd share the workload. How bizarre for a woman not to work or be the only one to do the cooking and washing. It just wouldn't work for most couples. A house wouldn't function properly. "Is this how you see it? Would you expect your future wife not to work and be restricted to the traditional housewife role?"

"I don't have that tunnel-vision. For me it's more about the money and the value I attach to that."

Emily sighed. This was going to be a tricky one. "Maybe we need to start with something small."

"It's crazy when you've lived your whole life with what you thought were model parents. You can't change that thinking over night."

"How about if we're going out we make an agreement beforehand who's going to pay so there's no embarrassing scenes in public? And if I want to buy you dinner then you accept graciously."

"Agreed. I think I can do that."

Emily kissed him on the cheek. The bigger issues around male-female traditional roles would be harder and take a lot more work.

"There's something I need to tell you," Ricky said. He sought her hand and she clung tightly to it. "It's about Vanessa. And I know how you feel about her. Do you want me to go on?"

Emily nodded. Although she didn't want to even hear her name, Vanessa had been a part of Ricky's life and maybe whatever was coming next would help her understand Ricky more.

"I fell in love for the first time in high school. Grace and I just seemed to fit. We were inseparable in our last year at high school. We promised to get married, but two weeks out from the end of the school year Grace died. She had contracted meningitis. And it all happened so quickly. Within twenty-four hours she was gone. She left this massive hole in my life but somehow, I pulled myself together and got on with it. I dated, but it just felt like I was going through the motions. Then I met Vanessa. We went out for six months. Our mutual attraction was gambling, then she fell pregnant."

Emily winced.

"I married her because it was the right thing to do. But I didn't love her the way I'd loved Grace."

So Ricky had a child? Emily's mind was racing.

"Vanessa lost the baby at three months and that's when the gambling escalated for both of us. We drifted apart unable to help each other in our grief. And as time went on I felt more and more like I was stuck in a loveless marriage. I filed for divorce and left Auckland to start a new life."

"You've certainly been dealt some blows," Emily said.

"I know, and I have you to thank for suggesting getting counselling, which is helping me understand why I gamble. People gamble when they've experienced loss: Like Grace, the baby and, to a certain extent Vanessa, but more so how she cleaned me out. There's been this inner conflict that I've been grappling with for ten years. The light bulb has kind of gone off. One of the side effects of not gambling is acting out the conflict in other ways. And for me, it's these old-fashioned values of what used to be that I somehow seem to desperately need to hang onto. The more I've lost, the more helpless, guilty and stressed I've felt and I try to resolve those emotions through gambling."

"That makes a lot of sense. So you're trying to fill a gap inside you, with gambling?"

"In a nutshell. See, I've got a lot of unresolved issues," Ricky said.

"We're working through them. We can do this together." Emily gave Ricky's hand a squeeze.

"You've been really good to me, Emily."

"Hey, I'm not going to walk out on you. I know how that feels. I'm here to help and it's not out of pity."

Ricky pulled Emily to her feet. "There's one more thing."

"I don't know whether I can cope with any more revelations," Emily joked.

The pain on Ricky's face deepened. "I've never loved anyone like I loved Grace."

Emily's heart jolted. How could she compete with a dead high school sweetheart?

"Until now," he added, tucking a strand of hair behind her ear. "You're good and kind and I'm so lucky to have you."

Emily hugged Ricky hard. In that tiny moment it could've fallen apart, but here was someone who finally loved her for everything she was. She gently eased herself away from Ricky.

"You know there's some old-fashioned values that I'd love for you to keep," Emily said.

"Oh, what are those?"

"I love how you open doors for me and pull out my chair before I sit down and the rose you gave me on Valentine's Day was very romantic."

"Typical. A woman who wants to pick and choose."

"Hey, it works both ways. You won't get upset if I open a door for you?"

Ricky gave her a cheeky grin and cocked his head to one side. "No. Just not in public."

And they both dissolved into laughter.

Chapter 29

The thread of hope that Ricky was continuing to work on his issues brought Emily out of her grief. With something to focus on other than her own problems, a little spark returned within her.

Ricky had let it slip that it was his birthday and it didn't take long for Emily to come up with the perfect present.

They were huddled together over his kitchen table one night after work. Emily had offered to cook him dinner. After dinner she presented him with a box.

"Happy birthday," she said, wrapping her arm around his waist.

He obviously wasn't used to getting presents. His eyes glowed like a five-year-old receiving his first rugby ball, and he ripped the paper off just like a five-year-old too.

"A cell phone," he exclaimed.

"Now we can finally communicate like normal people."

"Normal people?"

"You know. And it's one of those pre-paid things so you can completely control how much you spend."

Ricky's brow furrowed.

"Is something wrong?" Emily asked. God, was it going to be about money again? "You're mad because I've spent money on you?"

"No, no." Ricky was quick to answer. "Quite the opposite. I can't remember the last time someone bought something for me. And I'm not cross about the money."

"Oh, so. I'm your sugar mummy?"

Ricky pulled her close. "Yip. Good enough to eat." He sealed his statement with a long, sultry kiss.

***

The weeks passed into June, the start of winter, and on one dewy, misty evening, David rang.

Emily hadn't spoken to him since the funeral. She'd never been the one to instigate contact with him and was even more reluctant to do so with the unresolved issue of the barely-built house still the elephant between them. However, she couldn't keep avoiding him forever so, when it was his number that flashed up on her cell phone, she braced herself and answered.

"Hey, sis."

"Hey, David. How's things?" She closed the aromatherapy magazine she'd been reading.

David, never one for small talk, got straight to the point. "You'll be getting a letter soon from Nana Rose's lawyers. It explains the provisions of her will."

"Okay."

"It's a bit complicated. But the guts of it is that Paix has been left in a family trust to us grandchildren with decisions regarding the upkeep and running of the property to be made solely by you." Was that a touch of bitterness in David's voice?

"What? Why?" Emily asked.

"You were always the favourite grandchild."

"But what about Mum and Dad?"

"They always knew what the will stated. They inherit Nana's cash and assets, which are quite large. Her and Grandpa Thomas's days farming were quite profitable. Anyway, as I said you'll be getting a letter soon so it's up to you to make sure Paix carries on. Don't stuff it up."

Her heart thudded dully. He was never going to let her forget what a hash she'd made of her house building project, but she'd show him. She would look after Paix as if it was her own and keep Nana Rose's spirit alive. She closed her eyes and breathed in. Was that a hint of lavender in the air? She could picture the brown grass waving in the summer wind. The rope swing gently swaying. The smell of cheese scones and raspberry jam.

Her phone rang again making her jolt. It was Ricky.

"Hi," Emily said.

The replied "hi" was flat.

"Is something wrong?" she asked.

"Can I come over?"

"Sure."

"I'm five minutes away."

Emily hung up. Concern was etched in Ricky's voice. Had something bad happened?

When she opened the door the buoyant Ricky of weeks past had been replaced by a dark cloud of gloom.

"Come in," Emily said, holding the door open.

Ricky had big black circles under his eyes making him look strained and worried.

"The girls have gone to the movies. Here, sit down. I'll make us a drink." She made tea and a coffee. *Had Ricky suffered some kind of setback?* She was beginning to understand how precarious being in a relationship with someone who had a gambling addiction could be. Most of the time Ricky's moods were good, but he seemed to have hit a low point. She handed the coffee to him. "You've had a bad day?"

"It wasn't work. I've just come from a counselling session." Ricky dug the heel of his hands into his eyes.

"Oh."

He collapsed back against the couch. "Sometimes these sessions take so much out of me."

"You want to talk about it?"

"I'm done with the talking but I'm trying so hard to keep that promise of me sharing with you."

"Well, we can just sit," Emily offered, reaching out for Ricky's hand.

"This session I think I've had a breakthrough. Do you know what it's like to be totally absorbed in something, feeling on a high when you're doing something?" His eyes gleamed with life and a little of the cloud parted.

"I guess the closest I've come to that is being at Paix or making cosmetics that actually work."

"Well, gambling's very much like that. I never really thought about it in that way. But it's like a drug. The thrill of winning, a pokie machine's flashing lights and spinning reels are almost hypnotic. On a bender I blew five-thousand dollars in one go once. I'd sometimes play the pokie machines daily, stuffing money into them, flushing it away. I'd put in five dollars, then ten dollars, then fifty dollars. I'd be standing at these machines in a zombie-like state. There's even a special name for it, the 'zone'. You become detached from reality.

"The counsellor says I've probably used gambling to self-soothe emotions of loss, loneliness, and relationship problems. I've used it as an escape to another place, another time so I didn't have to deal with what I've been feeling for so many years. And those messages that flash up on the machines saying, 'You're a winner', 'You've won' have a subliminal effect on the brain. But we've been working through the healthier choices I can make when I feel the urge to gamble."

"Go on," Emily encouraged. This was the breakthrough she'd been hoping for with Ricky. He was finally opening up, really opening up.

"If I feel the urge to gamble, I need to talk to someone."

Emily squeezed Ricky's hand. "You know you can talk to me any time."

"I know, thank you. I have this card that has these suggestions on it." Ricky pulled out the card and handed it to Emily.

"The whole zone thing is about the rush of adrenaline I get when I gamble. The same rush I get when I do wood chopping. Now I understand why I like the sport so much, the sense of achievement I get when I do it," he explained, his voice getting louder.

Emily's mind drifted back to the summer days when they went to the wood chopping competitions. How animated, alive, and wired Ricky had been leading up to, during and after he competed. It made a lot of sense.

"The counsellor said that wood chopping is good therapy for me, something that can challenge me in a good way," Ricky continued.

Emily gulped. She still wasn't all that comfortable about the wood chopping thing, but she needed to put her feelings about that aside.

"I know how you feel about wood chopping, but I really want to commit to it. I know it can help me," Ricky said.

"And I need to put my reservations aside. I will cross my fingers, shut my eyes and hope you don't cut your foot off." She half-smiled.

Ricky smiled back. "That's going to be my goal. I'm going to save my money so I can buy my own axes. After I pay you back, of course."

This was good for Ricky and she'd do all that she could to help him achieve that goal. She'd never brought up the small amounts he was slowly paying her back. She hadn't wanted to put any extra pressure on him. What was important was that Ricky was now taking responsibility for himself, his past and future actions.

"Oh, there is something else you can help me with. Have a look at the card and see what it says about what I should do after a stressful day," Ricky said.

Emily scanned the card. "Ah!" She laughed. "A massage."

"And I've got my own special masseuse."

"Well, don't think you're getting it for free. I haven't given you a massage since that first awkward encounter way back in February."

Ricky pouted. "And here I was thinking you were one-hundred precent committed to helping me."

"That's just plain bribery. You'll make an appointment like everyone else." She poked him in his side.

"And that, my lavender lass, is why you'll run a very successful business. Can I at least get a discount?"

Chapter 30

Emily leant back against the pillows on her bed and rubbed her feet that ached after a full days' work. Propping her notebook up against her knees, she doodled. Lately her drawings had expanded from potential labels and logos for her cosmetics, to fields, a swing and Paix. The more she drew the more the idea that had been forming began taking shape. Her pencil slashed here then, there. Yes, this could be an answer. Would Kyle go for it?

She texted Kyle inviting him to come up for the day the next time he was in the district. His answer came back promptly; he was going to be at his house on Saturday. He could come up on Sunday. Perfect. She had the rest of the week to formulate her plan.

She hadn't seen Ricky for a couple of days. With diminishing daylight and declining weather, he'd told her the builders were under pressure to complete a set of houses and that he'd be too tired to see her tonight. His counselling sessions had reduced from two to one a week and he remained positive that he could get on top of his addiction.

She texted Ricky. Thank God he now had a cell phone!

Are we on for some time together over the weekend?

He was normally pretty good at texting back quickly. But her phone remained silent as she switched off the light.

When Ricky finally texted her back on Friday he claimed that after a full-on week of work, could he take a rain check and catch up on Sunday? Sunday? Why not Saturday? He hadn't mentioned that he was either building or had a catering gig on. Something niggled and crept inside making her shudder.

Well, it would give her some time to go over the house plans. She pulled open the top drawer where she'd normally kept them. They weren't on top. Maybe they'd gotten buried. She pushed a couple of other folders aside. No, they weren't there. She opened the second drawer. More papers. *I really must have a tidy up.*

After five minutes of fruitless searching in her room, she moved out to the lounge. Someone had tidied up and shoved a whole lot of magazines, newspapers, old bills and junk mail in the coffee table drawer, but they weren't there either. She scratched her head. Had she'd left them at the bank? The lawyers? Perhaps she was thinking too hard about it. Or she'd overlooked an obvious place. Not to worry. They'd turn up somewhere.

On Saturday morning she set out for a walk. The clean, fresh alpine air invigorated her as she walked into town, stopping to grab a tea at Café Steam.

"You've come at a good time," Linda said. "The ravenous breakfast customers have come and gone and I'm catching up before the brunch lot arrive." She placed her hand over the small of her back.

"You really must come in so I can give you a massage." Emily glanced around the near-empty café. She pulled up her usual stool, sipped on her pomegranate tea while she caught up on the local news.

"Oh darn. Not them again." Linda narrowed her eyes as she stared out the window that fronted the street.

Emily swivelled around. Four men were hanging around two old vehicles. "I think I've seen them before."

"Yep, they're the ones who were here a couple of months ago." Linda moved over to the window to get a closer look. "Drugs," she whispered.

And the more Emily looked, the more the figures took on a sense of familiarity. Not only were they the same guys who Ricky and Vanessa had been conversing with they were the same ones who had beat up Ricky.

"It's bad news if they're back in town," Linda said, shaking some sugar into a bowl. "My police contact tells me they're not only trying to sell drugs here, they're stealing electronics, cell phones, iPads, and laptops, so make sure you lock the house and your car against those slippery thugs."

Emily swallowed the last of the lukewarm tea down her throat. *Let's hope they don't cross paths with Ricky.* She'd never asked him what the altercation was that she'd broken up. She'd rather not know. Ricky didn't need any diversions or temptations. Not now. Not when he was doing so well, trying to start a new life. She didn't want any trouble for herself either. She'd wait in the café until the guys left. Should she warn Ricky they were back? She'd find a way to bring it up when she saw him tomorrow.

***

On Sunday morning Emily received a text from Kyle to say that he'd be at her house by lunchtime. That would give her the morning with Ricky. But Ricky had texted to let her know that he wouldn't be able to see her until early afternoon. She stared at his text, her suspicions once again aroused. *Why was she getting fobbed off?* The excuses were mounting. Was this just another phase Ricky was going through in his recovery? Was he losing interest in her? The bothersome worry that hung over her like a cloud wouldn't go away.

With a free morning, she filled in time by vacuuming and making another unsuccessful attempt to find her house plans. She made a pot of vegetable soup for lunch and put some bread rolls in the oven to warm.

Kyle turned up just before noon. He gave her a quick hug. The cap he wore in summer had been replaced by a black beanie; his blonde curls wrapped around the edges. He placed his gear on the table, took off his coat and hung it over the chair. "I've brought Faithful with me. Would it be all right to let him out of the ute?"

"Sure. Bring him round the back and I'll get him a bowl of water."

They chatted over lunch, finishing off with scones lathered in Nana Rose's peach jam.

"How's Paix looking?" Emily asked.

"This is the first weekend I've been up in a while. I can see someone's been tidying up the yard. I had a nosey through the windows and there's been some cleaning up going on inside too."

"That'll be the family sorting things out," Emily said. It was the first time that she could talk about Paix without a lump in her throat. "There's something I want to talk to you about, which is why I asked you here."

"Oh, sounds intriguing." Kyle put his empty plate down.

There was a knock on the door.

Emily excused herself and opened the door to Ricky.

"Hi, I wasn't expecting you till a bit later," Emily said.

"Well, I can go away and come back again," Ricky said, pointing towards the street.

"Don't be silly," Emily replied, pulling Ricky inside.

Ricky wrapped his hands around Emily's waist and pulled her close.

She breathed in the woody, alpine scent that was always Ricky. He had wood flakes on his jersey. He planted little kisses on her neck, working around to her lips. She responded eagerly, her head floating upwards, her chest tight, her knees weak.

Ricky's mouth was hot on hers. She gently pushed him back and Ricky's eyes widened with the sudden rejection.

"We'll have to pick this up later," Emily whispered. "I've got company."

"Who?"

"Kyle's here."

"What's he doing here?"

Do I detect a hint of jealousy in Ricky's voice? "I invited him. Come and say hello."

Emily took Ricky by the hand and led him into the lounge. The guys exchanged 'hellos' and 'how ya doings'.

"I've just got something I need to talk to Kyle about. How about you help yourself to some lunch? There's some soup, bread rolls and scones," Emily said.

"Sounds good."

She left Ricky in the kitchen and wandered back to the lounge.

"So what's the thing you want to talk to me about?" Kyle asked.

Now that the time had come to lay out her plan, a wave of uncertainty seeped through her. She licked her lips then briefly outlined the provisions of Nana Rose's will.

"You know how I was always trying to get Nana to think about selling Paix so she could live simpler. She always refused. She was stubborn like that. But I'm glad she dug her toes in. I can't imagine how I - or the family - could ever part with Paix.

It's part of us, and now I've been entrusted its care and maintenance."

"And how are you going to manage its upkeep?" Kyle asked, leaning forward.

The front door had closed and Ricky had wandered around to the back. Faithful, in his old gait and a tail that wagged lazily, nuzzled Ricky's leg. Ricky mussed up Faithful's fur. Ricky's dog-talk drifted through the open window as he picked up a stick and threw it. It was not a play day for Faithful who just stared at where the stick had landed.

"Silly mutt," said Ricky, roughing up the fur. "I wonder what Toto's doing now. Do you think she misses me, boy?"

Toto, the dog Ricky had to give away. Emily swallowed hard. It was heartbreaking to watch Ricky pine for his beloved dog. Faithful was bringing back painful memories for him.

"Emily?"

"Mmm, what?"

"You were telling me about Paix."

"Oh, yes." She shook her head. "Well, you know how you've been going on about needing more grazing land?"

Kyle nodded.

"What would you say to dividing up the back part of Paix? This would give you the extra land you need and it would reduce down a heap of work for me."

Kyle leant back on the couch and rubbed his chin. "You know, I'd always wanted to put a very similar proposition to

Nana Rose, but every time I thought about bringing it up she'd always say how much she loved Paix and how she'd never be able to part with it."

"So you think it's a good idea?"

Faithful woofed. He'd finally decided to play catch the stick after all.

"It's one that I'd very seriously consider. But I know there's more to it than just reducing the size of the land to make it more manageable."

"Now I know why you're a smart investor," Emily said. Kyle was smart. He could sniff out when there was something more at stake. "I thought that with my share of the proceeds from the sale of the land I'd have enough money to pay off my debts and start saving money again so I can finish off my house."

"Good thinking, Emily."

"So you'd go for it?"

"Absolutely. Why don't we work out some of the details now?"

Yes! Progress. Emily sat down.

The front door closed again and Ricky walked into the lounge. "That's a fickle dog you've got there," he said.

"Yeah, but a faithful one. It seems that dog has been my constant companion since I can't remember when. It's true what they say about a dog being a man's best friend."

"I understand." Ricky's eyes misted over.

"Let's go and do some figures, Emily." Kyle cocked his head towards the kitchen.

"Sure. I'm eager to find out just how much money this could be worth."

Kyle fired up his laptop and together he and Emily did some rough calculations based on land values, bank and lawyers' fees, how much Kyle was willing to pay for the land and the split four ways of the proceeds. Preliminary figures were looking favourable for Emily. A warm glow spread through her. Finally something was coming right. She'd cracked a way to start moving on again.

"I'll need to pass this across my lawyer, but this will work well for me. I can increase my sheep count with more land." Kyle rubbed his hands together. "I'll make a note in my calendar to get onto the lawyer next week." Kyle moved the laptop bag out of the way. "If I could just find my phone." He moved the bag back the other way. "Um… strange." He patted his trouser pockets.

"Not there?" Emily asked.

"No. Maybe I put it in my jacket pocket." Kyle leant over and turned out his jacket pockets. No phone. "I've probably left it in the car. I'll go have a look."

While Kyle went back out to the car, Emily had another look on the table.

"I can't see it," Ricky said, moving the laptop back again. "It's probably in the car like Kyle said."

Kyle came back without a phone. "That's strange. I know I had it with me when I left." He frowned.

"I'm sure it'll turn up," Emily said.

"Hmm," Kyle replied, his eyes scanning the room.

"See. I never had to worry like this when I didn't have a cell phone," Ricky added.

Emily poked him. "But you must admit life is easier now you've got one."

"A wee bit." Ricky grinned.

"I'd better make tracks." Kyle popped his laptop back in the bag. "Thanks, Emily. Lovely to see you again. I'll let you know how I get on with the lawyers, but it should be all good."

Emily and Ricky walked Kyle and Faithful out to the ute.

"Thanks for coming up. I'll let you know if your cell phone turns up," Emily said.

"That'd be good."

Emily waved Kyle off.

"I'd better go too," Ricky said.

"What? You've just got here. We were supposed to spend some time together. We've hardly seen each other all week."

"I know. I promise I'll make it up to you."

"What do you have to do that's more important than us?" Emily's voice threatened tears. She couldn't understand why Ricky kept giving her the brush-off.

"I'll explain later." Ricky gave her a quick peck on the cheek and trotted down the path.

"Wait! What do you mean 'explain'? Ricky!"

But it was too late He'd disappeared out of sight. Emily clenched her jaw and fought back tears.

She walked back inside. Kyle's missing cell phone played on her mind. She wasn't sure he had brought it inside. So maybe he'd left it at home. Something caught in her throat and the room tilted. What had Linda said earlier about those thugs? They were stealing electronics. Ricky. Had Ricky got himself mixed up with them again? She put her hand to her head to stop it from thumping. No. Please. Not again. Could this explain why he'd wanted to leave so quickly? Maybe she should follow him and see where he went. She paced back and forth. Ricky was up to something and it wasn't good. The excuses he'd been giving her when he said he couldn't or didn't want to see her. What was it Ricky had said? *Gamblers feel the need to be secretive.* Ricky was being secretive. Was he gambling again? Was this what it was like to be with a gambler? Always on guard. Watching. Reading into excuses that could ultimately be lies. She sat down because the more she moved the more everything tumbled in her head. She picked up her pad and doodled: stars, trees, the sun, hills, mountains, lavender. Everything kept coming back to lavender. With all that had been going on she'd not had time to make any products.

She needed to do something to keep her mind off things. She grabbed the key to the salon and within minutes she was setting out the ingredients to make a new batch of lavender butter and body cream. She placed the recipe book that Nana Rose had given her on the bench and smoothed the papers over, releasing a subtle scent of lavender. Nana Rose's voice appeared to come out of the pages. *"Go on, Midge. You've got the secret now. Go make me proud."* And I will Nana. She straightened up, lifted her head and set to work gathering and measuring out the ingredients, particularly the one that would make the difference, the coconut oil. Once the cream was done, she'd stored the new cosmetics away from the light in a cool place in thoroughly sterilised jars. She could feel it. This time it would be a success.

***

When Emily got back to the house that night, she'd missed dinner, and was too tired to cook so she made herself a sandwich.

Marie and Andrea were watching a movie.

"Come and join us," Marie called out from the lounge.

"I'll be there in a minute," she yelled out over the voices from the TV. It sounded like a chick flick. Marie laughed and Andrea yelped.

Above the noise a cell phone rang out a tune.

"Who's that?" Marie frowned.

"Not mine," Andrea said. "Your cell phone's ringing Emily."

Emily cocked her head. "No, it's not mine."

"Mute the TV," Marie said.

Andrea clicked the button. The TV was reduced to moving images and the cell phone rang on, then stopped.

"Are you sure it's not one of yours?" Emily said.

"Did you change your cell phone ring?" Marie asked Andrea. "You're always doing things like that, then forgetting it."

Andrea laughed. "No. Don't be mean. Anyway, it's stopped."

And then on cue it began ringing again.

"It's coming from the dining area," Marie said, leaning over the couch.

Emily turned in that direction. It wasn't on the table. Peering under it, towards the back and wedged in between the cushions that lined the bench on the back of the wall, the blue light from a cell phone glowed.

Scrambling under the table and straining to reach, her fingers wrapped around the cell phone. She pulled it out just as it stopped ringing. The phone looked familiar. It was Kyle's, but how had it gotten between the cushions? It must've fallen out of his pocket when he'd slung his jacket over the chair. She would let Kyle know she had his phone and figure out a way to get it to him.

That meant that Ricky hadn't taken the phone. She put her head in her hands and exhaled. Why had she jumped to conclusions? Connecting Ricky with the missing cell phone and those guys in town. This was not the way a relationship should be – if she could not trust him or trust herself then she'd made the wrong decision. At least she didn't have to worry anymore as to whether Ricky was a thief, but it still didn't explain why Ricky was being so secretive and evasive. She'd have to persist and not let him make excuses. Enough was enough. It was now just a matter of pinning him down again.

Chapter 31

Emily had finished her morning appointments and was walking into town to buy her lunch. It was the end of the following week and life had taken on a slow burn. Each day a little bit died within her. Ricky hadn't contacted her, and her texts and calls to him had gone unanswered. If he was no longer interested in her then she'd reached the point where she didn't even have the energy to drive out to his house and find out what was going on. Christine had an appointment with her after lunch. She'd give it one more shot and ask her if she knew anything.

When Emily returned from lunch, Christine was already waiting for her and she was not happy.

"Look. Just look at my arms." Christine had her sleeves rolled up.

Emily took a closer look. Christine's skin looked like she'd had a bad case of sunburn. Medium-sized blisters and raised red bumps covered both arms.

"Come with me," Emily said, in a low voice. She didn't want the other three customers who were in the waiting room to witness what could become an angry rant from Christine.

Emily escorted Christine into her treatment room and offered her a seat. "Let me take a look." She gently touched Christine's arm.

"It's that product you gave me. This old tough weathered skin of mine can put up with anything but that cream – whew! There's something bad in it."

Emily gulped. She should never have forced Christine to buy the cream when she'd had her doubts about it, but she'd let Lisa bully her into selling the awful stuff. But no more. First, she'd sort Christine out.

"God, I'm so sorry. I've got some cream that will sooth the itching. Bring the one I sold you back and I'll give you a refund." Emily gently rubbed some cream into Christine's arm.

"Just make the itching stop," Christine pleaded. "I'm going out of my mind. You know, you girls shouldn't be selling this product. I've written a letter of complaint."

Emily half-smiled. At last someone had taken action and that might finally convince Lisa this product wasn't natural – far from it.

"Here, take the cream with you and here's my cell phone number. If the itching gets too bad and the cream's not helping, give me a ring. I'll call you later this evening to see how you're going."

"I already feel some relief. Thanks, love. Ricky's lucky to have you, you know."

"I haven't seen much of Ricky lately. I think he's losing interest. Something's not right. He must be doing a lot of over time."

"Oh, he'll be back to his old self again, once he's got the latest sorted."

"Latest..? Latest what?"

"Never you mind. Anyway, I'd better get back and see what my boys are up to," Christine said. She seemed to be in a hurry to leave.

"Is it the latest house you're talking about?" Emily persisted.

"It's best you not ask questions. Now I'll see myself out."

Before Emily had the chance to say anything else Christine was gone. She frowned. She didn't understand. *Ricky. Latest. What?*

She focused on the Nature Own's products that she'd displayed on one of the shelves. She could no longer use products that were injuring people and making false claims. She could no longer work in an environment of red that was against the calming colours she knew would sooth her customers. And she could no longer work with someone who was a bully. She would always be thankful for Lisa for giving her her first job after her accident, but it was time to move on and take charge of her life. If that meant taking a big risk, she'd work through the consequences somehow.

With trembling hands, she picked up the rubbish bin and one by one put all the Nature One's cosmetics in the rubbish tin.

Pulling a piece of paper out of a drawer, she sat down to write her resignation letter.

"This leaves me in a bind," Lisa said, releasing the letter.

Emily watched it leave her hand and float down onto the desk. "I've given a week's notice, which is what my contract says but I can stay longer till you find a replacement."

"I'm going overseas at the end of next week. It's a sales trip for Nature's One."

Good luck with that. Emily rubbed her forehead. Thank goodness she didn't explain in the letter the real reason for her resignation instead stating that it was just time to move on to other opportunities. Lisa was so wrapped up in her world that she hadn't even asked her what those opportunities were.

"That'll leave me two people down." Lisa tapped her pen against the desk. "I'll juggle the appointments. Andrea's looking for some extra work. She thinks Vinnie's about to propose."

They both laughed. Even though Emily had put up with Lisa's behaviour for as long as she could, it was good that she could still share a laugh with her.

Lisa put out her hand. "You're a good worker, Emily. I'll be sorry to lose you."

Emily accepted the handshake and a weight like rocks was lifted from her shoulders.

No doubt the bank would complain that she'd resigned from a well-paying job, but the money from the sale of some of Nana Rose's land would go towards helping cover the bills while she got her cosmetics business off the ground.

As she walked home after work, pulling her scarf tighter around her neck from the frosty night air, her step was lighter. If she could just get to the bottom of the elusive Ricky, life would be almost perfect.

***

"You resigned?" Marie's fork stopped mid-way in the air.

"I couldn't go on anymore. Not after Christine's allergic reaction. I can't sell a product that's causing people pain."

"What are you going to do now?"

"It'll give me some time to work on my cosmetics now that I've found the secret ingredient."

"And what's the secret ingredient?" Marie's fork resumed its path.

"If I told you it wouldn't be a secret. How's your study going?"

"Good. I might get you to check my latest assignment."

Emily cut the last of her chicken breast in half. "Sure. I have lots of spare time now that Ricky's dumped me."

Marie's face fell in shock. "When did that happen?"

"I'm not sure exactly, but he's been avoiding me, making excuses." Emily sighed. She sat up straight. Now that she'd said the words it sounded so final. And what her mind kept saying and she kept pushing away became more of a possibility. "I think he's seeing someone else."

"No!" Marie exclaimed. "Ricky wouldn't do that."

"How would you know? He went back to his ex-wife after he told me he wasn't seeing her anymore. Anything's possible. For all I know he might even be gambling again."

"I'm sure there's an explanation." Marie's face flushed red. She got up from the table so fast her chair rocked backwards and forwards.

Emily placed her knife and fork down on her plate.

"I've just remembered I've got something I need to do. I'll be back in five minutes." Marie disappeared into her bedroom.

Emily got up from the table. She was confused with the sudden change in Marie. One minute they'd been having a conversation and next it was like Marie couldn't wait to leave the room. She tiptoed down the hall.

Marie's bedroom door was half open. She was standing with her back to the door, talking to someone on her cell phone. Emily edged closer to the door.

Marie's voice was whispered and hurried. "You need to tell Emily."

Tell me. Tell me what?

"She's going to find out soon."

Black spots appeared in front of her eyes. She hung onto to the doorframe. Who was she talking to?

"Ricky, you have to tell her."

Oh God. Ricky and Marie. Why hadn't she seen it before? Right in front of her. That's why Ricky didn't want to spend time with her here because he was seeing Marie.

"It's not fair on her. She needs to know," Marie whispered.

Emily put her head in her hands, which were shaking like jelly.

"I'll let her know tonight… Okay… Tomorrow… I'll try and keep her here until then… It has to be done now… Okay… Bye." Marie swung round and her eyes met Emily's.

She didn't want to see Marie, now or ever.

"How long have you been standing there?" Marie asked, her voice unsteady.

"It doesn't matter. I know now what you and Ricky have been up to." Her voice caught.

A puzzled look crossed Marie's face. "How could you know?"

"All that sneaking around Ricky's been doing and you knew all the time and were a part of it."

"It was supposed to be a surprise."

"A surprise? Having an affair with Ricky behind my back. How low could you go? You're supposed to be my friend," Emily cried.

"An affair? No, Emily. You've got it wrong. Ricky and I aren't having an affair."

Emily wiped her eyes. "Well, what's going on? You obviously know something about what Ricky's been doing. Both of you have been keeping something from me."

Marie reached out for Emily's hand. "You have to trust me on this. Can you wait until tomorrow morning and not ask any questions?"

Emily sighed. "I don't know what's going on."

"You're not supposed to know what's going on. That's what the word 'surprise' means."

Emily sniffled. "I'm not sure I like this kind of surprise."

"Oh you will. Now, we're not to discuss anything more about this until tomorrow. OK?"

"I'm baffled," Emily said. "But if I only have to wait till the morning to end this big mystery then okay."

"Good, and as much as I like Ricky, I prefer my men to have hair on their heads and not on their chins, so he's all yours."

Emily hiccoughed a half-laugh. She shouldn't have suspected her friend of having an affair with Ricky. Marie wouldn't do that.

She said good night and climbed into bed. As she snuggled down under the covers a million questions flicked through her mind with a spark of emotions – worry, anxiety, excitement, but most of all, intrigue.

Chapter 32

Despite it being Saturday and her favourite part of the weekend – a long sleep-in – the unanswered questions from the previous day lingered.

By 7 am she could no longer bear the anticipation. She showered, dressed and ate her cereal.

Marie seemed in no hurry to reveal this 'surprise' and no amount of questioning from Emily would budge her further.

"Emily, stop," Marie said, after the zillionth question.

"I can't stand the suspense!"

"We'll leave the house at eleven."

"Where are we going? Am I dressed right?"

Marie smiled. "You look fine. And you'll have to find something to do until eleven."

Now that she didn't have the commitment of a job, she could do some of those much-needed tidying up jobs. She frowned. She still hadn't found the house plans folder so to take her mind off the waiting, she set about cleaning out her drawers and wardrobe.

By 10.30 the tidying was complete. Her renewed energy had been set off by the tingling of excitement that seemed to be dancing just under her skin, but still no house plans in sight.

"Okay, Emily. Are you ready to go?" Marie yelled out from the lounge.

At last! She couldn't stand it anymore.

"We'll take my car," Marie said. "Let's go."

Where were they going? She hadn't been asked to pack anything so it wasn't a weekend away somewhere. A million scenarios - new ones and ones that kept reappearing time after time - kept flicking around in her head as Marie drove the car out towards Hillview. They crossed over the bridge lined with lavender bushes. Marie turned the car into a cul-de-sac and pulled up outside Emily's unbuilt house. Except it wasn't unbuilt. She hadn't visited the site for couple of months. What with Nana Rose's passing, work, focusing on Ricky's quest to wellness and her financial issues, visiting it had fallen by the wayside.

Staring, she climbed out of the car. She blinked twice. *Am I dreaming?* Her house was completely finished. The walls were up, the roof was on and someone – Christine? - was hanging curtains in a room.

The front door opened and Ricky walked out. A huge smile covered his face from ear to ear.

"I'm not sure I understand what's going on," Emily said, clasping her hands to her chest.

"It's your house," Ricky said. "Ninety nine percent finished. We haven't completely finished but, um, things were getting dicey Marie told me, so we've been working like crazy this morning to get things finished."

"Come on," Marie said, grabbing Emily's hand. "Come and have a look at your new home."

Everything was surreal as she was led through the front door. The entrance continued straight into an open plan lounge, dining area and kitchen. Huge windows let in the lukewarm winter sun. Pots of herbs lined the big bay window. A dining table with seating for six had a dark blue tablecloth thrown over it and a vase with the delicate blossoms of winter sweet sat in the centre of the table.

"And here's the lounge!" Marie said.

A big, blue couch and comfy chairs surrounded a coffee table displaying the latest magazines. A TV hung on the wall across from the couch.

Marie unlocked the sliding door. "Out here on the patio you can entertain your guests, like us. And you have to see the bedrooms."

Emily followed Marie down the hall, unable to speak.

"So there are two double bedrooms and two single bedrooms," Marie said.

In the first bedroom, Christine was hopping down off a stool. "Ah, so today is the big reveal."

"We couldn't keep it a surprise any longer. She was onto us," Ricky said. His smile still huge.

"I hope you like the curtains. We've tried to keep it with the whole feel of the house, light and open," Christine said.

Emily merely nodded. She couldn't believe what was happening. Somehow her house had been built without her knowing about it. Her house was not just a fantasy anymore.

She touched the dark blue duvet on the bed just to make sure it was real.

Linda was in the next bedroom fluffing up pillows.

"You're in on this too?" Emily managed to say.

"A-ha. But I'll need to sit down soon. My back is killing me."

"It's about time for refreshments anyway," Marie said. "Let's go out to the lounge. I'll make some coffee."

Emily followed Christine, Linda, Marie and Ricky back down the hall touching the walls as she went, making sure it wasn't all going to suddenly disappear. They sat down while the aroma of freshly plunged coffee filled the air.

"Well, tell us what you think?" Christine said.

"I'm in shock," Emily replied.

"Do you like it?" Linda asked.

"I love it. It's exactly the way it's supposed to be."

Marie placed a cup of tea in front of Emily and a plate of biscuits on the table.

"How did you know what I wanted? How did you build it right?" Emily asked.

"Have you forgotten the late night conversation we had about your perfect house-" Christine started.

"-and the one's we had about colouring and furnishings-," Linda added.

"-plus the ideas I had to ensure the house captured most of the sunlight." Christine popped a biscuit into her mouth.

"But what did you have to build from?" Emily asked.

"Remember that folder you've been carting around for months with the plans in them?" Marie winked at Emily.

"The one I can't find. Oh! You took my file!"

"I did," said Marie, hands on her hips.

"You minx! I've been looking forever for that folder."

"Got ya." Marie poked her tongue out. "Do you want to show Emily the best bit?"

Ricky got up from the table and cocked his head. "Follow me."

Another surprise? "What else can there be?"

Ricky walked Emily out through the sliding doors and round to the side of the house to a separate prefab. Ricky pushed open the front door revealing a front desk with a computer and a chair. Behind it were three rooms.

"I don't get it. It's not quite a sleep out. It's like an office," Emily murmured.

"Well, you're partly right. Come and take a look."

Ricky led her into a room that had been set up with a massage table. Candles burnt softly in white frosted glasses. Photos of fields of lavender hung on the wall. She'd seen this scene somewhere before.

"Is this what I think it is?"

"Yip. This is where you can run your own massage business, which is quite timely since I've heard you don't have a job anymore."

Emily covered her mouth with her hands. "I don't believe this. It's exactly how I'd envisioned it. How did you know?"

"Remember the night we went out for dinner and you were all excited about what your own massage therapy rooms would look like?"

"And I drew a plan on a serviette, which I couldn't find later..."

"See." Ricky snapped his finger. "You blinked and suddenly it was in my pocket."

"God! Between you and Marie I'm going to have to nail everything down."

The massage table had a dark purple chenille blanket over the white sheets, the same one she'd seen earlier in the year at Cache.

As she looked around, the reality sunk in. Here was her house, a chance to run a successful massage business and the man responsible for all of it, the one she now knew loved her like no other, standing in front of her.

Emily threw her arms over Ricky's shoulders. "I don't know how to thank you. It's a dream come true." She kissed him full on the mouth, her desire raging. Ricky was full of surprises but this one would forever go unbeaten. Ricky responded with a passionate soul searching kiss. She'd gone so long without his touch he was doing things to her that were threatening to send her out of control. She returned his kiss deeply. She was falling, swirling into a vortex.

"Hey," Ricky said. "Someone might come looking for us. We don't want to give them a show if we end up naked on the floor."

"There's nothing more that I want right now." Emily massaged the base of Ricky's neck.

"If you turn around look what you can see."

Emily released herself from Ricky's grip. Out of the back window, the old gum tree stood proud and tall. There was something hanging from one of its branches. "Is that what I think it is?" she asked. She moved on outside, over the path and towards the tree, its leaves rustling in the wind.

Two long pieces of rope hung from the tree with a board across the bottom. It was a swing.

"Here, my lavender lass, you can swing away to your heart's content and think of Paix and all its precious memories."

"This is just too much." Tears trickled down Emily's cheeks. "You've put so much thought into this. Why would you do this?"

"Because I love you, Emily. You've got me through a difficult time, you've stood by me when a lot of people did me over."

"You didn't have to build me a house. Dinner would've been fine."

Ricky chuckled. "Oh, Emily, you deserve so much more than that."

Emily gave the swing a gentle push. She was just about to sit on it when Marie yelled out through the window that the were about to crack open a bottle of champagne.

"I guess we should go help them drink it," Ricky said, Emily's wrapping herself around his arm.

As they walked towards the house, Emily looked over her shoulder at the swing, still moving gently. Soon, she promised herself. *Soon, I'll ride the swing.*

Chapter 33

After the initial shock of the surprise, it finally hit home what they had actually pulled off. Ricky explained that he had organised the Misty Springs community to help provide donated or discounted furniture and appliances. Christine had arranged her builders to supply free labour on Saturdays.

"So all those excuses you were making and here I was thinking you were up to no good, you were building my house?" Emily asked.

Ricky and Emily were sitting in the lounge watching the sun disappear behind Red Hill. Everyone else had left, eager to enjoy a sunny winter's afternoon at home.

"I didn't really think that part through. And I kept running out of excuses. That's why Marie and I had to delay you finding out as long as possible," Ricky said.

"I can't believe you did all this without me finding out or without anyone else letting it slip."

"Everyone knows what a bad deal you got when Gardenway Homes collapsed. They were more than happy to help. They're a good bunch of people here. They love to root for the underdog. The challenge was to get the frames up and then the roof on before winter set in."

Emily pictured Ricky night after night banging in nails, measuring, and sawing to build her house. The Saturdays that he'd been evasive about what he was doing, he was working on finishing touches or supervising the interior with help from Marie. And the workmanship was perfect. At his insistence, later that afternoon she went back around the house, inspecting the work, Ricky following closely behind, double checking.

"It had to be the best for you," Ricky said.

"But what about the money? Even with you doing a lot of the work and the discounted rates, there must be some costs somewhere."

"There are. I went to see Farrah, your lawyer. I explained to her what I was trying to do. She couldn't tell me a lot because of client confidentiality, but she mentioned something about the sale of some land that might be able to cover the costs."

Kyle's lawyers had obviously been in touch with Farrah.

"They'd hinted that there'd be enough money to cover the expenses with a minor loan from the bank," Ricky continued.

So Kyle's buying part of Nana Rose's land had worked out. She'd be able to tell her family, especially David, that the house would be completed after all and she hadn't completely stuffed things up.

"When do you think you'll move in?" Ricky asked.

"As soon as I can. I can't wait to have my own space." Emily jumped up, spread her arms out and twirled around and around in the centre of the room. "I'll be able to do what I want, when I want and you'll be able to sleep over."

Ricky put a hand out to stop Emily from spinning. "I'd like that. How would you like to go away for the weekend? Christine has a bach in Aqua Bay. She's offered it to me, us. You're going to be busy with the house and the business soon so let's spend some time together."

"And you could probably do with some R and R after all the effort you've put in here."

"One weekend without having to work would be heaven."

"Let's get away soon. Next weekend," Emily said. She grabbed Ricky's hand. "I can't wait any more."

"I'll check with Christine," Ricky said. "In the meantime, how would you like to explore your new premises?"

She didn't need an invitation. She spent the rest of the afternoon showing Ricky what she'd do here, what she'd put there, made a slight adjustment to a vase on the other side. He just followed her around with a bemused smile.

Emily could do nothing more than smile back.

***

She spent the week slowly moving her belongings into the house. She surveyed her new bedroom, biting down on her knuckles unable to contain the excitement that this was finally home... her home.

As she wandered over to the Serenity Day Spa and "in the excitement of the past week, she'd forgotten about the new batch of body butters and creams she'd made.

363

"I'm surprised Lisa hadn't thrown them out," Emily said, as she opened the cupboards

"I think she was too busy getting herself organised for her trip," Marie replied.

Emily carefully pulled out the jars from the cupboard and placed them on the table. "I'm almost too scared to open the lids."

"I'll do the countdown. 1... 2... 3..."

Emily picked up a jar and gently opened the top. She'd been expecting to see mould - green, and furry bits - but the top of the cream was pristine white. Nothing green! Nothing furry!

"Oh God! I think I've done it," Emily squealed.

"Let's see." Marie took the jar from Emily, inspected it and passed it to Andrea who took a sniff.

"It smells all right," she said.

"Maybe it's just one." Emily opened the lid on another jar. This was the same as the first one. No mould – clean, white product.

"I can't believe it. I've done it," Emily said. "The coconut oil and making sure the environment is right was the secret." *Thank you, Nana Rose.*

"Can we try it?"

"Go ahead," Emily said.

Before long all three of them had their hands and arms plastered with body cream.

"I know we're not going to get any nasty break-outs with this," Emily said.

"You're onto a winner here," Andrea said, wiping the excess cream off with a tissue.

"I think I have the perfect name for the body butter," Emily said, placing the lids back on the three jars. "It took me three attempts to get the formula right so I think I should call it Potion No. 3"

"Perfect. As long as no-one asks what happened to potions one and two," Andrea said. The girls laughed.

Emily surveyed the jars. Finally, at last, her formula had worked. A deep warmth filled her, and she clapped her hands. The first step to making something successful had been completed. She couldn't wait to start her other products. The body butter, body cream and lip balm made for a good base for her to build on.

***

Kyle rang her the following Friday to touch base regarding the final details of Nana Rose's land. Both the lawyers were happy that the i's had been dotted and the t's crossed.

"You sound happy, Emily," Kyle said, his voice taking her to Paix.

"I am. Things are going well with Ricky. We're going to Aqua Bay this weekend. My house is finished, and I've now got three really good products I can sell to kick off the business. It's going to take me a while to make any money from that side of things, but it's a start."

"I've been thinking about your business. I'm really surprised that the bank turned you down. Why don't you drop off some of your products at my house on your way down? I'll show them to my business partner. I think I could convince him to invest in your business. To start things off for you," Kyle said.

"Really? You'd do that?"

"You've put up a sound financial business case and apart from that, your enthusiasm and positive attitude will make you a winner."

"That's very generous of you. I feel like all my Christmases have come at once." *Wow!* Kyle was willing to give her a chance. And he wasn't just doing it because they were friends; he really believed in her.

While Emily was packing her bag for the weekend, Marie rang her.

"We're having a slow day. We're shutting the salon early and having a pampering session. Why don't you come over and we can give each other a massage. I'd kill for one right now."

"Great idea. I can't remember the last time I've had a massage."

Before long Emily, Marie and Andrea were happily painting their nails, giving each other facials, waxing and massaging.

"Oh, I so needed that," Emily said, when Marie had finished giving her a full body massage. "I feel all floaty and relaxed. I could go to sleep right now."

"Oh, no you don't. Not until you give me my massage."

Emily prepared a lavender, lemongrass and bergamot oil blend and began kneading and stroking Marie's back.

They finished the afternoon with a glass of wine toasting Emily's new cosmetics, and her last night with the girls before she moved into her new home.

They all walked back to the house together. The cold night air had turned frosty and little plumes of steam escaped from their mouths as they chatted about their day.

Emily pulled her hat harder down on her head and wrapped her scarf tighter around her neck. Rather than the cold air freezing her, it was somehow invigorating, sending little cold jolts through her spine reminding her she was alive, well and had everything to look forward to.

***

Christine had given the all clear for the weekend Ricky and Emily could have the bach.

Emily picked Ricky up in the morning. "Is that all you have?" she asked, when he threw his small backpack in the boot.

"I don't own many clothes," Ricky said. "Look at your bag! Three times the size. We're only going to be away for less than forty-eight hours."

367

"A girl has to pack for all eventualities. Hurry up and hop in. I checked the weather report and it's not looking too good. There's a south-westerly building up that's supposed to bring, rain, snow and a tonne of wind."

"Okay then; let's go." Ricky jumped in the car.

They stopped off at Paix on the way. Emily had a quick look over the property. Kyle had already moved the boundary fences forward in preparation for the upcoming lambing season. Inside Paix, most of Nana Rose's personal belongings had been packed away and just the furniture remained. After she got the business established, she'd come back and sort through some more stuff. The attic hadn't been touched and there would be a goldmine of memories and mementoes stored away.

They popped next door to Kyle's. He'd left a note on the door saying he was out getting some feed but to leave the products in the cooler in the garage.

Before long they were back out on the road.

"The wind's picking up," Emily said, as she peered harder out the window.

"And here comes the rain," Ricky replied as a sheet of rain smothered the car.

"Let's hope the weather's better in Aqua Bay."

But it wasn't. As Emily drove into the small seaside community, the wind had grown stronger, slightly shaking her wee hatchback.

"Okay. Where's Christine's bach?" Emily asked.

"Down by the waterfront. Take the first left into the township and then follow the esplanade around. It's number twenty-two".

They continued through the main street.

"They're really protective of their environment here," Ricky said, as he read the writing on the billboards out loud. "Save our dolphins, Stop seismic surveying."

"They have Nerissa Taylor to thank for that. Apparently these Americans were going to do some seismic surveying looking for oil and Nerissa has worked hard to keep them out. Ah, here we are."

She pulled up outside a white wooden bach with light blue panels surrounding the windows giving it a seaside feel. The driveway was sprinkled with stones and broken shells and lavender bushes bordered the path.

"See everywhere you are, lavender seems to follow you," Ricky said, pulling the bags out of the boot. He unlocked the front door and Emily followed him inside.

Ricky dumped the bags down in the small lounge area and set to work to light a fire in the log burner.

Emily looked around. The lounge and small kitchen was sparsely furnished but cosy. Wicker furniture had blue blankets thrown over them and the walls were lined with photos of old boats and seagulls. Worn Turkish rugs laid across the wooden floors. The lounge doors looked out over the currently murky grey sea. The wind was whipping up white caps and spray was scampering across the waves.

"This place shouldn't take too long to warm up," Ricky said, brushing his hands clear of bits of wood.

"I'll just go and have a look at the rest of the place," Emily said.

There wasn't much else to look at. A tiny bathroom and two small bedrooms completed the house. One of the bedrooms had a big old-fashioned poster bed which took up most of the room. A huge blue duvet covered the bed. Emily turned the cover back to reveal four blankets. The wind whistled around the house singing out that winter had well and truly arrived. It was a perfect day just to lie back and listen to the force of nature.

She couldn't resist. The bed looked cosy and inviting. She kicked off her shoes and dived underneath the covers. Through the window she watched the tree branches sway vigorously one way in unison, then with a change in the wind direction sway back the other. The wind roared. Leaves were plucked away. Gaps in the trees widened, confused as to which way to bend. Large raindrops battered the window and the rain on the roof beat down steadily, hypnotising her. She snuggled further under the blankets. The effects of yesterday's massage remained with her. Her arms and legs were floppy, any tension seemingly melted away into a peaceful and calm ocean in complete contrast to the whirlwind and rain outside. She closed her eyes and drifted off…

"Where are you?" Ricky called out, bringing her back.

"In here," she yelled.

Ricky's footsteps grew louder as he entered the room. "I can hardly see you. You've buried yourself under the covers. Isn't it early for bed?"

Emily threw back the covers. "How about you find out how cosy it is in here?"

Without a word he climbed into bed beside her and spooned her, wrapping his strong arm over her side and pulling her in. "You smell divine."

She hadn't showered that morning, too eager to make a start on their weekend. The massage oils from yesterday were still on her skin – coconut oil and shea butter. The sweetly intoxicating scent had penetrated her skin and clothes, the warmth of her body seemed to enhance it more.

"You smell like a flower shop," Ricky whispered in her ear.

Emily brought her hand up to cradle his head against hers.

"I just want to hold you," he said. He pressed his body against the length of hers and squeezed her gently.

The wind and rain belted against the window. As it strengthened she could feel him harden against her back. She rolled over to face him and gazed into his eyes.

"I want you so bad," Ricky said. "I can't wait any more." His brown eyes deepened in the fading light.

Emily pulled the jersey over Ricky's head, then in a confusion of arms and legs, clothes were discarded and thrown out of the bed.

Finally, at last, they were naked.

Ricky kissed her hard on the mouth.

Emily responded with all the eagerness that had been lying dormant for so long as he moved on top of her covering her body.

His hands stroked her legs, the roughness of his skin sending electric pulses through her from head to toe.

She traced his biceps with her fingers down, down, until both hands cupped his butt, pulling him closer to her. Any moment they would melt into each other. Ricky's hot mouth moved down across the base of her neck to the curve of her breasts. His mouth closed over a nipple and he sucked greedily. His beard tickled her, intensifying the sensation. The burning and tingling increased everywhere. She guided his head towards her other breast. Ricky's tongue traced around the nipple teasing the outside, lingering. She moaned; she was on fire.

His touch was exquisite. His tongue flicked over the tip of her nipple and she just about died. His mouth found hers again, wet and hungry and she gasped. She opened her legs wide ready to receive this man she'd waited so long for.

He entered her gently and then began a delicious stroking in, out, in, out until she couldn't stand it anymore. She brought her knees up and Ricky plunged deep inside her. She gasped and let out a shattering moan.

The wind cried out and the rain pounded on the roof.

Ricky, slick with sweat, and with the scent of coconut and shea butter rising between their bodies, plunged one final time and exploded bringing her up and over the edge with a shuddering force so strong stars burst behind her eyes.

She panted and Ricky let out a long sigh. He slowly withdrew and then collapsed alongside her.

She turned to him, drowsy, but complete. "That would have to be the best sex I've ever had."

"Mmm," Ricky said, kissing her nose, cheeks and eyelids.

And in the afterglow, just before she drifted off to sleep, Ricky picked up her left hand and kissed the stubs one by one. His lips were as light as butterfly wings, but it was the most gentle, soothing touch she'd ever known.

***

They made love again and again. Between periods of their dozing, the rain had eased and the wind had dropped, but every time the storm seemed to be losing its strength, it would fire up again, and with it, another round of love making.

"Okay, I'm done," Ricky said. "I think we've made up for lost time."

"I don't know." Emily traced a finger across Ricky's chest. "Those cold showers you told me to have just didn't do it for me."

373

"Well, it's certainly a relief not to hear someone on the other side of the wall doing what we were doing."

"Or be interrupted by a train at the wrong moment."

They laughed at their 'near misses, but agreed it had been worth waiting for.

"Speaking of a shower," Emily said, leaning back on her elbows. "Do you want to check it out?"

"Hopefully the water will be hot enough by now." Ricky swung his legs over the bed.

"Otherwise it'll be another cold shower," Emily replied, but she couldn't have cared less.

***

After their warm showers, the wintry weather had moved on and a weak sun peeked out between the clouds.

They drove back into town, found a cosy restaurant/bar that was packed with the Saturday night crowd and managed to get a table just on the fringe.

"I think we're lucky to get this." Ricky pulled out her chair for her.

"At the moment I don't mind either way. I'm starved," Emily said, studying the menu intently. "And I'm paying."

Ricky smiled back at her and not one word of protest escaped from his mouth.

Before long they were tucking into seafood chowder and bread. They both ordered chicken and finished off with apple crumble and ice cream.

Ricky patted his stomach. "I couldn't possibly eat another thing."

"You need to keep your tank topped up. We've a long night ahead of us," Emily teased.

The smile that had started to pull at Ricky's mouth disappeared. His eyes lost the merriment that had been there since that afternoon.

"What's wrong?"

"Nothing." Ricky's leg jiggled up and down.

"There's something wrong. Please tell me."

"Can you hear it?"

Emily frowned at the noises that were coming from every corner of the bar – glasses clashing, people laughing, chairs scraping across the floor, and loud music pumping. She shook her head, confused. What was it she was supposed to be hearing?

"There," Ricky said.

From the corner, metal coins banged against a tray as someone won at the pokie machines. She could just make out the carnival-like music announcing the win. The realisation of what that meant to Ricky hit her.

"God, it's like the Pied Piper summoning me," Ricky said, his eyes darting back and forth.

"I hadn't even thought..."

"We should leave," Ricky said. "When I hear those awful pokies it only reminds me of the mess I'd made of my life."

Emily took Ricky's hands. "Then we'll have to find you a new theme song."

When they got back to the bach, it was warm and toasty.

Emily was hardly inside the door when Ricky drew her to him. He buried his head in her hair. "You still smell heavenly," he whispered.

She planted a kiss on his mouth and licked her lips. "And, I think that's apple crumble I can taste."

Clothes were pulled off and thrown on the ground again. Somehow Emily found herself on top of the bed. Ricky hovered over her. She shut her eyes and waited for bliss to take hold.

***

Sunday dawned fine. After a lazy morning in bed they hired mountain bikes and biked the 10 km Ocean Track, stopping off for lunch at the Blue Penguin Cafe. They held hands as they went for a long, leisurely walk along the esplanade. The song of the sea was gentle as it rippled over the stones. Salt lingered in the air and clouds caressed the mountains that bordered Aqua Bay.

Emily held Ricky's hand tight. He rubbed his finger back and forth across her stubs and somehow it forged a bond. The sad story that lay there could now be left behind, welcoming the promise of good things to come. She stared out of the grey-blue sea that went on forever. Her life had changed in so many ways - positive ways - and with Ricky beside her they could help each other recover from past wounds. There were now only good things to look forward to – at long last.

Chapter 34

"You're still glowing," Marie said, as she and Emily unpacked boxes in Emily's new house.

"Well, I'm not going to deny it. It was a fantastic weekend if you know what I mean."

"I do believe you're blushing." Marie handed Emily some towels.

Emily opened up the cupboard in the hall.

"I've been thinking about opening my own business soon. I wondered whether you'd like to help me with the marketing side. I can't pay you much to start off with, not until I get some clients, but I've kept all my sketches and have been playing around with logo ideas," Emily said.

"Hey, I'm happy to help and don't worry about payment. Just pay me with massages," Marie said.

Emily stood on tiptoes to put the last of the towels on the shelf.

"Here, let me," Marie said. "What do you think about having a grand opening day? I could design some flyers and distribute them around town. You could offer some specials and start selling your cosmetics."

"That's a great idea." Emily collapsed an empty box. "I'm so excited. I can't believe I'm that much closer to my goal."

"You've worked hard and have overcome all sorts of things. I know the last few months have been difficult for you. I'm keen to hear what you're going to call the salon."

"Let's have a chat about that tomorrow. There's something else I'd like to talk to you about. It's to do with Ricky."

"No. I don't want a ménage trois."

Emily laughed. "Ah, no. This one does involve getting dirty, but not in the way you're thinking."

The next day Emily outlined her plan to Marie, which somehow ended up having the code name Operation Dirty. She'd checked with Christine that Ricky would be working all day Saturday. She rustled up as many people as she could, including Marie, Andrea, Linda and a few of the locals and some of Ricky's woodchopping mates. She collected buckets, mops, rags, gardening tools, cleaning products, brooms, pans and shovels.

Early on Saturday morning Emily and the Operation Dirty gang set to work on Ricky's house. Half of them set to work outside. Lawns were mowed, knee-deep weeds pulled out, kerbs tidied, and overgrown branches trimmed back. Emily gave the veranda a good sweep ridding it of twigs, spider webs, stones and dead insects. She'd bought some colourful pots decorated with yellow, red and purple polyanthus which instantly brightened up the entrance to the house.

Inside Marie and Andrea were busy working on hanging new curtains.

"Lordy," Linda said as she vacuumed the floor. "Ricky won't recognise the place when he sees it."

Emily smiled. And that was exactly the reaction she wanted from him. She cleared up the dirty plates in the sink, and as she was about to put the kitchen scraps in the rubbish tin a business card lying on top of the pile caught her eye: *SPCA, Christchurch,* scribbled across the top in Ricky's handwriting was the word *Toto* and a drawing of a sad face. *Was this where Toto had ended up? Ricky had said something about having to leave Toto in a kennel.* She picked up the card, brushed it off and put it in her back pocket.

She turned around and surveyed the room. Everything was taking shape and the inside was now looking more like a home. Outside, the house really needed a coat of paint but there was only so much she could do.

But there was one last thing she had to do. Christine had just arrived and warned her that the boys would be finished in an hour and Ricky would be getting dropped off. "So what is it that needs fixing? Christine asked.

"The gate. It's fallen off one hinge and it has a high-pitched squeal every time you open it," Emily said, swinging the gate back and forth.

"Okay, I get the story." Christine covered her ears.

Emily watched as Christine heaved the gate back on to its pin, used some tools to make it secure and applied some CRC lubricant.

Emily rocked the gate back and forth. Silence. "Fantastic."

"It really needs replacing, but it will do for now."

Everyone finished tidying up and amongst the 'goodbyes' and' see you laters', Emily promised to put on a barbecue in the summer to say thank you.

And then she was alone. The yard looked new and clean. She wandered up the path to open the front door. The old mustiness inside had disappeared and was replaced by the crisp, winter air. The sun poured in through the entrance.

She looked up as a car pulled up outside and Ricky got out. She waved. Ricky would be rapt at what she'd done.

But as he walked down the path his face was stony and his lips were drawn together tightly. He stood with his hands on his hips, surveying the yard.

An icy chill started at the base of her spine and slowly travelled up her back stopping at the edge of her scalp.

In five big steps Ricky was inside the house. He looked around, the expression on his face unchanged.

Emily swallowed hard.

"What's been going on here?" Ricky asked.

"I wanted to thank you for what you did, building my house. The least I could do was help you make your home a little more liveable."

"I don't need your help," Ricky said, scratching his goatee. "I'm capable of cleaning up. I just haven't had the time because my attentions have been elsewhere."

Meaning her. "But that's precisely why I did it. To help you. We all did something to help."

"What do you mean 'we?'"

"Marie, Andrea, Linda. Even Christine-"

"So everybody knows how hopeless I am at keeping house? How poor I am?"

"No, nobody thinks that. And people can see the state of the house from the road. It isn't a big secret. We've tidied up the yard for you and it looks so much better."

"I don't need your help, Emily. Stop meddling." He brought his hands up to his head. "Grrr!" He brushed past her, down the footpath, and slammed the gate behind him with a loud clang. The sharp metal twang reverberated through her with such a force she jumped. The gate hadn't latched and it swung back open again.

Her feet somehow moved and she slumped down on the edge of the veranda. Tears trickled down her face and she wiped them away angrily. She'd only been trying to help Ricky. *Why does he think what I've done is so bad?* But worse, he'd walked away. Walked away from her. Left her. Just like so long ago when Josh had left her. She would be alone and have to start again. To start over. She looked down at her two remaining fingers, the unsightly stubs. The day she'd lost those fingers had changed the course of her life. But would she have to go through this every time she got close to someone, who almost accepted her for who she was, only to be disappointed when he left? She'd put her all into her relationship with Ricky. They'd built up trust together and Ricky had walked out on her, rejected her.

She let out a sob, but she was strong; she could handle this. She'd been rejected before. She'd just pick herself up and start over – again. Marie was right. She had worked hard despite so many obstacles. She was in her new house, about to open her salon and sell her cosmetic products. The only thing that was missing was someone who would be by her side and travel the journey with her.

Emily lifted her head. *But not to worry. I can do this myself.* Tears blurred her sight. Greens and browns mixed with the blue of the sky merged into a watery haze. She wiped both eyes with the heels of her hands. When her vision cleared, someone was standing on the path in front of her. She blinked. Ricky reached out and placed a hand on her shoulder.

He knelt down in front of her.

He'd come back.

"I made an arse of myself, didn't I?" he whispered.

Emily nodded.

The face that had been flushed with anger moments before was now ghostly pale.

"You walked away," she managed to choke out.

"I did, but I came back. To apologise for being such an unthankful git." His eyes pleaded with her.

"Please explain to me what I've done wrong."

Ricky cradled Emily's hand in his. "You've done nothing wrong. It's just me. Every time you do something for me I can't believe how lucky I am. You're not out to take anything from me, only to give. And that's still taking some getting used to."

"I wouldn't take anything from you." Emily sniffed.

"I know."

"But why has something like this set you off?"

"I should've been maintaining the yard and house. No excuses. I've neglected my responsibilities."

"You had a good reason for that. You've been building my house, working and attending counselling sessions. You've had a lot on your plate."

"That's no excuse for letting things go."

"It's okay to ask for help. That's what people do."

"I'm trying, Emily. Please be patient."

She squeezed his hand and a reassuring squeeze came back setting their relationship in stone, setting her tears flowing again.

"Hey, now." Ricky's coarse fingers wiped the tears that were forming in pools under her eyes. "It's not that bad."

"You don't know what it's like to see the person you love walk away. That's already happened to me and the loss was immense. Watching you do that just now brought back memories. I thought you'd gone. That it was over."

"No. Emily. It's not over. I'm here for the long haul if that's what you want. I know it's not easy, but we're getting there. I've been going to the counselling sessions. I haven't gambled in a long time. Things have been difficult for you, but you've moved mountains. And I love everything about you. Will you stay with me, Emily?"

Emily stared down the path that moments before had led Ricky right back to her. He'd come back, through the open gate. This was it. She could leave Ricky and all his flaws behind right now. He wasn't the realtor or the financial banker. He wasn't tall, dark or had good blonde-surfer boy looks. He wasn't going to help her pay back her debts, but he built houses with his bare hands, he pulled chairs out for her and opened doors. He was determined to involve himself in a sport where in one misguided move he could chop his feet off. And he munched on liquorice allsorts and she liked that. He was different, he was caring and he loved her. All of her – not because of guilt but for love.

"I'm here for the long haul too," Emily said.

A smile broke out on Ricky's face. A smile that was returned with more certainty about the future than before.

Emily spent the following week working with Marie on designing a logo for her business, putting the final touches on signage, preparing advertising, making more cosmetics, and moving the last of her gear into her house.

She prepared her massage rooms till they were just the way she had wanted them, had always dreamed of. She'd purchased some purple throws from Cache. Marie hung up some gorgeous photos and some fairy lights and popped some candles into little glass jars. They were all set for the grand opening on Saturday - an opportunity for Emily to showcase the newest business to the Misty Springs community.

She'd also made a call to the SPCA in Christchurch. "I'm ringing about a dog that was left with you about eight months ago," Emily said, tapping the business card on the table. *Please let Toto be there.*

Emily gave the lady some more details. It seemed that the SPCA had been inundated with dogs over the Christmas period and some had been transferred up to the Culverden SPCA. She dialled their number and the phone was answered by a clear speaking woman.

"Yes, I do remember that day. Lovely thing she was. Just let me pull up our records."

Emily held her breath while the lady, Sue, seemed to take forever.

"Toto, yes. Toto was picked up by a nice family so she's got a new home now."

Emily stopped tapping, and her shoulders slumped forward. Well, what had she expected? That Toto would still be there after all this time?

"Oh, wait. Hang on. There's a note here," Sue continued. "Family had to move overseas and they've given Toto back. She came in last weekend. I've been away sick, which was why I didn't know about it. I certainly would've remembered such a sweet-natured dog."

Emily's head bolted upright. "Could I come see her tomorrow?"

"Sure. We're open until six pm."

"I'll be there around lunch time."

She'd found Toto and she was going to bring her back to Ricky. She'd seen how much Ricky had missed Toto and patted every dog he came across. The misery in his eyes when he saw Kyle and Faithful together almost tore Emily's heart in two. Maybe getting Toto back for Ricky would help him and give him something to focus on that could help in his recovery.

She'd just hung up when Marie rang.

"Emily, quick. You have to come over to the salon."

"Why? What's happened?"

"We've got big news. You're not going to believe this." Marie was almost yelling.

"Okay. Give me five minutes and I'll be there."

When she walked into Serenity Day Spa, Marie and Andrea were huddled over the reception desk.

"Read this." Andrea thrust a letter into Emily's hands.

Words jumped out at her as she quickly scanned the contents. "… clients … complaints… false claims… not natural… high chemicals and synthetics… must not sell this product…"

"You were right!" Marie exclaimed. "Nature's Own was falsely claiming itself as being natural. Lisa must cease sales."

"Finally." Emily breathed out. Lisa shouldn't have been making her, Marie or Andrea sell these products.

"You stood up to Lisa, Emily. She pushed it too far and it's landed her in hot water," Marie continued.

"And that's not all. It seems she must've known something like this was about to happen. She sent me an email this morning from Paris saying she's not coming back and she's put the salon on the market," Andrea added.

"You're joking," Emily said.

"Look for yourself. Here's the email."

It was true. It seemed Lisa didn't want to come back and face the music, the email was an excuse, stating that she'd had enough of the business, had got the travel bug and had fallen in love with Hunter.

"Well, there you go." Emily sat down on the chair. "What are you two going to do then?"

"We'll wait it out. See who buys the business."

"Why don't you come and work for me? I haven't any clients yet but we could see about bringing some of Lisa's clients over. None of us have a restraint of trade contract."

Marie and Andrea looked at each other and smiled.

"We'd love to come and work with you. Actually we were hoping that when you got yourself established you'd offer us a job," Marie said.

"Don't get too excited yet. I need to work through the financials. I might not be able to pay you much to start with."

"I don't care," Andrea said. "I'd much rather work for you than Lisa. Besides it's the perfect opportunity to play with your lovely creations."

Was it too soon to take on staff? With Serenity up for sale, selling it would only open up more business opportunities. She could make this happen. "How are we going with the advertising?" Emily asked Marie.

"I'm only hearing good things. Of course, all the females around town said they'd be there on Saturday and I'm coercing the guys to come in and at least buy their other half a gift voucher. Which reminds me. I'd better get onto that."

"Will you be okay if I leave you to follow up on anything that needs to be done tomorrow? I'm off to Culverden to collect a dog."

"A dog?" Andrea said. "An addition to your home already."

"It's not for me, but I'll tell you all about it when I get back. I appreciate the extra work you're doing to help me - both of you."

"No worries," Andrea said. "Free products will go down a treat."

Emily waved good-bye. *What would I do without friends like Marie and Andrea?* If someone had said six months ago she'd have not only a massage therapy business but her two best friends working for her she wouldn't have believed them. It was all working out and the next part of the plan would hopefully reunite two lost friends.

***

If she was to get to Culverden and back before Ricky finished work, she needed to leave by 8 am. She hauled herself out of bed and pulled on a pair of jeans, a number of thermal layers and a warm jersey.

Marie and Andrea had already left for work and had stoked up the log burner so the house was toasty and warm.

She poked her nose outside the door. There had been a good frost overnight; the lawn was crispy white and her breath came out in clouds. She would have to watch the roads, be careful of any icy patches, particularly in the spots that the sun never reached.

The drive to Culverden was uneventful and she pulled into the township just before 11 am. The SPCA was down a long road on the other side of town. She walked into the reception area and was greeted by a confusion of animal noises – dogs barking, cats meowing and a budgie squawking out, "Get that phone". Goldfish glided obliviously in the huge fish tank.

"Hi," Emily said to the woman behind the counter. "Are you Sue? The one I was talking to about a dog called Toto?"

"Yes, it was. Come and have a look."

Emily followed Sue outside across to a large concrete building where the barking grew louder.

"We're just given the dogs their lunch."

Emily walked past cages and staff who were dishing out dog food.

"Toto's down the end." Sue stopped outside the last cage where a dog was sleeping in the back. She had her head on her two front paws. "Is this the dog you're looking for?"

It was the dog in the photo Ricky had shown her. "This is definitely Toto. Here, girl."

Although the cage was clean, being confined to a space couldn't be pleasant for Toto. She looked up, her sad eyes saying it all – a dog who'd been given away, not understanding why, separated from their master and living in a dog shelter. She clambered to her feet and walked slowly, tail barely wagging, over towards Emily.

"How you going? How'd you like to come and live in Misty Springs? I've got someone who's going to be very pleased to see you," Emily said, patting her.

"She's a lovely dog. Very placid with a good nature. It's a shame she hasn't a home to go to."

"Oh, but she does. I'm taking her back to her owner."

"Well, I'm pleased to hear that. Dogs and their owners shouldn't be apart."

Sue opened the cage, put a collar round Toto's neck. "Unfortunately we don't have enough staff to walk the dogs every day, so she'll be eager to get out." She handed the leash to Emily and Toto took off at a quick pace.

Back at reception Emily and Sue came to an agreement over payment for Toto plus Sue gave her some dog food, biscuits and a few toys.

"You're going to make someone's day," Sue said.

"I sure hope so." Emily grabbed the dog goodies and Toto, picking up that she was going somewhere and leaving the SPCA behind, she woofed and jumped into the passenger seat without any encouragement.

Emily pulled out of the driveway and started on the journey back to Misty Springs with Toto staring out the window and looking all around. She put her face hard up against the side window.

"Oh, I forgot. Dogs like to have their noses out the window."

Emily opened the window and Toto stuck her head out, the wind instantly whipping up fur, and bending her ears back. She laughed as Toto stuck her nose high in the air, inhaling in the sweet smell of freedom.

They made good time and as much as she wanted to stop off at Paix she kept on driving. She tooted the horn as she drove past. Toto brought her head back down inside the car, circled once on the seat and woofed again.

"Not long to go. Not long to go."

By 4 pm she'd reached Ricky's. The fading light making it difficult to work outside, he'd be finishing work around about now.

Jumping out of the car, Toto followed close at her heels sniffing here, there and everywhere. She was like a child in a toy shop. New smells, new sights, new places to explore.

Emily opened the front door and got the fire going in the newly-cleaned chimney. She looked around at the new curtains, the more modern duvet cover which Christine had brought and the shelves with an odd collection of mismatched cups and plates donated by the locals. The house had a more lived-in feel, the cold and starkness that had once been here vanished and replaced by colour.

She unpacked the dog food, filled Toto's new bowl up with water, and placed it outside on the porch.

Toto lapped up the water sending puddles of waves over the side.

Emily sat down on the step. The last time she'd sat here she'd watched Ricky walk away after the clean-up job, the angry man who'd found it hard to accept that it was okay for people to help him. He'd come back and she replayed that scene again in her mind.

Ricky swung the gate open.

"Hey, I didn't expect to see you here," he called out. He was carrying two bags of groceries.

"You carried those all the way from town? Your arms must be nearly breaking."

Toto, who'd gone off to explore something behind the house, came bounding around the corner.

Ricky dropped the groceries to the ground. "Toto?"

Toto flew into Ricky's arms. "Toto! My God, it is you. What…"

Emily walked down the path and knelt down beside Ricky and Toto.

"I found Toto, Ricky. I've brought your dog back to you."

"Em…" Ricky choked on his words.

"You don't have to say a thing. Toto can help you."

"I don't know what to say." Ricky's eyes glazed over with tears. Toto stretched up against Ricky, demanding his attention.

"You spend some time with Toto while I go start dinner," Emily said.

"Thank you," he whispered.

Emily picked up the groceries and walked up the path. At the top she stopped and turned around.

Toto was on her back, all four legs up in the air while Ricky rubbed his hands over her stomach, muttering something. Toto jumped onto her feet, woofed and wagged her tail furiously.

Ricky picked up a stick and threw it. "Go fetch, girl."

Toto bounded off, running so fast she overshot the stick. She turned, grappled with it, securing it in her mouth then bounced back to Ricky.

"Good girl." Ricky ruffled Toto's fur.

His smile was ridiculously broad and satisfied. It caught on as she made her way into the house, her own smile tugged at her lips and widened. Toto had come back home. To Ricky's home.

Chapter 36

Emily didn't need any excuse to get up early on Saturday. She was out of bed at 7 am. So much to do. Today was opening day at her salon.

She dressed, ate quickly, and padded out to the prefab to warm up the inside. The prefab faced north and would soon capture the morning sun. She switched on fairy lights, lit some candles and turned on some music where the soothing sound of pan pipes filled the reception area. She had displayed her new range of body butters, lip balm and body cream, which now had the simple names of Potion No. 1, 2 and 3. She'd done up little sample pots of body butter for people to take home. Marie had designed a fantastic logo and labels for the products – a simple stylised bunch of lavender – black stalks, purple flowers.

She took one look at the two rooms. Everything was exactly how she'd always visualised it. Running her hand over the purple blanket, she repositioned the gerbera on the pillow. Picking up her box of aromatherapy oils, she chose rose, grapefruit, sandalwood and neroli, mixed them up and placed them in the oil burner. Soon the rooms were filled with the heavenly fragrance. She breathed in a big sigh of contentment. This was it. Her life, being completely in control.

There was a knock on the door.

"Ricky."

"Morning."

Emily tilted her head to receive his kiss. "You're the first here."

"Well, be prepared. Marie and Andrea are right behind me and they're bringing a gaggle of women."

"Great. That's just what I need."

Ricky stood back and looked up at the name on the back wall. "That's a lovely thought Emily."

Emily followed his eye up to the sign. There was the name of her business – The Lavender and Rose Day Spa. "Lavender for me and Rose, after Nana Rose." She swallowed over a lump in her throat. If Nana only could be here today…

"And she'd be so proud of you," a voice came from behind her, echoing her thoughts.

"David! What are you doing here?"

"Marie invited me. And I needed to see what mess you're going to get yourself into this time."

Emily gasped. *Was David going to be forever reminding me of the mistake I'd made?*

"Hey, only joking. I have complete faith in you, little sis."

"For crying out loud, David. Give me some credit for once."

"Honestly. I wish you all the best." David leant forward and kissed her on the cheek. "I'm proud of you too."

"Thank you."

Emily introduced David to Ricky.

Hands covered her eyes from behind. "Guess who?"

Emily removed the hands and spun round. "Kyle. Oh my God! You knew about this too?"

"A-ha." His face broke out into a cheeky grin.

"I'm so glad you've come," Emily said. "Marie, come and meet Kyle."

She introduced Marie to Kyle and smiled. There was a spark that jumped between the two of them. Kyle and Marie as a couple would be perfect.

"Let me show what we've done," Marie said, leading Kyle down the hall.

"I'll grab a moment with you later," Kyle said over his shoulder. "My partner and I want to invest in your business."

If my smile could get any wider it would completely encircle my face.

David and Ricky had retreated outside as the entrance way began overflowing with 'oohing' and 'aahing' women.

Andrea and Christine took the women on a grand tour.

"Well, where do I sign up?" Linda asked. "I really need someone to have a go at my back."

Emily sat down behind the reception desk and opened up the booking calendar which was empty. "You're officially The Lavender and Rose Day Spa's first appointment." She wrote the day and time down on an appointment card and handed it to Linda.

***

Opening day was a success. Fifty people, mainly women, had come through the doors. Twenty onward appointments had been made and all the sample potions had gone.

They locked the doors to the spa at 5 pm and Emily, Marie, Andrea, Ricky, David and Linda went down to Strawberry Desert for a meal. Celebrations went on to almost midnight.

Bone weary, but on a high from all the excitement, Emily climbed into bed. Here she was in her new home with the promise of a successful day spa just metres away. She let out an enormous sigh of relief as her eyes began to close. But there was so much to do. She had a full schedule of appointments next week, new batches of potions to make up and then there was...

***

She jumped. What had woken her? She tilted her head. Something sharp had hit the window. *Must be the wind whipping up things.* She put her head back down. Whop! Something hit the window again like a tiny stone. She looked at the clock – 6.07. She moaned. More sleep needed. Another whop. This time she sat straight up.

"Emily!" Someone was outside calling out her name. "Emily, are you awake?"

She stumbled out of bed and pulled back the curtains. In the moonlight Ricky's head gleamed up at her.

She opened the window. "Ricky, what on earth?"

"Quickly! You have to get dressed."

"What? No, I don't. I'm going back to bed."

"No, Emily, please. You have to get dressed. I need to show you something."

"At six in the morning? It's freezing out there."

"Please let me in."

"OK," she said crossly. *My only day to sleep in and he's got to get worked up about something.*

She unlocked the front door.

"You need to get dressed," Ricky said, as he came inside.

"So you keep saying. I don't understand… what's the emergency."

"Put on some warm clothes and your sneakers."

Emily grumbled. In the hall light she fumbled putting on her track pants, sweatshirt, windbreaker, woollen socks, beanie and scarf.

"Right. You have to drive us to the bottom of Red Hill," Ricky said.

"What-?"

Ricky put up his hand. "No questions."

Emily, still grumbling, locked up the house, started up the car and within five minutes they were at the base of Red Hill.

"What are we doing, Ricky?"

"Ah, remember no questions." Ricky grabbed her hand.

"Please tell me we're not going up Red Hill."

"Yes we are."

"But it's dark; we won't be able to see."

"It will be light soon. Here, take my hand."

She put her gloved hand in his and they started the switchback climb up Red Hill. The birds were just starting to twerp as tiny light streaks broke the night sky.

"Warming up?" Ricky asked.

"Yes, but I still don't-"

"Yes, okay, no questions."

The invigorating walk was warming her up. A slight wind throughout the night had prevented any frost settling.

Finally they reached the top of Red Hill as the sun peeped up over the hills in the valley below. The clouds skimming along in the sky glowed with a mixture of orange and pink.

Emily leant up against the rail.

The sky turned a cerise-pink, stayed like that for a heartbeat and then turned a fiery red.

"Wow!" she exclaimed, the hint of a breeze caressing her face.

"Perfect timing."

The last of the night receded behind them and dawn won. The sky was awash in a brilliant glow.

"Someone once told me the sunrises up here were better than the sunsets," Ricky whispered in her ear.

"Well, now I know that to be true."

"You shared your sunset with me, now here is our sunrise."

"Our?"

He plucked at her gloves, pulling them off.

"I'll freeze," she squeaked.

Ricky knelt down on one knee.

"Ricky, what are you doing?" A flutter of apprehension wavered in her chest.

Ricky pulled out a small box. "Emily, will you please marry me?"

The landscape was splashed in pink and orange and reflected back into Ricky's eyes. He flicked open the box and nestled in the soft, white tissue was a ring. "Here, give me your hand."

Emily placed her left hand in Ricky's. He slowly pushed the ring down her middle finger. It was a perfect fit. "Please say yes. I love you so much."

"Yes, yes, yes," Emily said. This was the last thing she'd ever expected. They'd never talked about getting married or much about the future but that hadn't mattered.

"I love you too." She threw her arms around his shoulders.

His mouth came up to meet hers, their warm breath intermingled and she melted into his kiss.

She brought the ring up to her face for a closer look in the strengthening daylight.

"Don't look too closely. It's only a cheapy. I couldn't afford anything too flash, but I promise I'll buy you a proper ring soon."

"It's okay, Ricky. I don't care if it only cost five dollars. It means the world to me."

As the township of Misty Springs started to stir, they walked back down Red Hill hand in hand.

***

They discussed making hot tea and coffee when they got back to Emily's.

"Come with me for a moment," Emily said, leading Ricky around the side of the house. She made her way over to the tall gum tree and sat down on the swing. Now was the time to take that first swing. "Push me."

Ricky pulled the ropes of the swing towards him and then let them go. His strong hand on the small of her back pushed her higher. Lavender that grew on the sides of the garden swished past her in a blur. A sparkle from her left hand caught the early light of the sun and she soared higher, feet pointing true north towards Misty Springs and Red Hill.

Connect with Casey
http://caseyfaehewson.com
Friend me on Facebook: http://facebook.com/caseyyaauthor
Follow me on Twitter: http://twitter.com/@caseyfae
Follow me on Pinterest:
https://nz.pinterest.com/caseyfaehewson/
Instagram: https://www.instagram.com/caseyfae8917/

Light My Way
(co-authored with Bob Boze)

Almost 7,000 miles separates two apple orchards, but it can't separate the bond of love two sisters, Ciara and Moira, have for each other. Nor, can distance prevent someone from doing everything he can to assure the person he cherished falls in love with the one man who will love and treasure her as he did.

A year after a long overdue visit ends in the tragic death of Ciara's husband, something draws her to the beach in Sumner New Zealand. Away from the orchard; the distraction she's used to try and forget.

Is it fate or something else that guides her and her dog Macintosh, to that beach, on that morning, for a walk? A walk that will change her life forever.

And what, or who, is it that brings Aidan, a Bonita Fireman, halfway around the world so that a stray volleyball can lead him to someone? Someone he's sure he knows. Someone that every sign, every gesture, every path, every beam of light keeps pointing to.

***

The authors invite you to enter this wonderful story of caring and friendship that quickly turns to love. A story guided not by fate, but perhaps someone watching over the one he was forced to leave behind. A story that suggests that love has no boundaries and that it doesn't end when one partner is no longer with us; that love and caring don't die when we do.

Available on Amazon, Barnes and Noble and iBooks.

Aqua Bay

Nerissa Taylor's heart lies in the spectacularly beautiful Aqua Bay. As an eco-tour guide she proudly showcases the pristine bay and dolphins she loves to the many tourists who visit the area.

All that is about to end as she prepares to move to the city and marry her fiancé, Scott.

Geologist Jackson Darnell arrives in the area to investigate oil exploration possibilities hiding behind a cavalier attitude to avoid the pain of his past.

When Nerissa and Jackson's paths cross, sparks fly and loyalties are tested.

As tensions rise, and she faces a frightening unresolved issue form her past, Nerissa is forced to question exactly what she wants in life.

How far will Nerissa go to protect Aqua Bay and the precious dolphins she loves?

Available on Amazon, Barnes and Noble and iBooks.

Haven River

Sixteen-year-old Luke Conway is in his last year of high school in the harbour-side town of Haven River.

Writing is Luke's life. All he wants to do is be a journalist and write stories about storm chasers.

But Ryan, Luke's protective older brother and guardian, has other ideas.

When Luke meets newcomer to town, the mischievous Jamie Pascoe, his world is turned upside down.

Tragedy strikes and Luke is catapulted down a path of self-destruction.

Can Luke overcome the odds pitted against him? To make Jamie proud of him. To hold on tight to his family. To follow his dream on his own terms.

Reviews for Haven River:

"A delightful story – which in my case – rekindles the delicate and precarious path of young love. The narrative explores a love of books and writing and overcoming major events in life, all skilfully woven into the plot.

A Satisfied Reader, Wellington, New Zealand

A warm, well written romance story that should be added to your "want to read" list. 5 stars!"

Bob Boze, USA

Available on Amazon, Barnes and Noble and iBooks.

Coming Sometime Soon!

Pacific Vines

Set against the stunning backdrop of a Marlborough vineyard

Ryleigh's love life is a mess so she decides to focus on her career as a Personal Assistant, but can she still find romance amongst the vines?

Freeway

A series of six novellas about love, life on the road, and learning to take risks.